# COLD BODIES ™

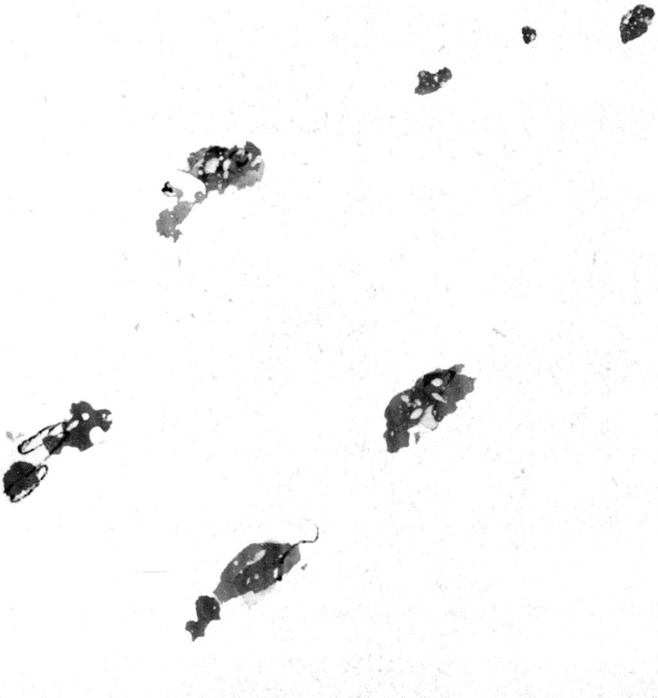

SCRIPT BY **MAGDALENE** VISAGGIO

ART BY **ANDREA** MUTTI    LETTERING BY **NATE** PIEKOS OF BLAMBOT®

DARK HORSE BOOKS

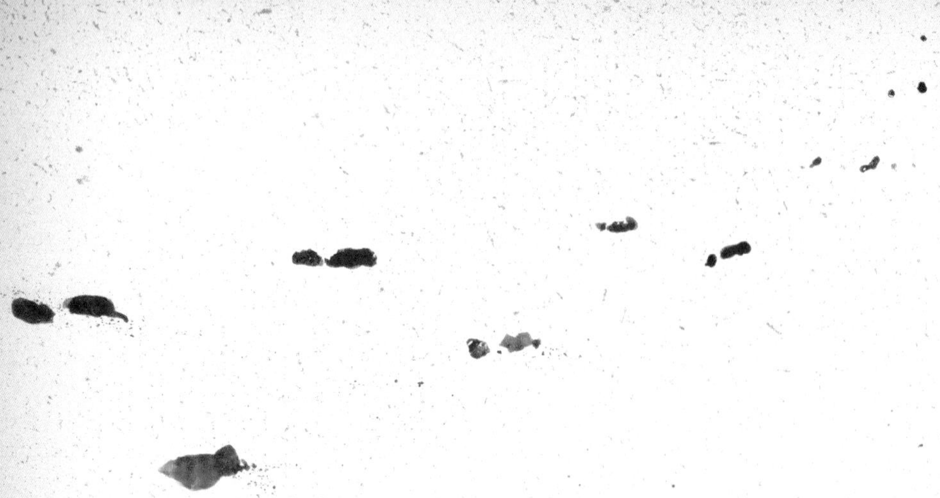

PRESIDENT AND PUBLISHER MIKE RICHARDSON EDITOR DANIEL CHABON

ASSISTANT EDITORS CHUCK HOWITT, KONNER KNUDSEN, AND MISHA GEHR

DESIGNER MAY HIJIKURO DIGITAL ART TECHNICIAN JOSIE CHRISTENSEN

EXECUTIVE VICE PRESIDENT NEIL HANKERSON CHIEF FINANCIAL OFFICER TOM WEDDLE CHIEF INFORMATION OFFICER DALE LAFOUNTAIN VICE PRESIDENT OF LICENSING TIM WIESCH VICE PRESIDENT OF MARKETING MATT PARKINSON VICE PRESIDENT OF PRODUCTION AND SCHEDULING VANESSA TODD-HOLMES VICE PRESIDENT OF BOOK TRADE AND DIGITAL SALES MARK BERNARDI VICE PRESIDENT OF PRODUCT DEVELOPMENT RANDY LAHRMAN GENERAL COUNSEL KEN LIZZI EDITOR IN CHIEF DAVE MARSHALL EDITORIAL DIRECTOR DAVEY ESTRADA SENIOR BOOKS EDITOR CHRIS WARNER DIRECTOR OF SPECIALTY PROJECTS CARY GRAZZINI ART DIRECTOR LIA RIBACCHI DIRECTOR OF DIGITAL ART AND PREPRESS MATT DRYER SENIOR DIRECTOR OF LICENSED PUBLICATIONS MICHAEL GOMBOS DIRECTOR OF CUSTOM PROGRAMS KARI YADRO DIRECTOR OF INTERNATIONAL LICENSING KARI TORSON

FSC
MIX
Paper from responsible sources
www.fsc.org  FSC® C169962

Published by Dark Horse Books
A division of Dark Horse Comics LLC
10956 SE Main Street, Milwaukie, OR 97222

DarkHorse.com

To find a comic shop in your area,
check out the Comic Shop Locator Service: comicshoplocator.com

First edition: June 2022
Ebook ISBN: 978-1-50672-266-5 | Trade paperback ISBN: 978-1-50672-265-8

10 9 8 7 6 5 4 3 2 1
Printed in China

Library of Congress Cataloging-in-Publication Data

Names: Visaggio, Magdalene, author. | Mutti, Andrea, 1973- artist. | Saam, Zakk, letterer.

Title: Cold bodies / script by Magdalene Visaggio ; art by Andrea Mutti ; lettering by Zakk Saam.

Description: First edition. | Milwaukie, OR : Dark Horse Books, 2021. | Summary: "Years ago, Denise Stokes was the sole survivor of the brutal Winter Man massacre, in which several young adults were slaughtered during a powerful blizzard in Wisconsin. Now, in present-day, Denise has tried to bury the past behind her, while the world around her has become obsessed with the murders through a popular film franchise called Snow Day"-- Provided by publisher.

Identifiers: LCCN 2021011168 (print) | LCCN 2021011169 (ebook) | ISBN 9781506722658 (trade paperback) | ISBN 9781506722665 (ebook)

Subjects: LCSH: Graphic novels.

Classification: LCC PN6727.V58 C65 2021 (print) | LCC PN6727.V58 (ebook) | DDC 741.5/973--dc23

LC record available at https://lccn.loc.gov/2021011168
LC ebook record available at https://lccn.loc.gov/2021011169

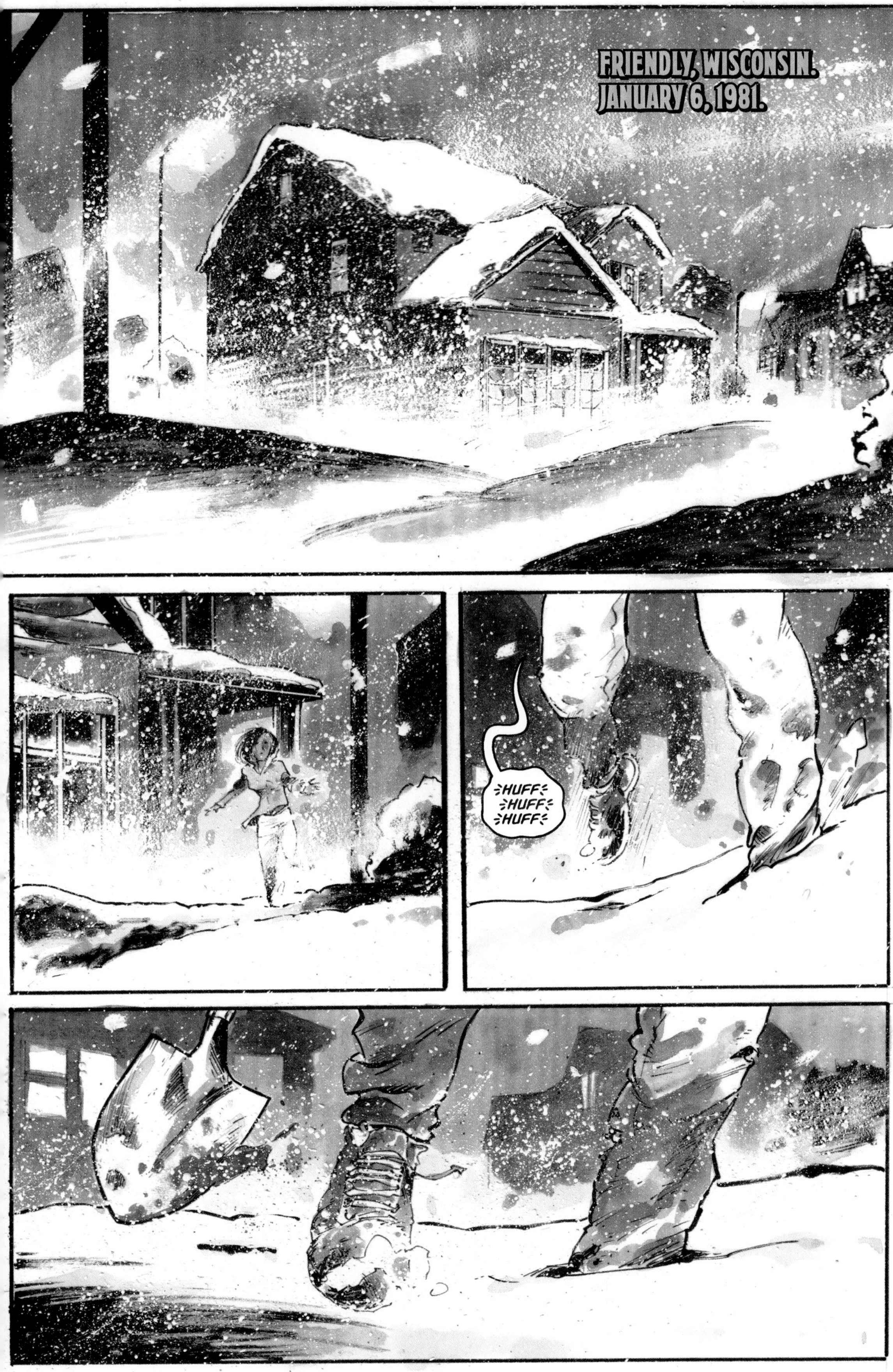
FRIENDLY, WISCONSIN.
JANUARY 6, 1981.
HUFF HUFF HUFF

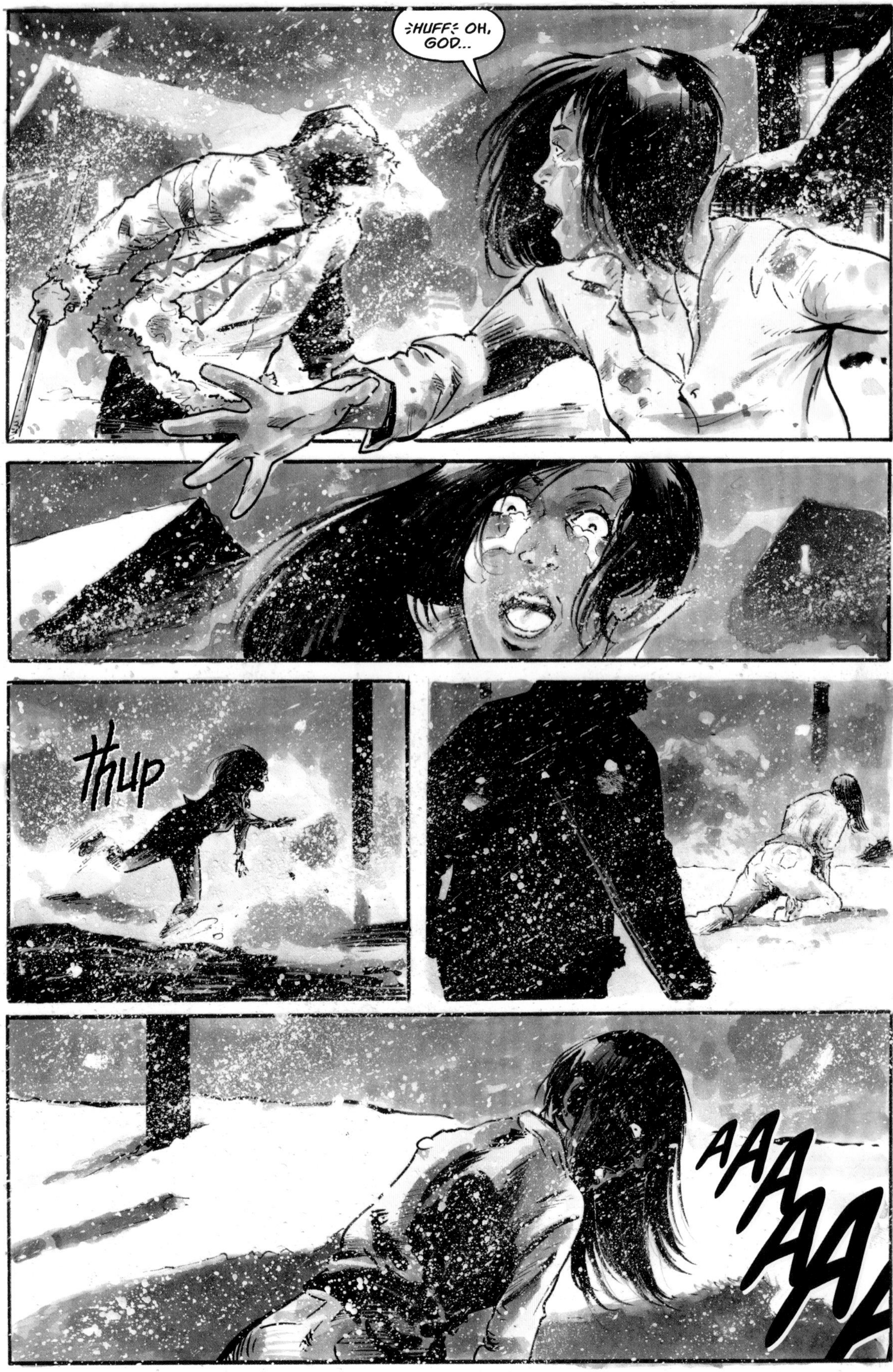

HUFF OH, GOD...
thup
AAAAAAA

HHN!

NEW YORK CITY.
JANUARY 5, 1996.

≈HUFF≈
≈HUFF≈
≈HUFF≈

JAMES.
COME ON.

WAKE
UP.

NNNNNNNNN.
LEAVE ME
ALONE.

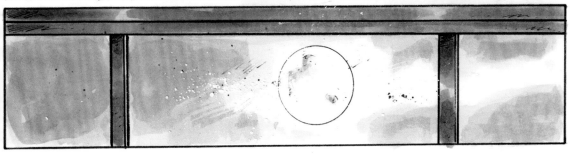

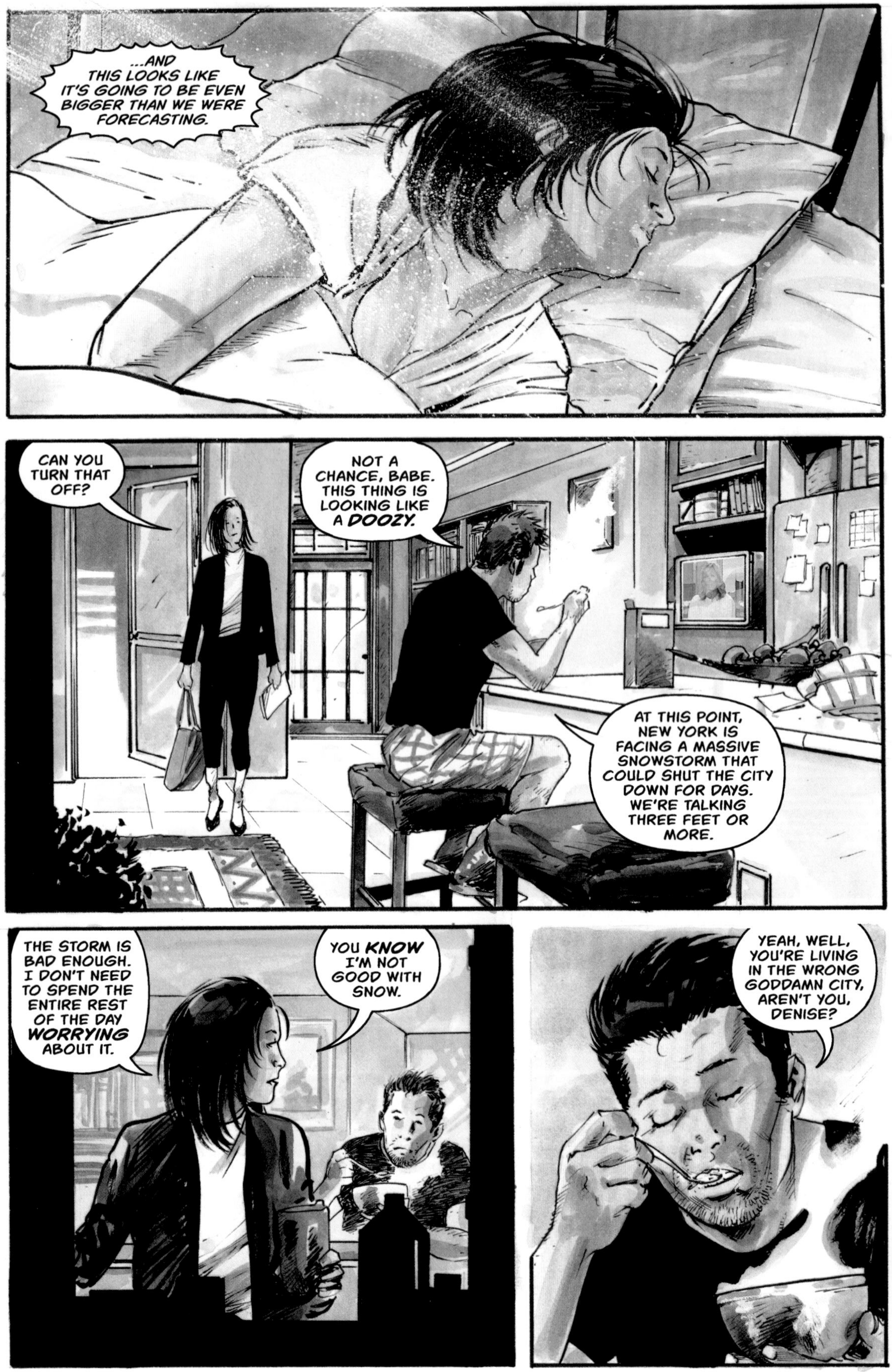
...AND THIS LOOKS LIKE IT'S GOING TO BE EVEN BIGGER THAN WE WERE FORECASTING.
CAN YOU TURN THAT OFF?
NOT A CHANCE, BABE. THIS THING IS LOOKING LIKE A *DOOZY.*
AT THIS POINT, NEW YORK IS FACING A MASSIVE SNOWSTORM THAT COULD SHUT THE CITY DOWN FOR DAYS. WE'RE TALKING THREE FEET OR MORE.
THE STORM IS BAD ENOUGH. I DON'T NEED TO SPEND THE ENTIRE REST OF THE DAY *WORRYING* ABOUT IT.
YOU *KNOW* I'M NOT GOOD WITH SNOW.
YEAH, WELL, YOU'RE LIVING IN THE WRONG GODDAMN CITY, AREN'T YOU, DENISE?

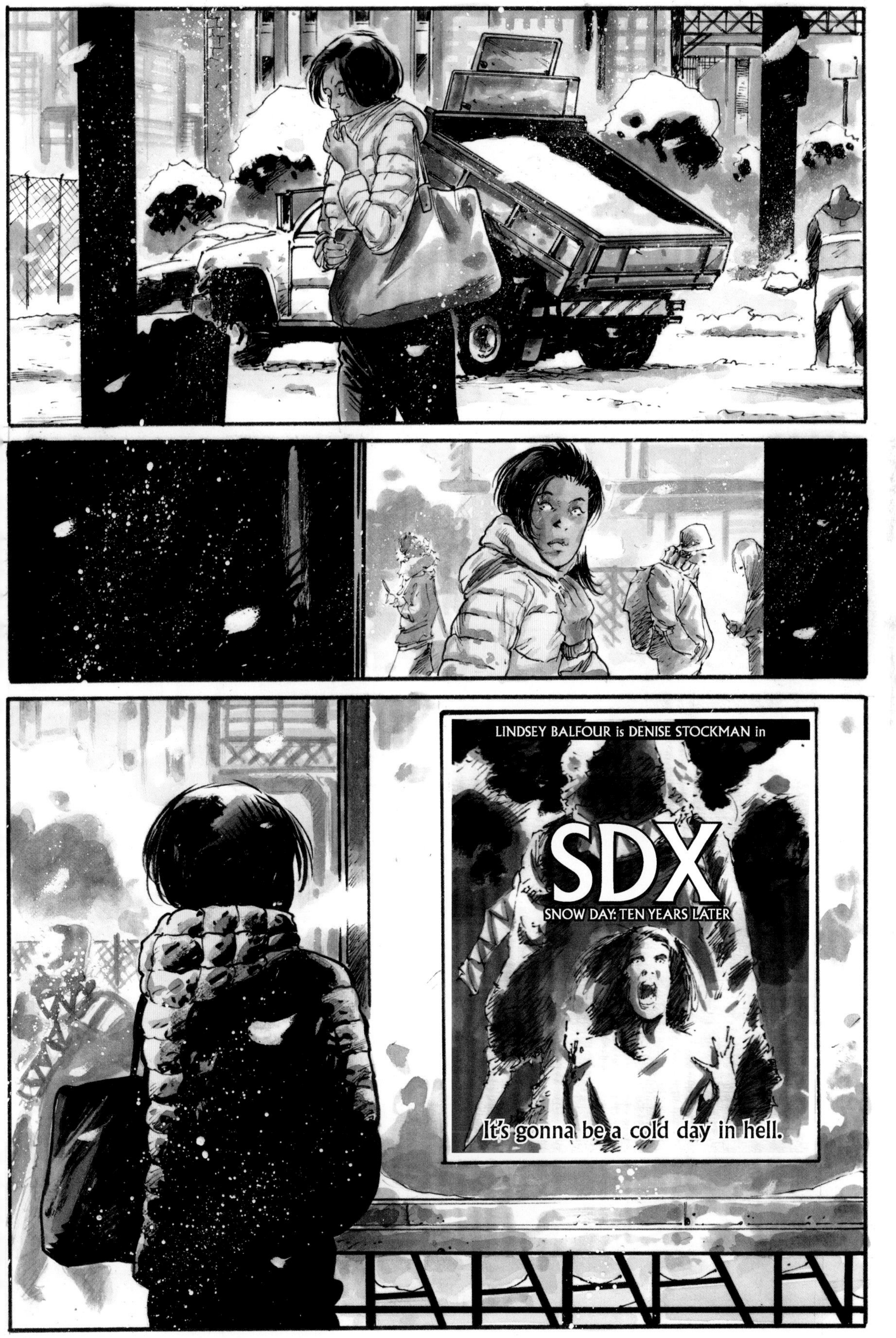
LINDSEY BALFOUR is DENISE STOCKMAN in
SDX
SNOW DAY: TEN YEARS LATER
It's gonna be a cold day in hell.

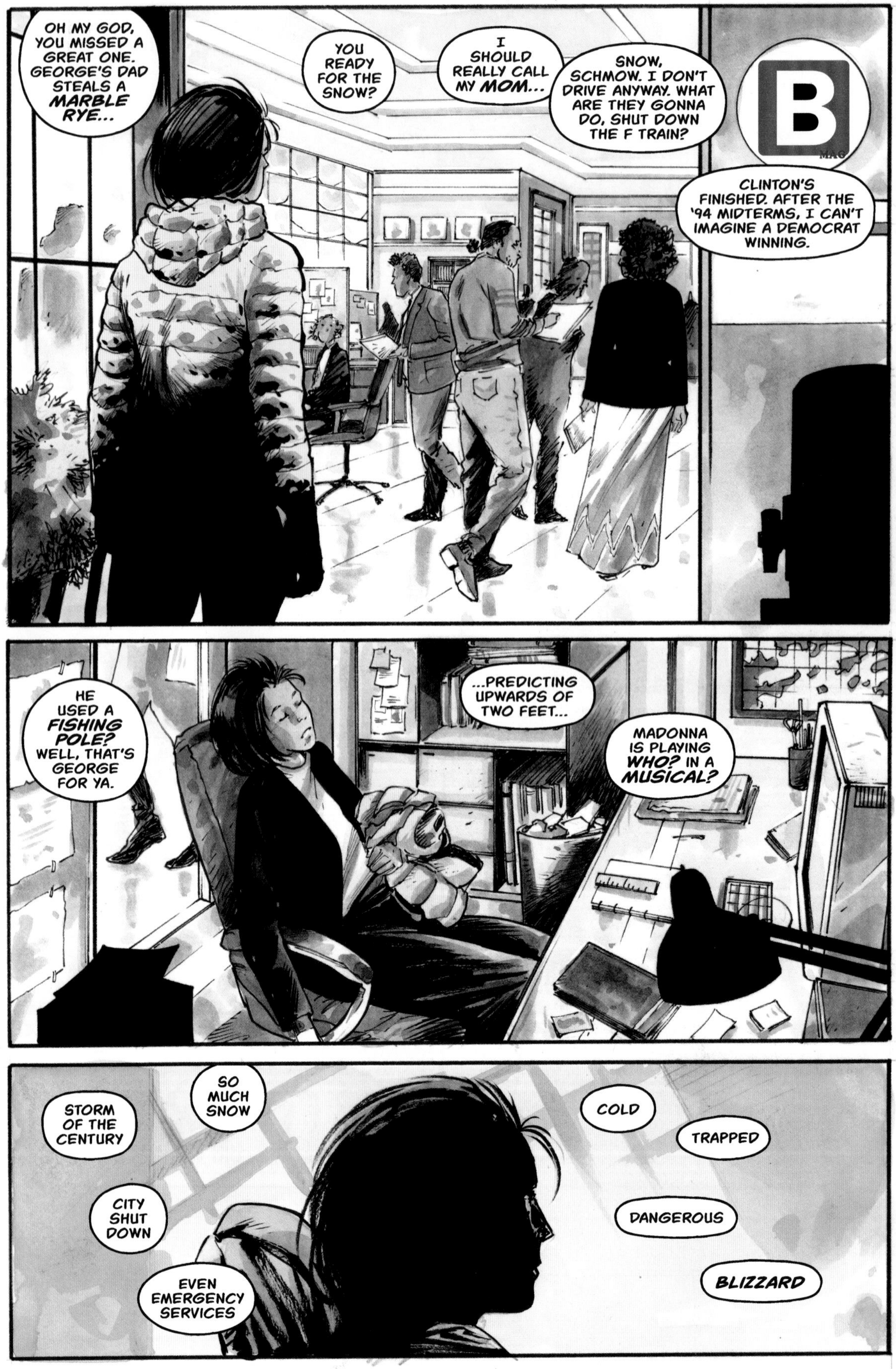
OH MY GOD, YOU MISSED A GREAT ONE. GEORGE'S DAD STEALS A MARBLE RYE...
YOU READY FOR THE SNOW?
I SHOULD REALLY CALL MY MOM...
SNOW, SCHMOW. I DON'T DRIVE ANYWAY. WHAT ARE THEY GONNA DO, SHUT DOWN THE F TRAIN?
B
MAG
CLINTON'S FINISHED. AFTER THE '94 MIDTERMS, I CAN'T IMAGINE A DEMOCRAT WINNING.
HE USED A FISHING POLE? WELL, THAT'S GEORGE FOR YA.
...PREDICTING UPWARDS OF TWO FEET...
MADONNA IS PLAYING WHO? IN A MUSICAL?
STORM OF THE CENTURY
SO MUCH SNOW
COLD
TRAPPED
CITY SHUT DOWN
DANGEROUS
EVEN EMERGENCY SERVICES
BLIZZARD

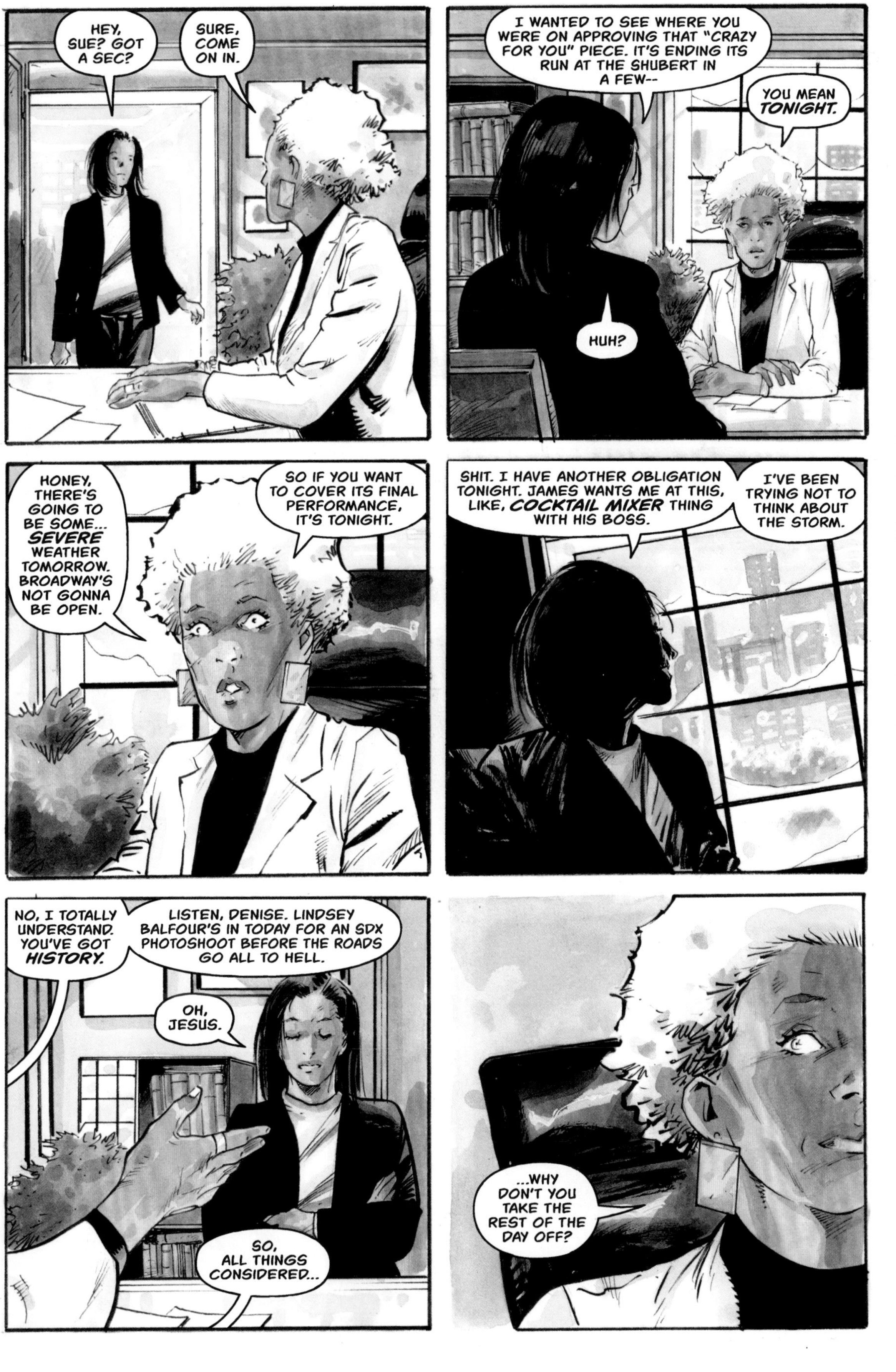
HEY, SUE? GOT A SEC?
SURE, COME ON IN.
I WANTED TO SEE WHERE YOU WERE ON APPROVING THAT "CRAZY FOR YOU" PIECE. IT'S ENDING ITS RUN AT THE SHUBERT IN A FEW--
YOU MEAN TONIGHT.
HUH?
HONEY, THERE'S GOING TO BE SOME... SEVERE WEATHER TOMORROW. BROADWAY'S NOT GONNA BE OPEN.
SO IF YOU WANT TO COVER ITS FINAL PERFORMANCE, IT'S TONIGHT.
SHIT. I HAVE ANOTHER OBLIGATION TONIGHT. JAMES WANTS ME AT THIS, LIKE, COCKTAIL MIXER THING WITH HIS BOSS.
I'VE BEEN TRYING NOT TO THINK ABOUT THE STORM.
NO, I TOTALLY UNDERSTAND. YOU'VE GOT HISTORY.
LISTEN, DENISE. LINDSEY BALFOUR'S IN TODAY FOR AN SDX PHOTOSHOOT BEFORE THE ROADS GO ALL TO HELL.
OH, JESUS.
SO, ALL THINGS CONSIDERED...
...WHY DON'T YOU TAKE THE REST OF THE DAY OFF?

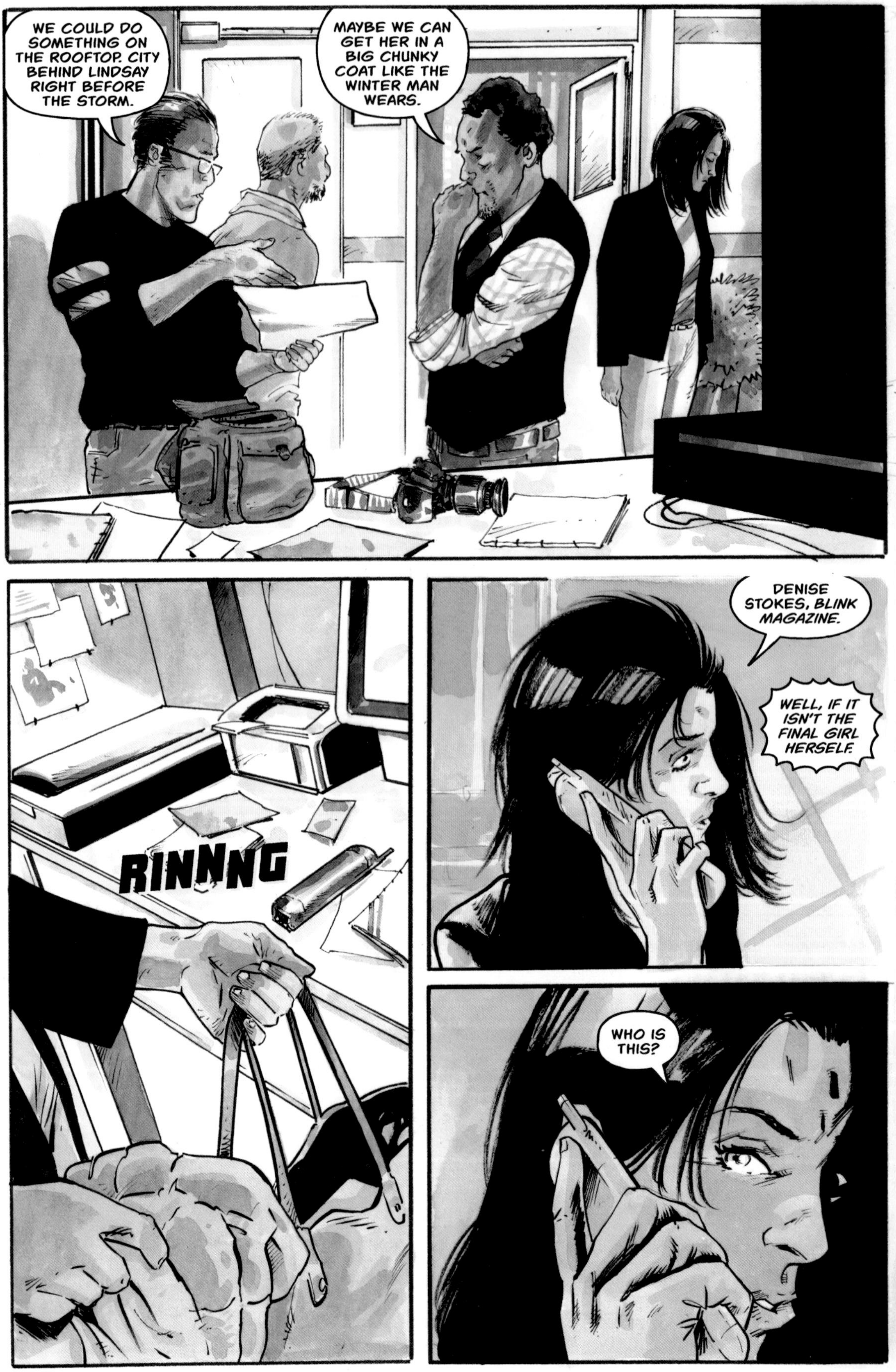
WE COULD DO SOMETHING ON THE ROOFTOP. CITY BEHIND LINDSAY RIGHT BEFORE THE STORM.
MAYBE WE CAN GET HER IN A BIG CHUNKY COAT LIKE THE WINTER MAN WEARS.
RINNNG
DENISE STOKES, BLINK MAGAZINE.
WELL, IF IT ISN'T THE FINAL GIRL HERSELF.
WHO IS THIS?

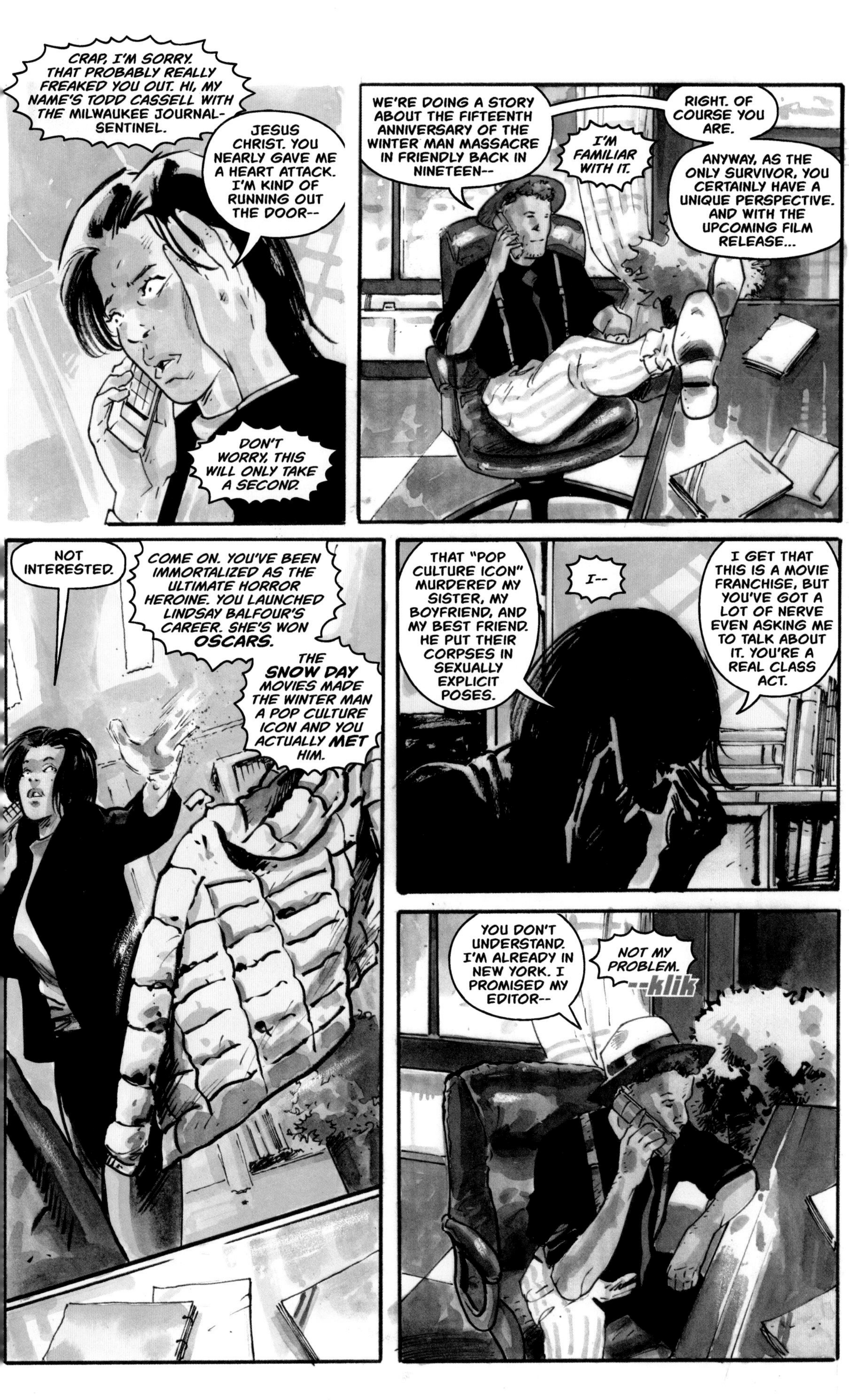
CRAP, I'M SORRY. THAT PROBABLY REALLY FREAKED YOU OUT. HI, MY NAME'S TODD CASSELL WITH THE MILWAUKEE JOURNAL-SENTINEL.
JESUS CHRIST. YOU NEARLY GAVE ME A HEART ATTACK. I'M KIND OF RUNNING OUT THE DOOR--
DON'T WORRY, THIS WILL ONLY TAKE A SECOND.
WE'RE DOING A STORY ABOUT THE FIFTEENTH ANNIVERSARY OF THE WINTER MAN MASSACRE IN FRIENDLY BACK IN NINETEEN--
I'M FAMILIAR WITH IT.
RIGHT. OF COURSE YOU ARE.
ANYWAY, AS THE ONLY SURVIVOR, YOU CERTAINLY HAVE A UNIQUE PERSPECTIVE. AND WITH THE UPCOMING FILM RELEASE...
NOT INTERESTED.
COME ON. YOU'VE BEEN IMMORTALIZED AS THE ULTIMATE HORROR HEROINE. YOU LAUNCHED LINDSAY BALFOUR'S CAREER. SHE'S WON OSCARS.
THE SNOW DAY MOVIES MADE THE WINTER MAN A POP CULTURE ICON AND YOU ACTUALLY MET HIM.
THAT "POP CULTURE ICON" MURDERED MY SISTER, MY BOYFRIEND, AND MY BEST FRIEND. HE PUT THEIR CORPSES IN SEXUALLY EXPLICIT POSES.
I--
I GET THAT THIS IS A MOVIE FRANCHISE, BUT YOU'VE GOT A LOT OF NERVE EVEN ASKING ME TO TALK ABOUT IT. YOU'RE A REAL CLASS ACT.
YOU DON'T UNDERSTAND. I'M ALREADY IN NEW YORK. I PROMISED MY EDITOR--
NOT MY PROBLEM.
--klik

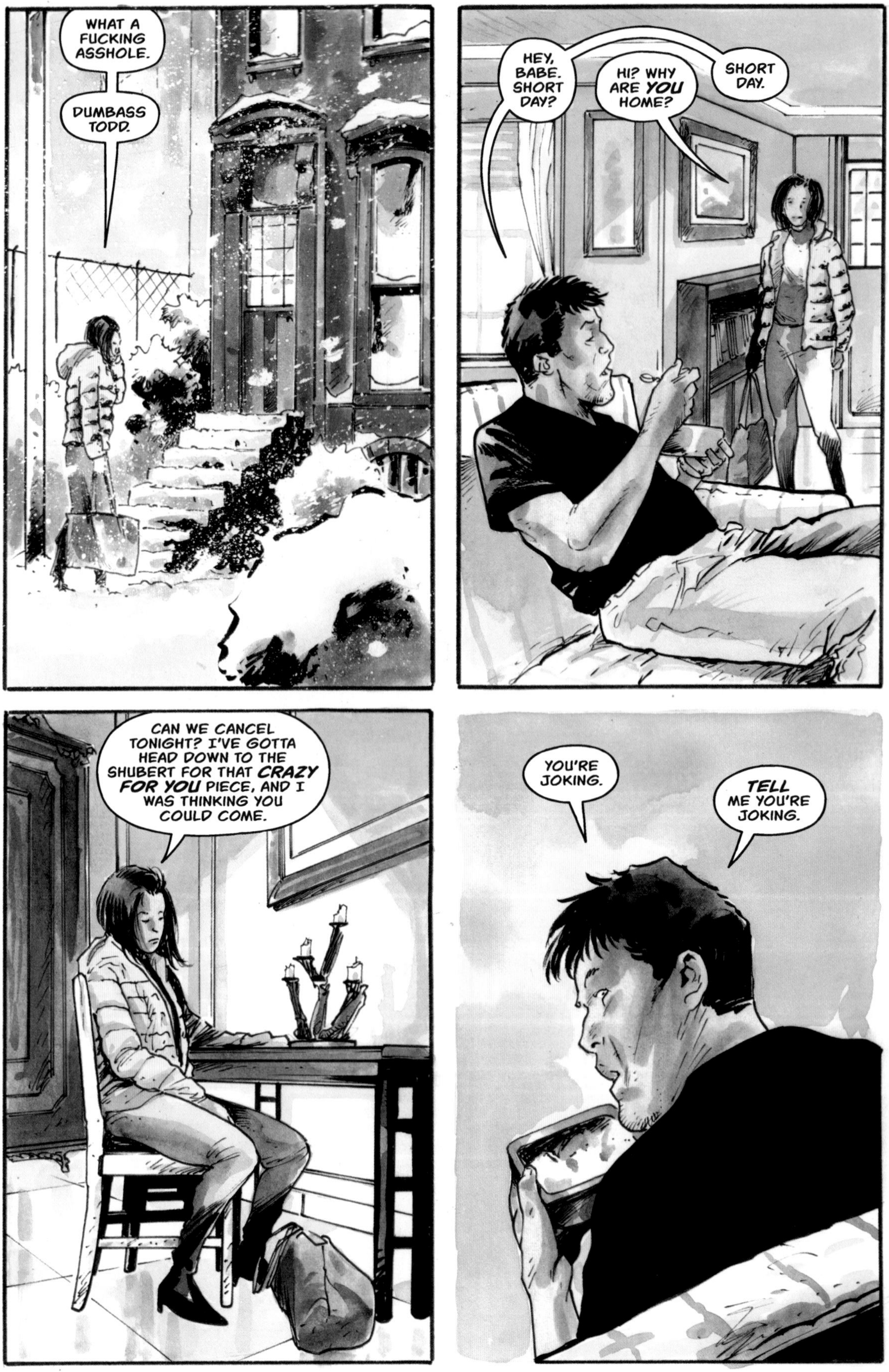
WHAT A FUCKING ASSHOLE.
DUMBASS TODD.
HEY, BABE. SHORT DAY?
HI? WHY ARE *YOU* HOME?
SHORT DAY.
CAN WE CANCEL TONIGHT? I'VE GOTTA HEAD DOWN TO THE SHUBERT FOR THAT *CRAZY FOR YOU* PIECE, AND I WAS THINKING YOU COULD COME.
YOU'RE JOKING.
*TELL* ME YOU'RE JOKING.

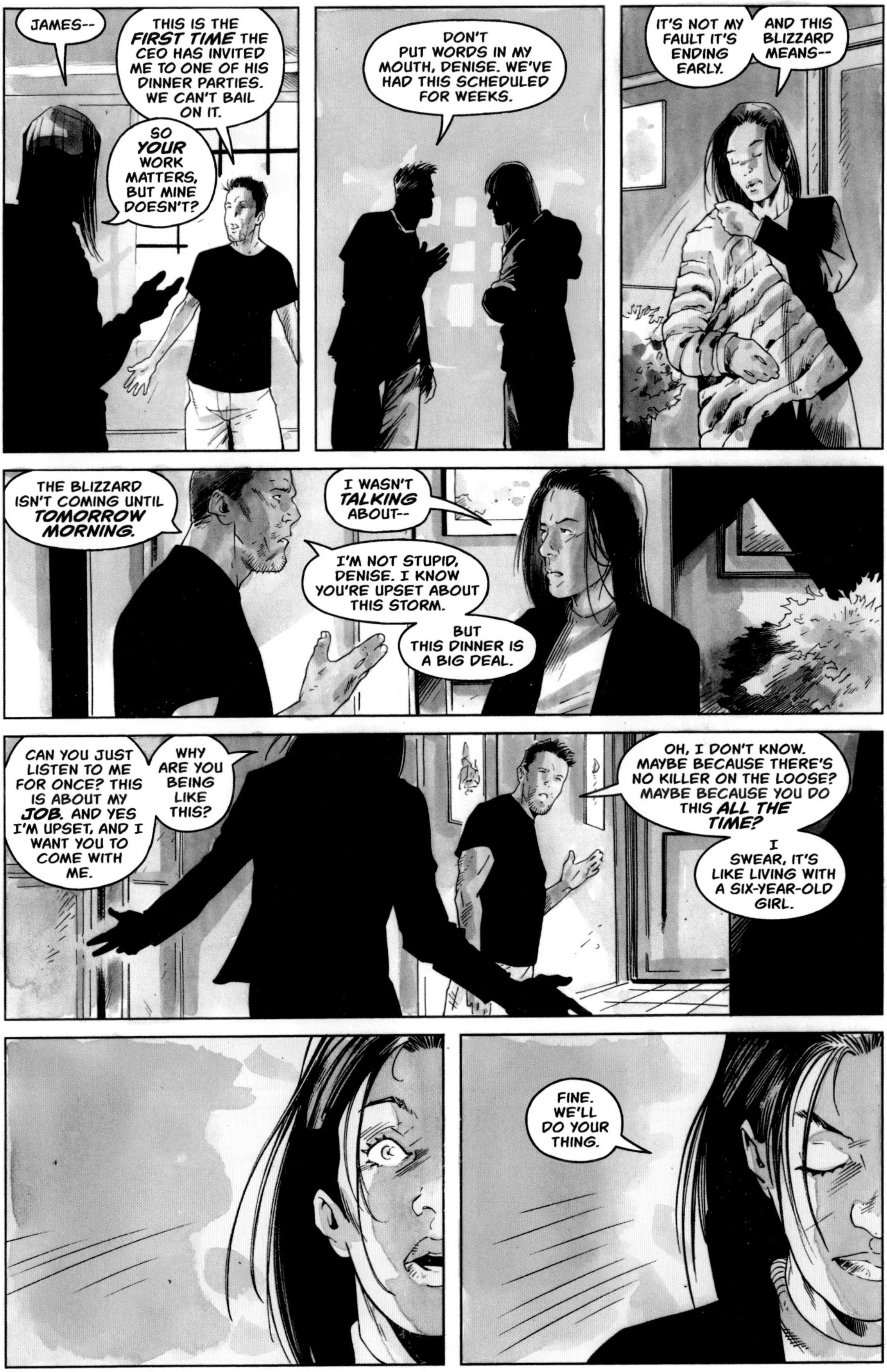
JAMES--
THIS IS THE FIRST TIME THE CEO HAS INVITED ME TO ONE OF HIS DINNER PARTIES. WE CAN'T BAIL ON IT.
SO YOUR WORK MATTERS, BUT MINE DOESN'T?
DON'T PUT WORDS IN MY MOUTH, DENISE. WE'VE HAD THIS SCHEDULED FOR WEEKS.
IT'S NOT MY FAULT IT'S ENDING EARLY.
AND THIS BLIZZARD MEANS--
THE BLIZZARD ISN'T COMING UNTIL TOMORROW MORNING.
I WASN'T TALKING ABOUT--
I'M NOT STUPID, DENISE. I KNOW YOU'RE UPSET ABOUT THIS STORM.
BUT THIS DINNER IS A BIG DEAL.
CAN YOU JUST LISTEN TO ME FOR ONCE? THIS IS ABOUT MY JOB. AND YES I'M UPSET, AND I WANT YOU TO COME WITH ME.
WHY ARE YOU BEING LIKE THIS?
OH, I DON'T KNOW. MAYBE BECAUSE THERE'S NO KILLER ON THE LOOSE? MAYBE BECAUSE YOU DO THIS ALL THE TIME?
I SWEAR, IT'S LIKE LIVING WITH A SIX-YEAR-OLD GIRL.
FINE. WE'LL DO YOUR THING.

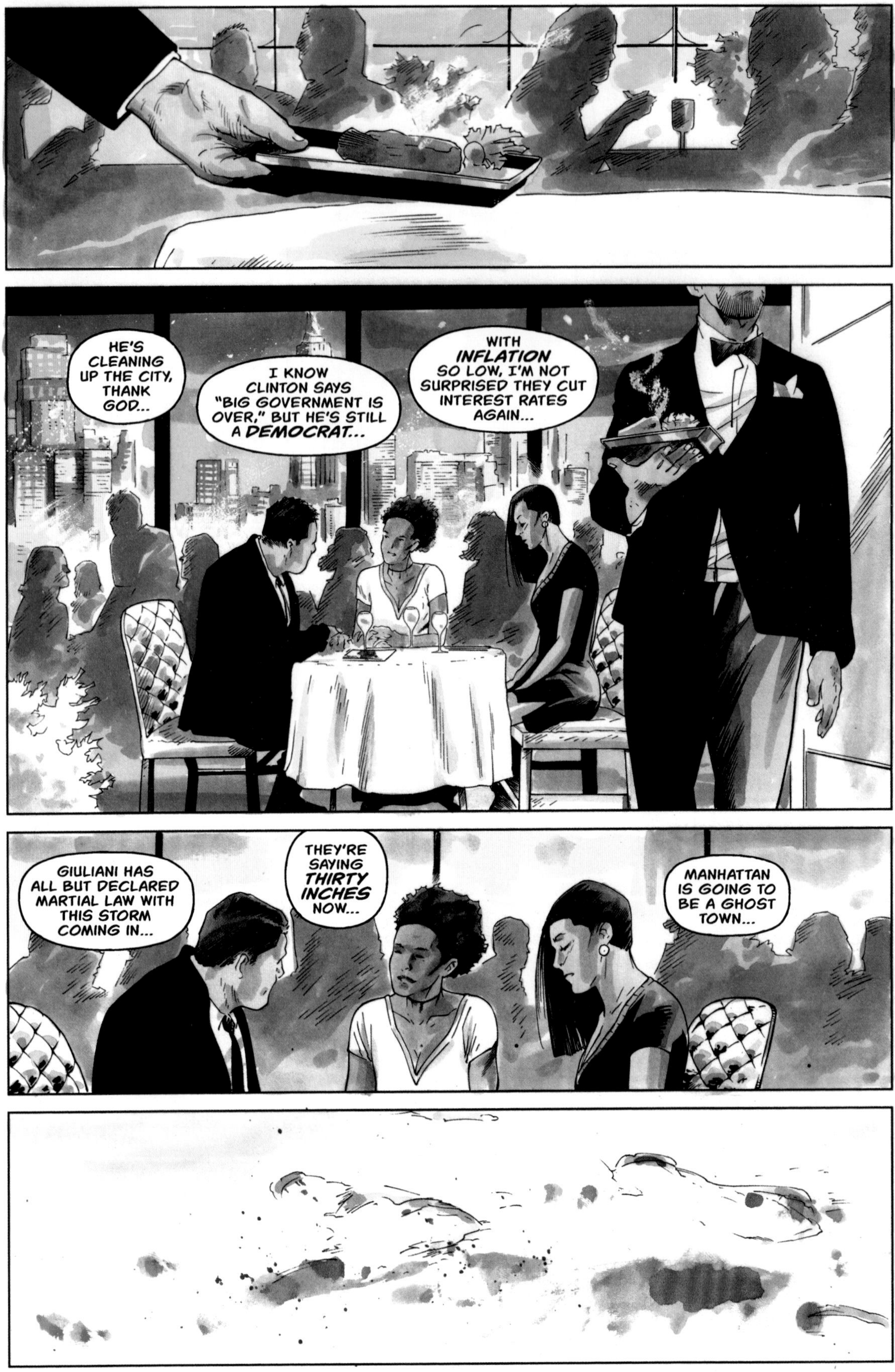
HE'S CLEANING UP THE CITY, THANK GOD...
I KNOW CLINTON SAYS "BIG GOVERNMENT IS OVER," BUT HE'S STILL A DEMOCRAT...
WITH INFLATION SO LOW, I'M NOT SURPRISED THEY CUT INTEREST RATES AGAIN...
GIULIANI HAS ALL BUT DECLARED MARTIAL LAW WITH THIS STORM COMING IN...
THEY'RE SAYING THIRTY INCHES NOW...
MANHATTAN IS GOING TO BE A GHOST TOWN...

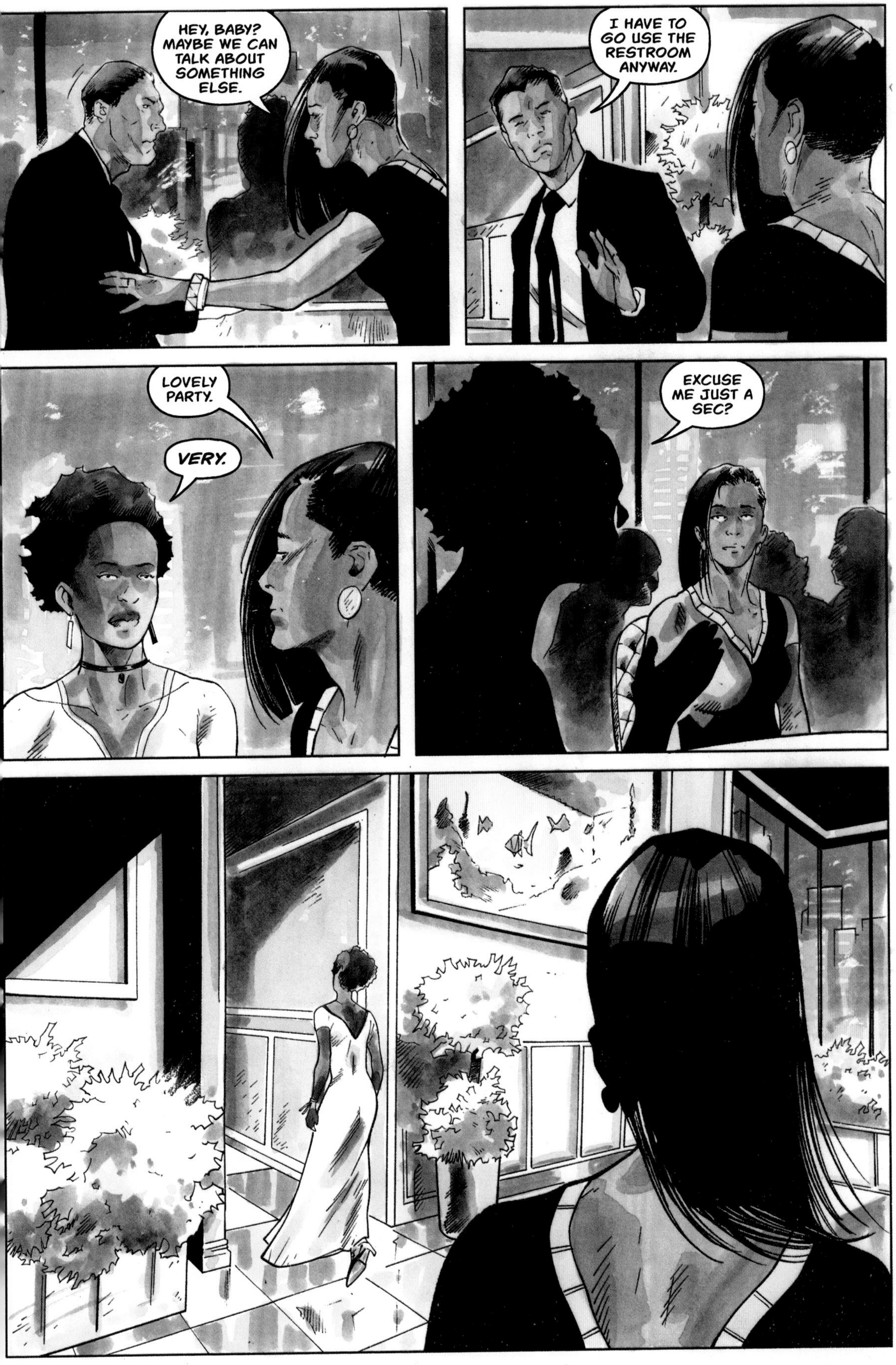
HEY, BABY? MAYBE WE CAN TALK ABOUT SOMETHING ELSE.
I HAVE TO GO USE THE RESTROOM ANYWAY.
LOVELY PARTY.
VERY.
EXCUSE ME JUST A SEC?

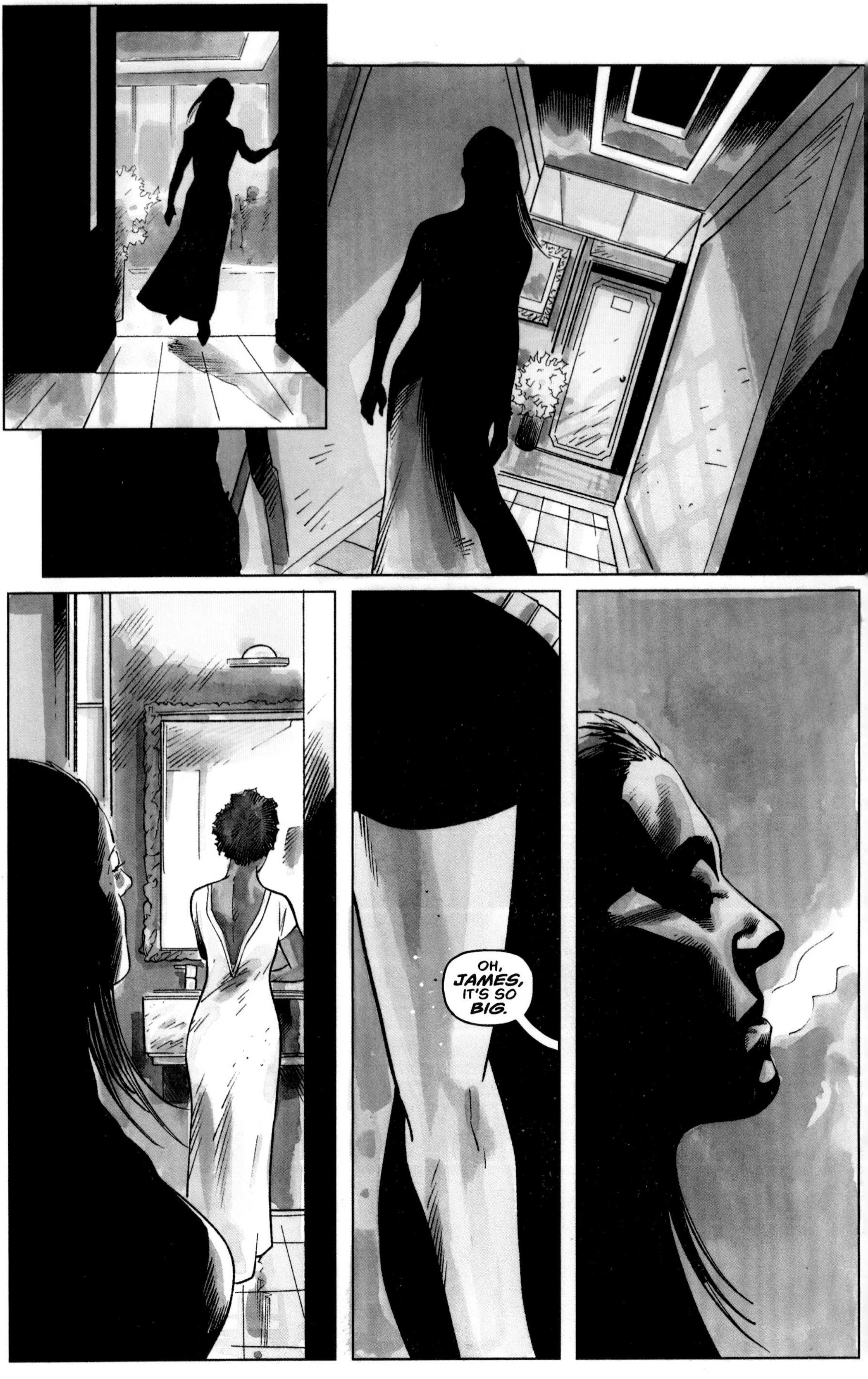
OH, JAMES, IT'S SO BIG.

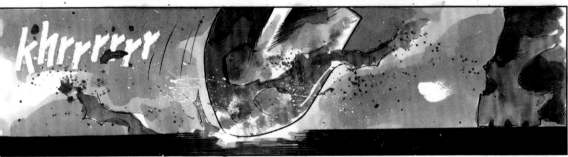

khrrrrrr

WHAT'S HER PROBLEM?

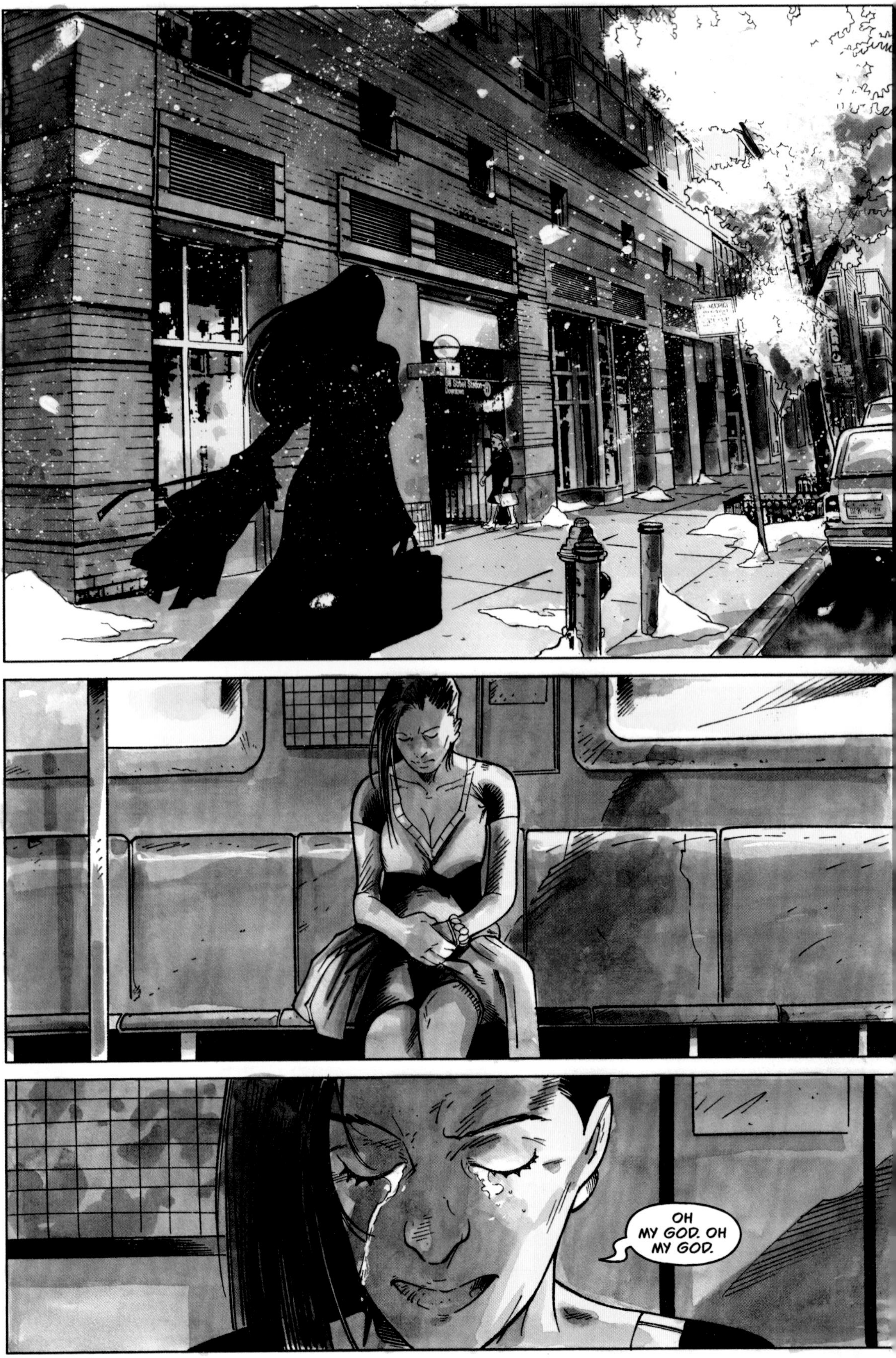
OH MY GOD. OH MY GOD.

DENISE...YOU HAVE TO HELP ME...

YOU...

YOU WERE...

...HE'S ALMOST...

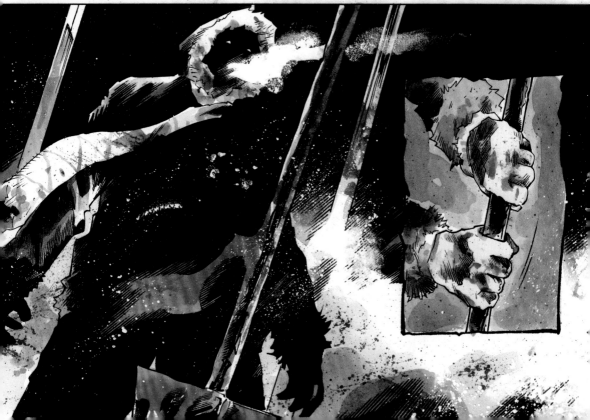

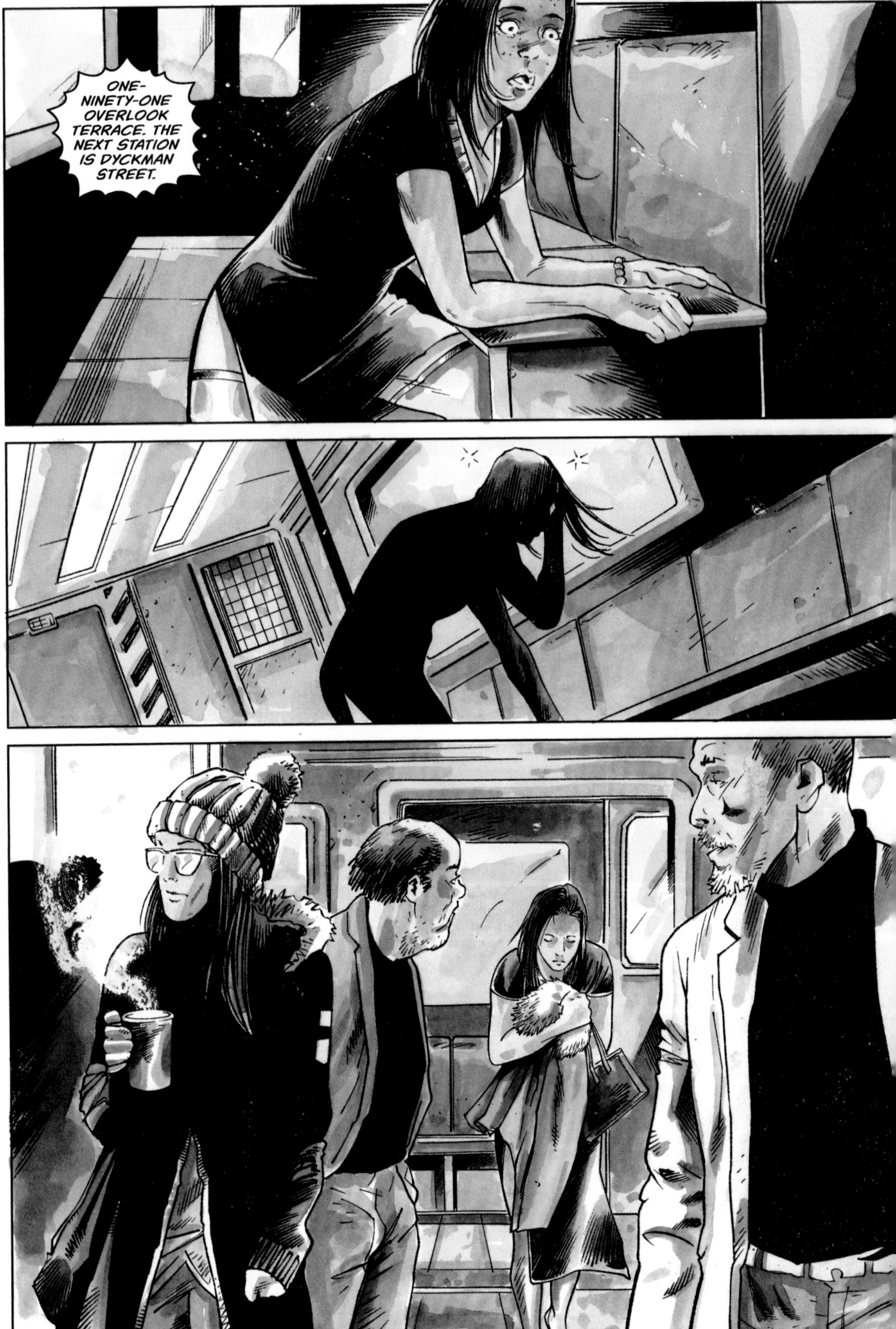
ONE-NINETY-ONE OVERLOOK TERRACE. THE NEXT STATION IS DYCKMAN STREET.

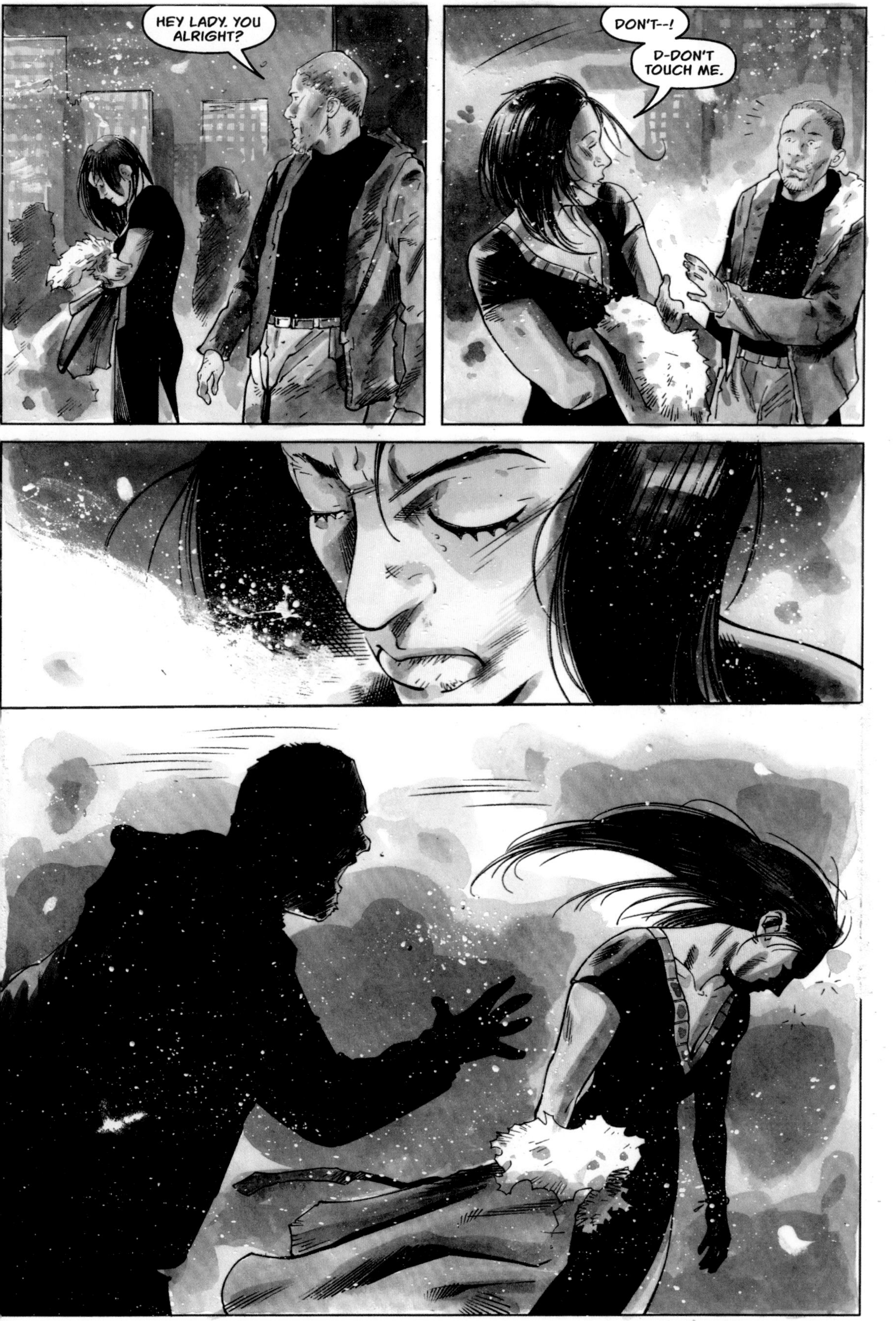
HEY LADY. YOU ALRIGHT?
DON'T--!
D-DON'T TOUCH ME.

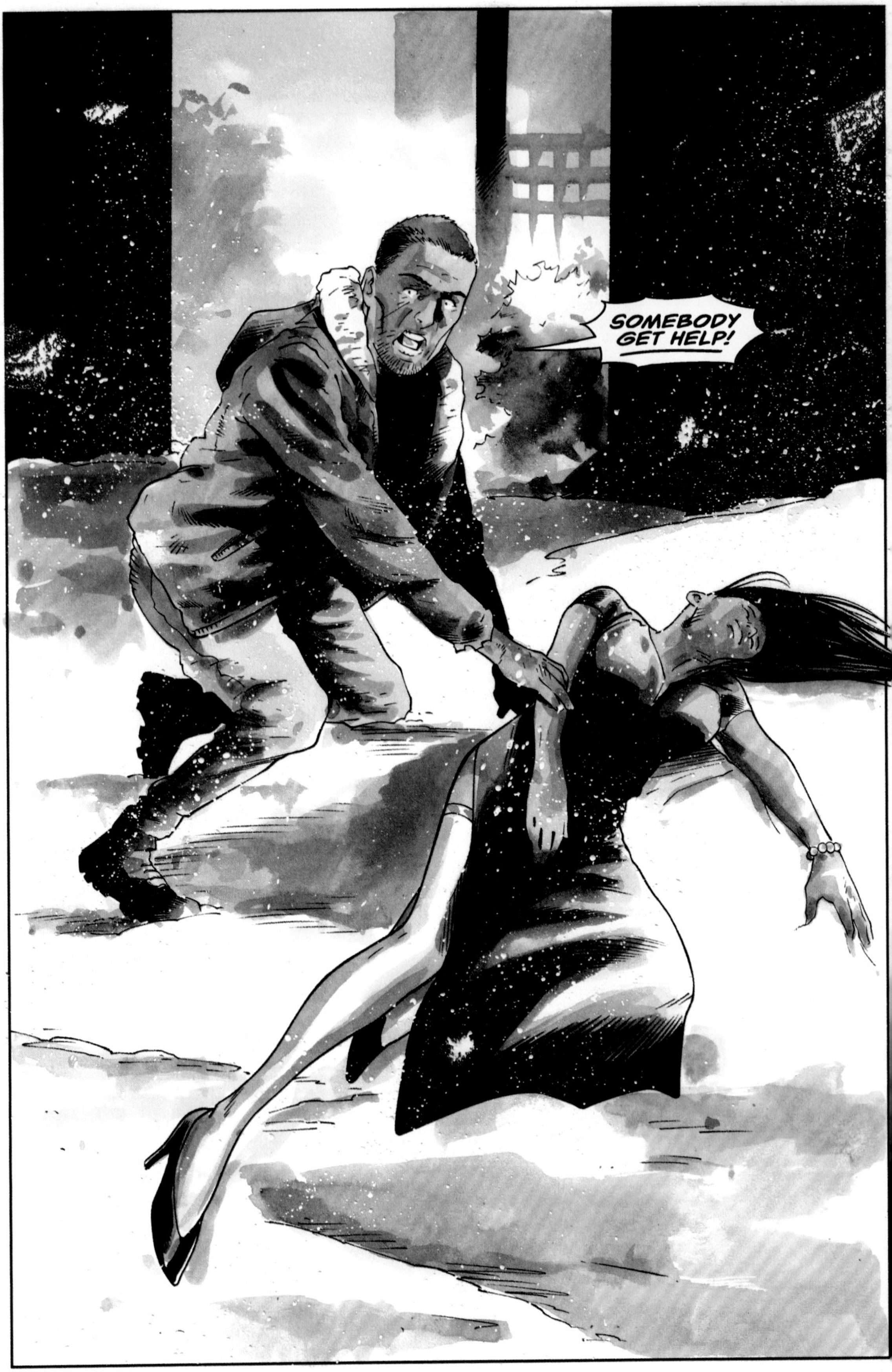
SOMEBODY GET HELP!

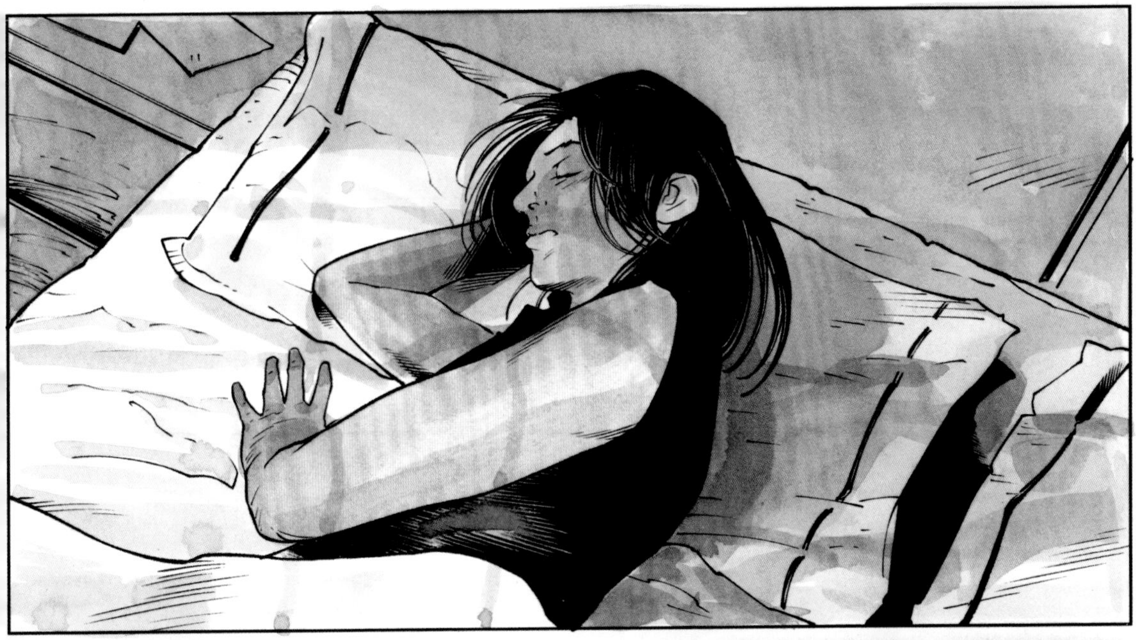

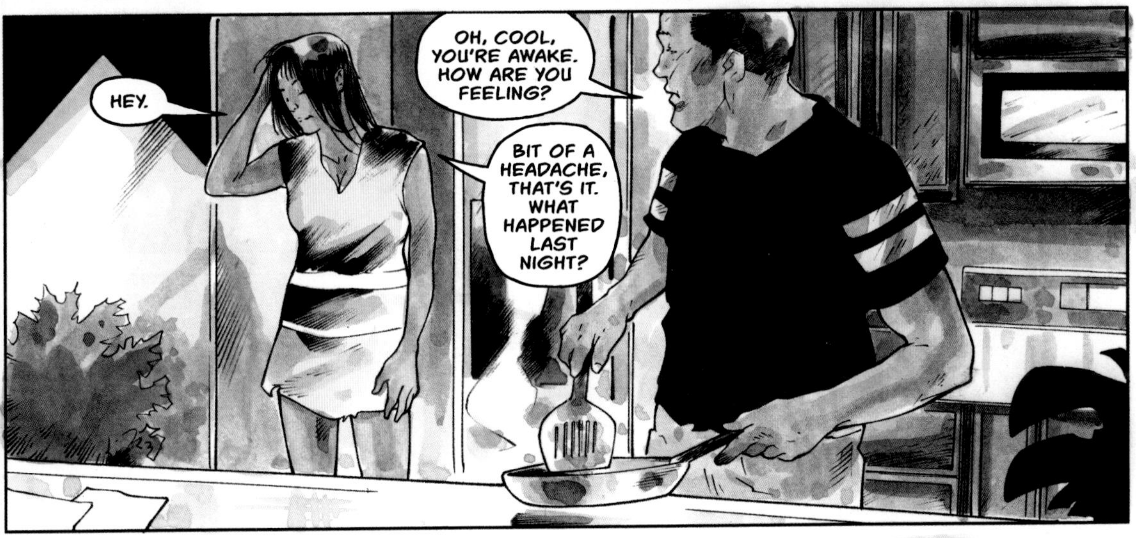
HEY.
OH, COOL, YOU'RE AWAKE. HOW ARE YOU FEELING?
BIT OF A HEADACHE, THAT'S IT. WHAT HAPPENED LAST NIGHT?

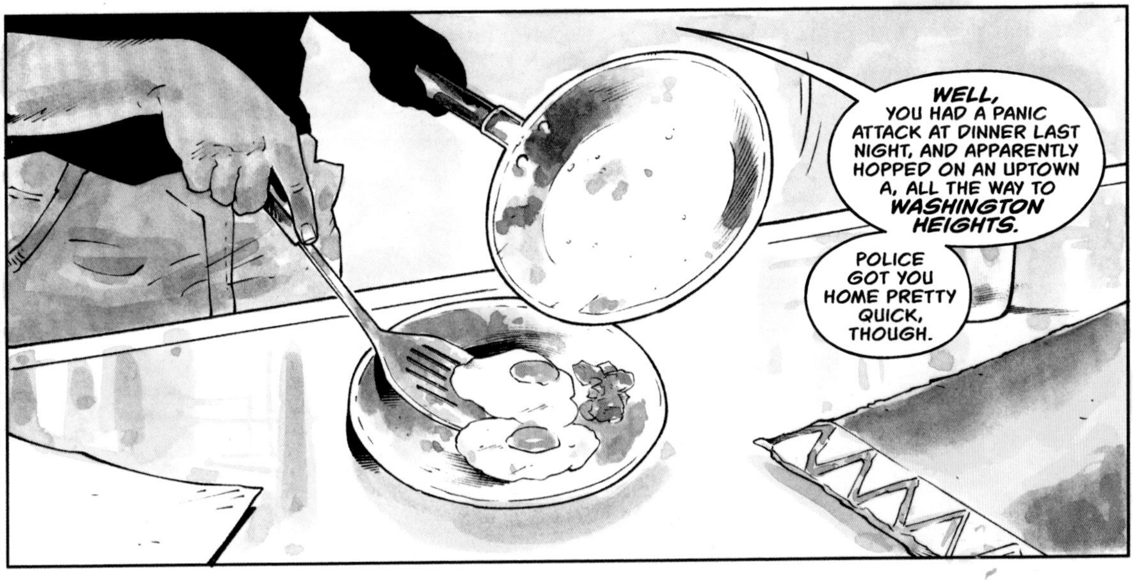
WELL, YOU HAD A PANIC ATTACK AT DINNER LAST NIGHT, AND APPARENTLY HOPPED ON AN UPTOWN A, ALL THE WAY TO WASHINGTON HEIGHTS.
POLICE GOT YOU HOME PRETTY QUICK, THOUGH.

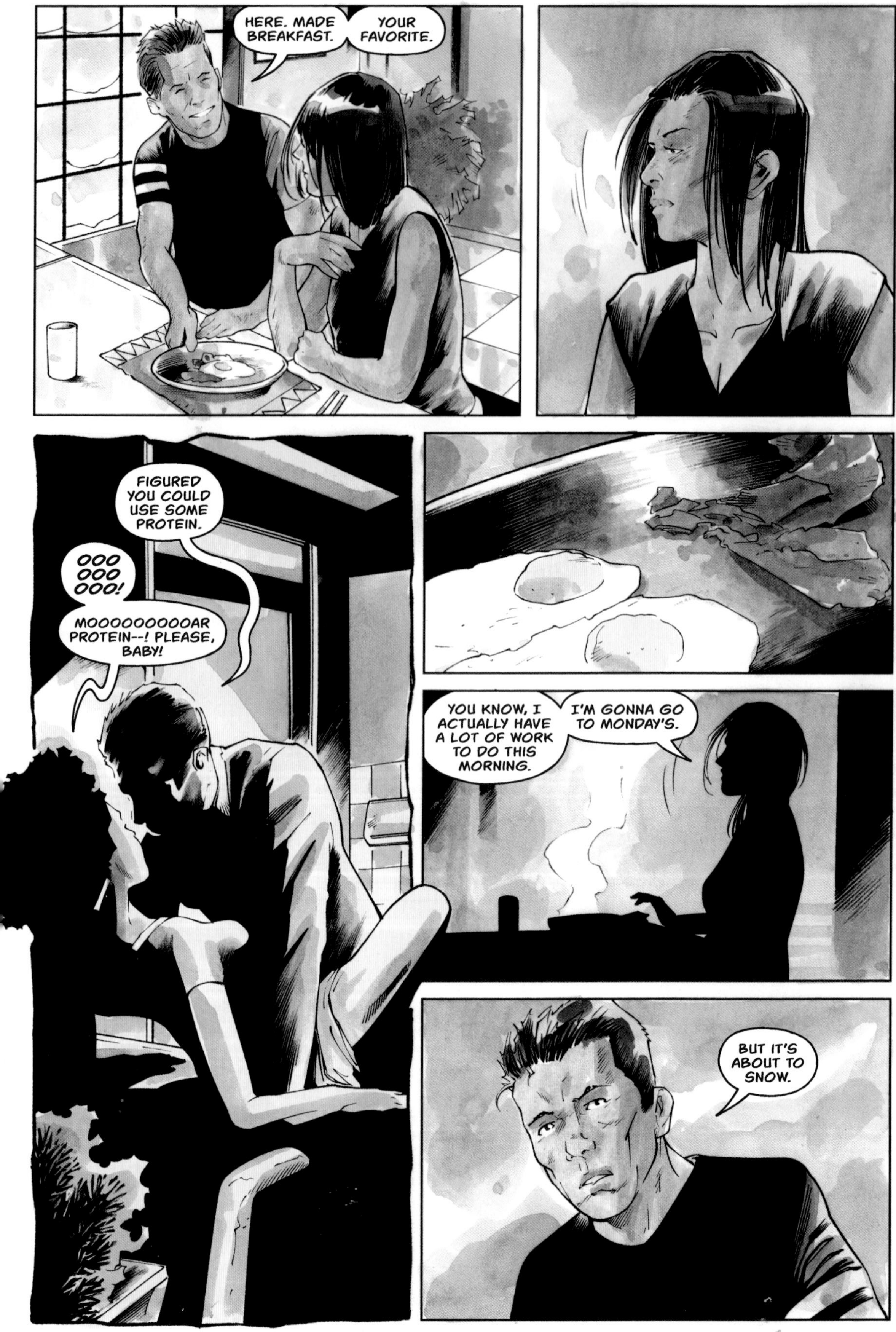
HERE. MADE BREAKFAST.
YOUR FAVORITE.
FIGURED YOU COULD USE SOME PROTEIN.
OOO OOO OOO!
MOOOOOOOOOAR PROTEIN--! PLEASE, BABY!
YOU KNOW, I ACTUALLY HAVE A LOT OF WORK TO DO THIS MORNING.
I'M GONNA GO TO MONDAY'S.
BUT IT'S ABOUT TO SNOW.

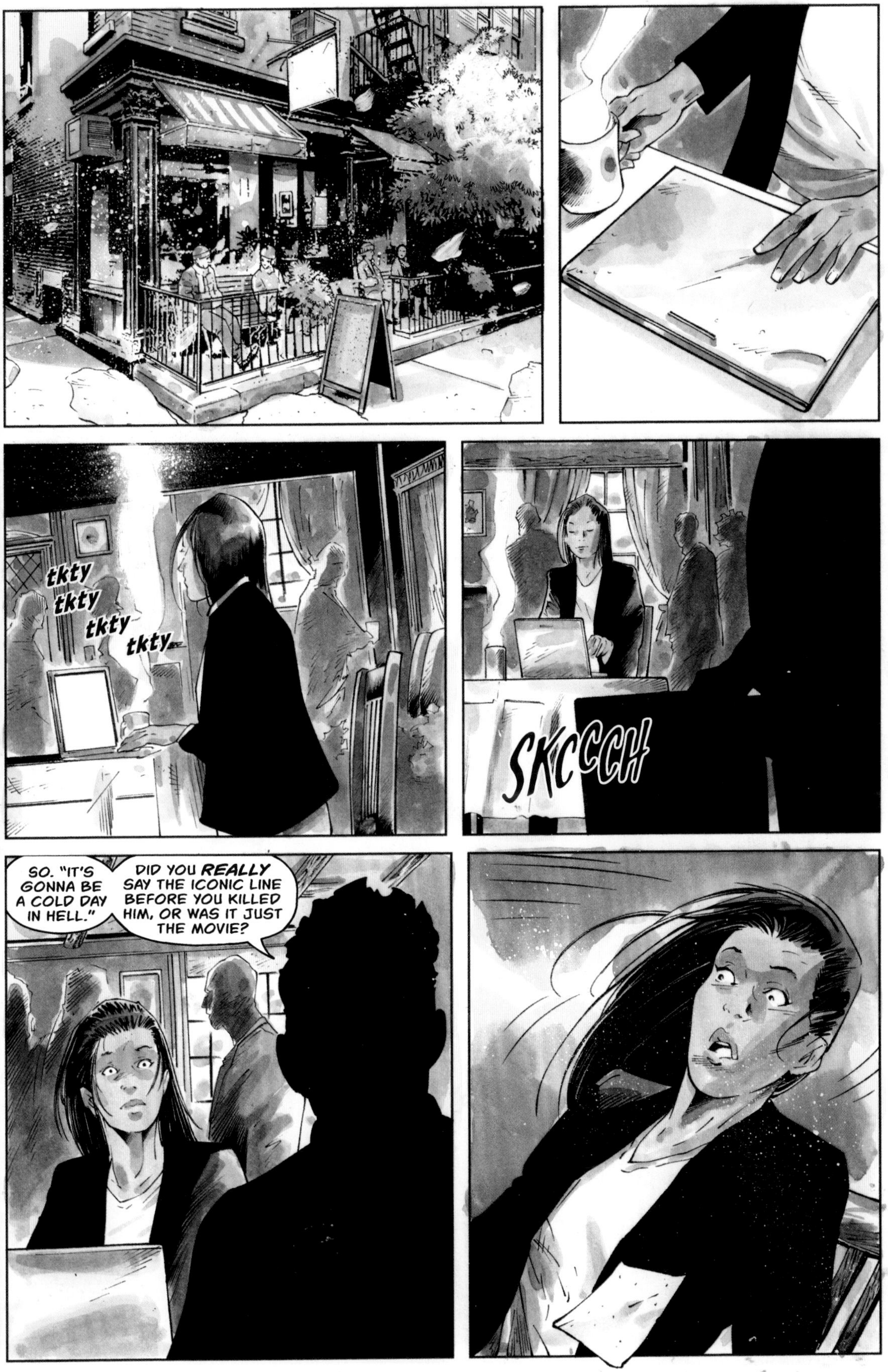
tkty
tkty
tkty
tkty
SKCCCH
SO. "IT'S GONNA BE A COLD DAY IN HELL."
DID YOU **REALLY** SAY THE ICONIC LINE BEFORE YOU KILLED HIM, OR WAS IT JUST THE MOVIE?

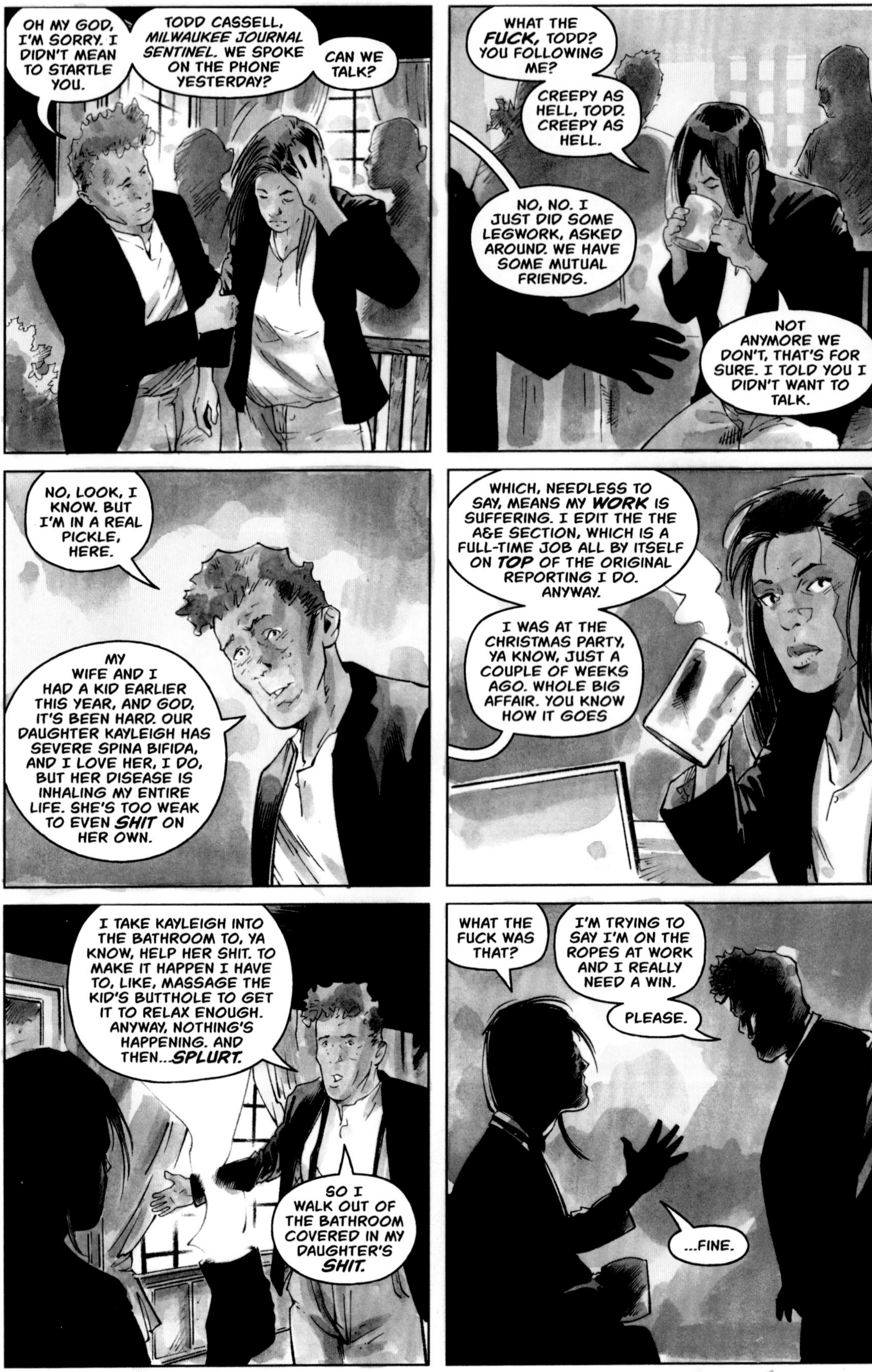
OH MY GOD, I'M SORRY. I DIDN'T MEAN TO STARTLE YOU.
TODD CASSELL, MILWAUKEE JOURNAL SENTINEL. WE SPOKE ON THE PHONE YESTERDAY?
CAN WE TALK?
WHAT THE FUCK, TODD? YOU FOLLOWING ME?
CREEPY AS HELL, TODD. CREEPY AS HELL.
NO, NO. I JUST DID SOME LEGWORK, ASKED AROUND. WE HAVE SOME MUTUAL FRIENDS.
NOT ANYMORE WE DON'T, THAT'S FOR SURE. I TOLD YOU I DIDN'T WANT TO TALK.
NO, LOOK, I KNOW. BUT I'M IN A REAL PICKLE, HERE.
MY WIFE AND I HAD A KID EARLIER THIS YEAR, AND GOD, IT'S BEEN HARD. OUR DAUGHTER KAYLEIGH HAS SEVERE SPINA BIFIDA, AND I LOVE HER, I DO, BUT HER DISEASE IS INHALING MY ENTIRE LIFE. SHE'S TOO WEAK TO EVEN SHIT ON HER OWN.
WHICH, NEEDLESS TO SAY, MEANS MY WORK IS SUFFERING. I EDIT THE THE A&E SECTION, WHICH IS A FULL-TIME JOB ALL BY ITSELF ON TOP OF THE ORIGINAL REPORTING I DO. ANYWAY.
I WAS AT THE CHRISTMAS PARTY, YA KNOW, JUST A COUPLE OF WEEKS AGO. WHOLE BIG AFFAIR. YOU KNOW HOW IT GOES
I TAKE KAYLEIGH INTO THE BATHROOM TO, YA KNOW, HELP HER SHIT. TO MAKE IT HAPPEN I HAVE TO, LIKE, MASSAGE THE KID'S BUTTHOLE TO GET IT TO RELAX ENOUGH. ANYWAY, NOTHING'S HAPPENING. AND THEN...SPLURT.
SO I WALK OUT OF THE BATHROOM COVERED IN MY DAUGHTER'S SHIT.
WHAT THE FUCK WAS THAT?
I'M TRYING TO SAY I'M ON THE ROPES AT WORK AND I REALLY NEED A WIN.
PLEASE.
...FINE.

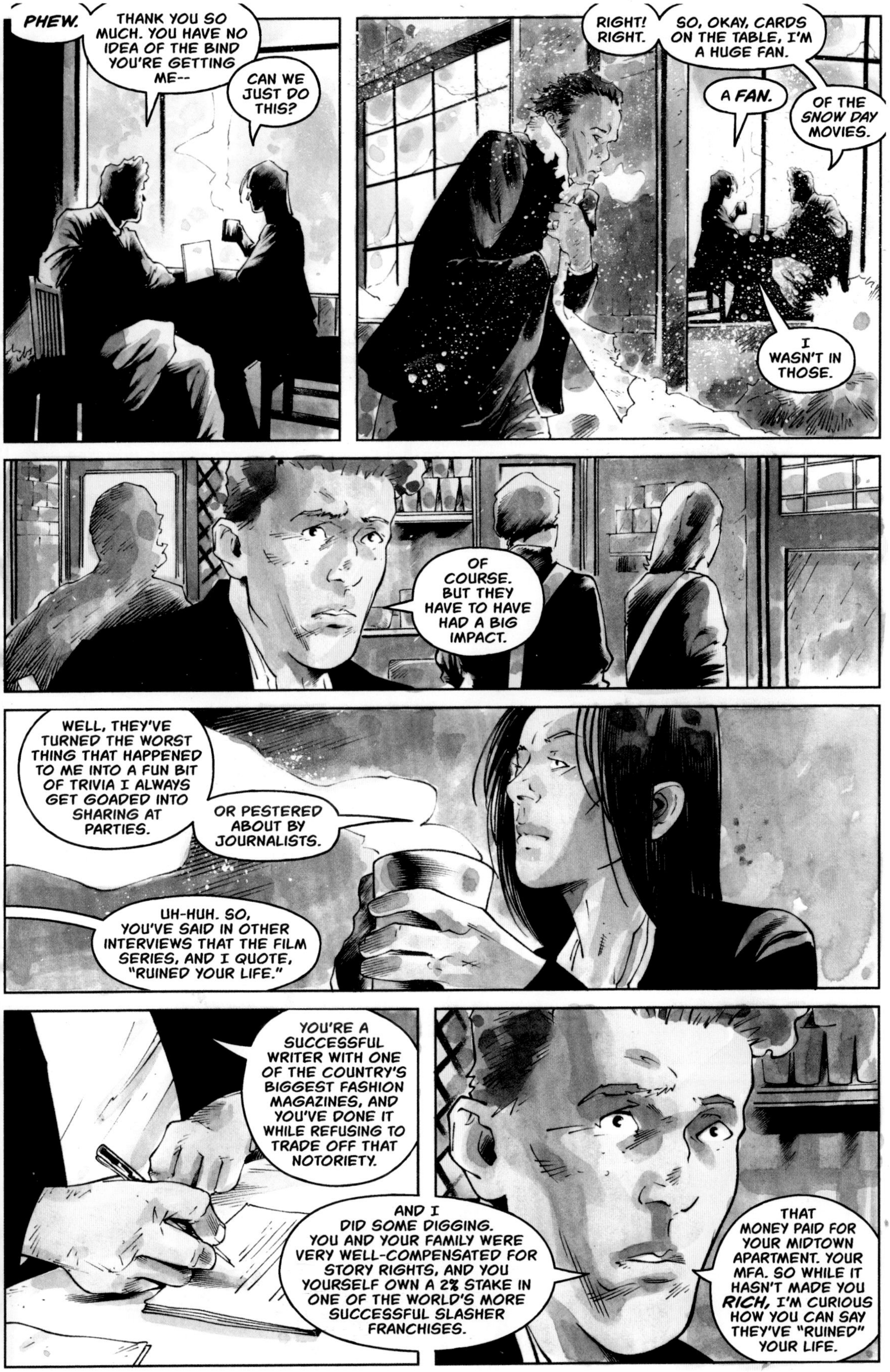

PHEW.
THANK YOU SO MUCH. YOU HAVE NO IDEA OF THE BIND YOU'RE GETTING ME--
CAN WE JUST DO THIS?
RIGHT! RIGHT.
SO, OKAY, CARDS ON THE TABLE, I'M A HUGE FAN.
A FAN.
OF THE SNOW DAY MOVIES.
I WASN'T IN THOSE.
OF COURSE. BUT THEY HAVE TO HAVE HAD A BIG IMPACT.
WELL, THEY'VE TURNED THE WORST THING THAT HAPPENED TO ME INTO A FUN BIT OF TRIVIA I ALWAYS GET GOADED INTO SHARING AT PARTIES.
OR PESTERED ABOUT BY JOURNALISTS.
UH-HUH. SO, YOU'VE SAID IN OTHER INTERVIEWS THAT THE FILM SERIES, AND I QUOTE, "RUINED YOUR LIFE."
YOU'RE A SUCCESSFUL WRITER WITH ONE OF THE COUNTRY'S BIGGEST FASHION MAGAZINES, AND YOU'VE DONE IT WHILE REFUSING TO TRADE OFF THAT NOTORIETY.
AND I DID SOME DIGGING. YOU AND YOUR FAMILY WERE VERY WELL-COMPENSATED FOR STORY RIGHTS, AND YOU YOURSELF OWN A 2% STAKE IN ONE OF THE WORLD'S MORE SUCCESSFUL SLASHER FRANCHISES.
THAT MONEY PAID FOR YOUR MIDTOWN APARTMENT. YOUR MFA. SO WHILE IT HASN'T MADE YOU RICH, I'M CURIOUS HOW YOU CAN SAY THEY'VE "RUINED" YOUR LIFE.

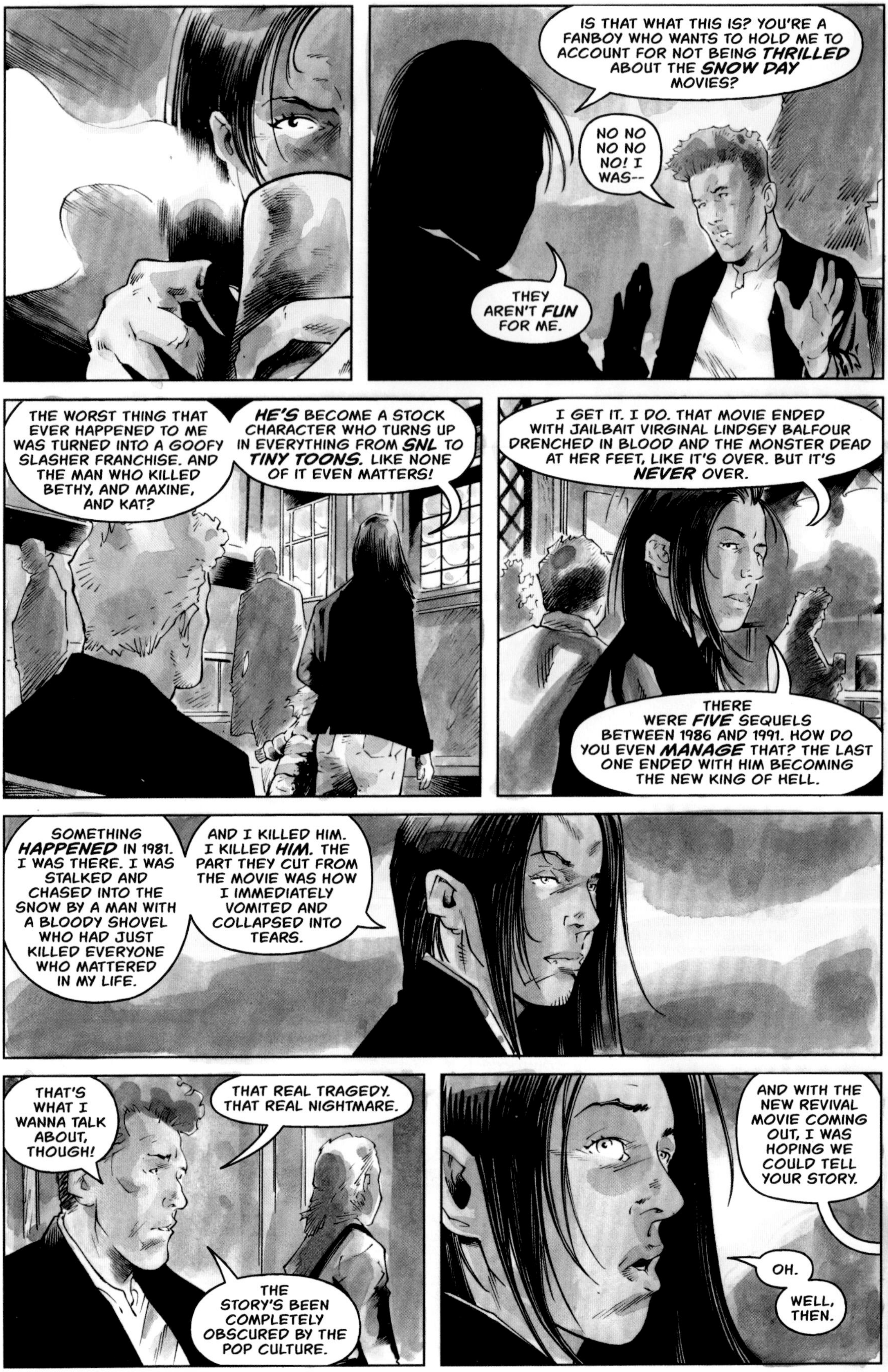
IS THAT WHAT THIS IS? YOU'RE A FANBOY WHO WANTS TO HOLD ME TO ACCOUNT FOR NOT BEING THRILLED ABOUT THE SNOW DAY MOVIES?
NO NO NO NO NO! I WAS--
THEY AREN'T FUN FOR ME.
THE WORST THING THAT EVER HAPPENED TO ME WAS TURNED INTO A GOOFY SLASHER FRANCHISE. AND THE MAN WHO KILLED BETHY, AND MAXINE, AND KAT?
HE'S BECOME A STOCK CHARACTER WHO TURNS UP IN EVERYTHING FROM SNL TO TINY TOONS. LIKE NONE OF IT EVEN MATTERS!
I GET IT. I DO. THAT MOVIE ENDED WITH JAILBAIT VIRGINAL LINDSEY BALFOUR DRENCHED IN BLOOD AND THE MONSTER DEAD AT HER FEET, LIKE IT'S OVER. BUT IT'S NEVER OVER.
THERE WERE FIVE SEQUELS BETWEEN 1986 AND 1991. HOW DO YOU EVEN MANAGE THAT? THE LAST ONE ENDED WITH HIM BECOMING THE NEW KING OF HELL.
SOMETHING HAPPENED IN 1981. I WAS THERE. I WAS STALKED AND CHASED INTO THE SNOW BY A MAN WITH A BLOODY SHOVEL WHO HAD JUST KILLED EVERYONE WHO MATTERED IN MY LIFE.
AND I KILLED HIM. I KILLED HIM. THE PART THEY CUT FROM THE MOVIE WAS HOW I IMMEDIATELY VOMITED AND COLLAPSED INTO TEARS.
THAT'S WHAT I WANNA TALK ABOUT, THOUGH!
THAT REAL TRAGEDY. THAT REAL NIGHTMARE.
THE STORY'S BEEN COMPLETELY OBSCURED BY THE POP CULTURE.
AND WITH THE NEW REVIVAL MOVIE COMING OUT, I WAS HOPING WE COULD TELL YOUR STORY.
OH.
WELL, THEN.

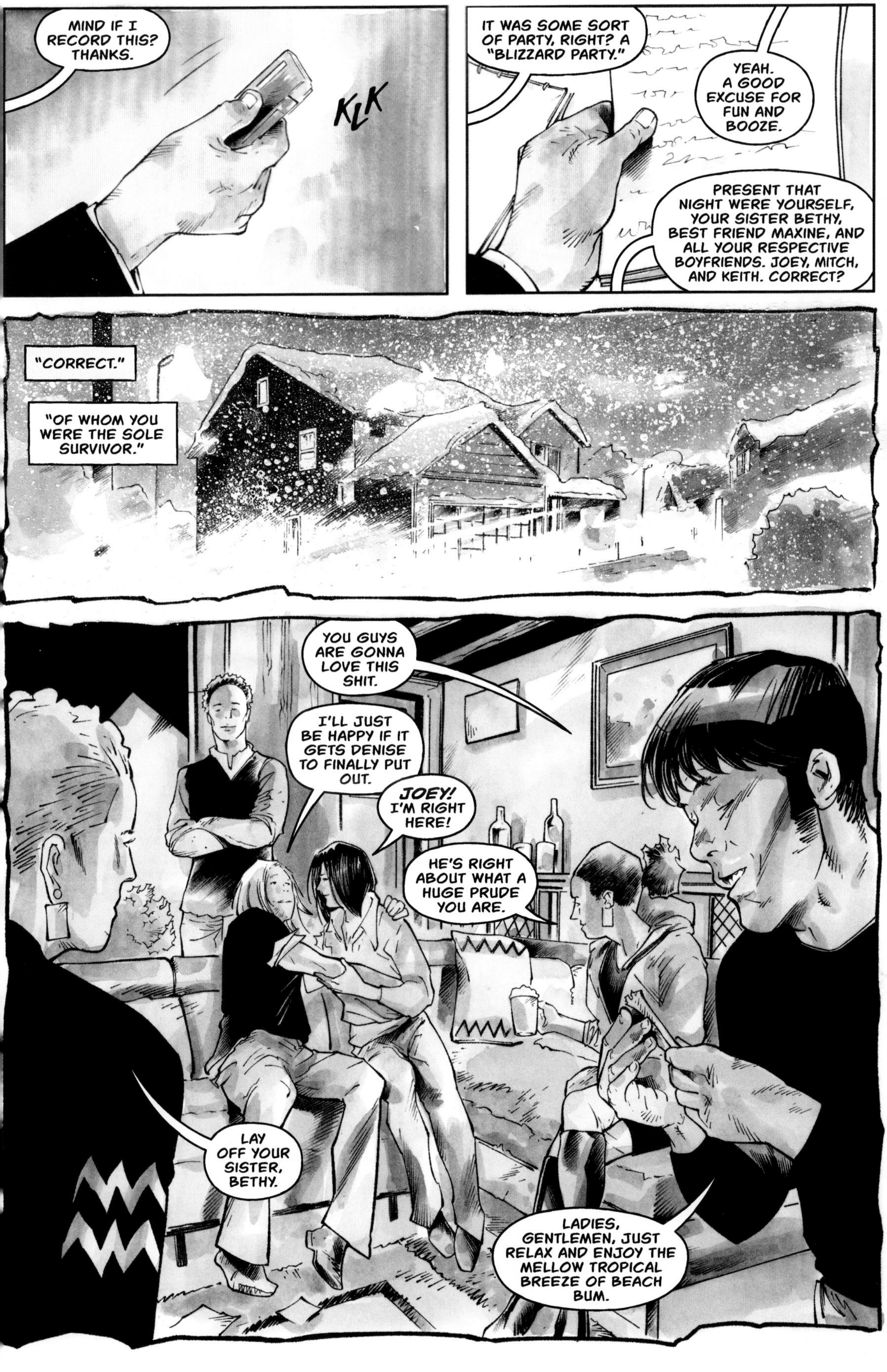
MIND IF I RECORD THIS? THANKS.
KLK
IT WAS SOME SORT OF PARTY, RIGHT? A "BLIZZARD PARTY."
YEAH. A GOOD EXCUSE FOR FUN AND BOOZE.
PRESENT THAT NIGHT WERE YOURSELF, YOUR SISTER BETHY, BEST FRIEND MAXINE, AND ALL YOUR RESPECTIVE BOYFRIENDS. JOEY, MITCH, AND KEITH. CORRECT?
"CORRECT."
"OF WHOM YOU WERE THE SOLE SURVIVOR."
YOU GUYS ARE GONNA LOVE THIS SHIT.
I'LL JUST BE HAPPY IF IT GETS DENISE TO FINALLY PUT OUT.
JOEY! I'M RIGHT HERE!
HE'S RIGHT ABOUT WHAT A HUGE PRUDE YOU ARE.
LAY OFF YOUR SISTER, BETHY.
LADIES, GENTLEMEN, JUST RELAX AND ENJOY THE MELLOW TROPICAL BREEZE OF BEACH BUM.

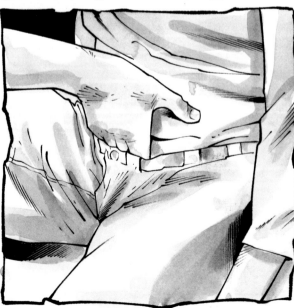

WHAT? WHAT *THIS* TIME?

JUST DON'T *WANNA.*

BUT I'M DOING ALL THE *WORK!*

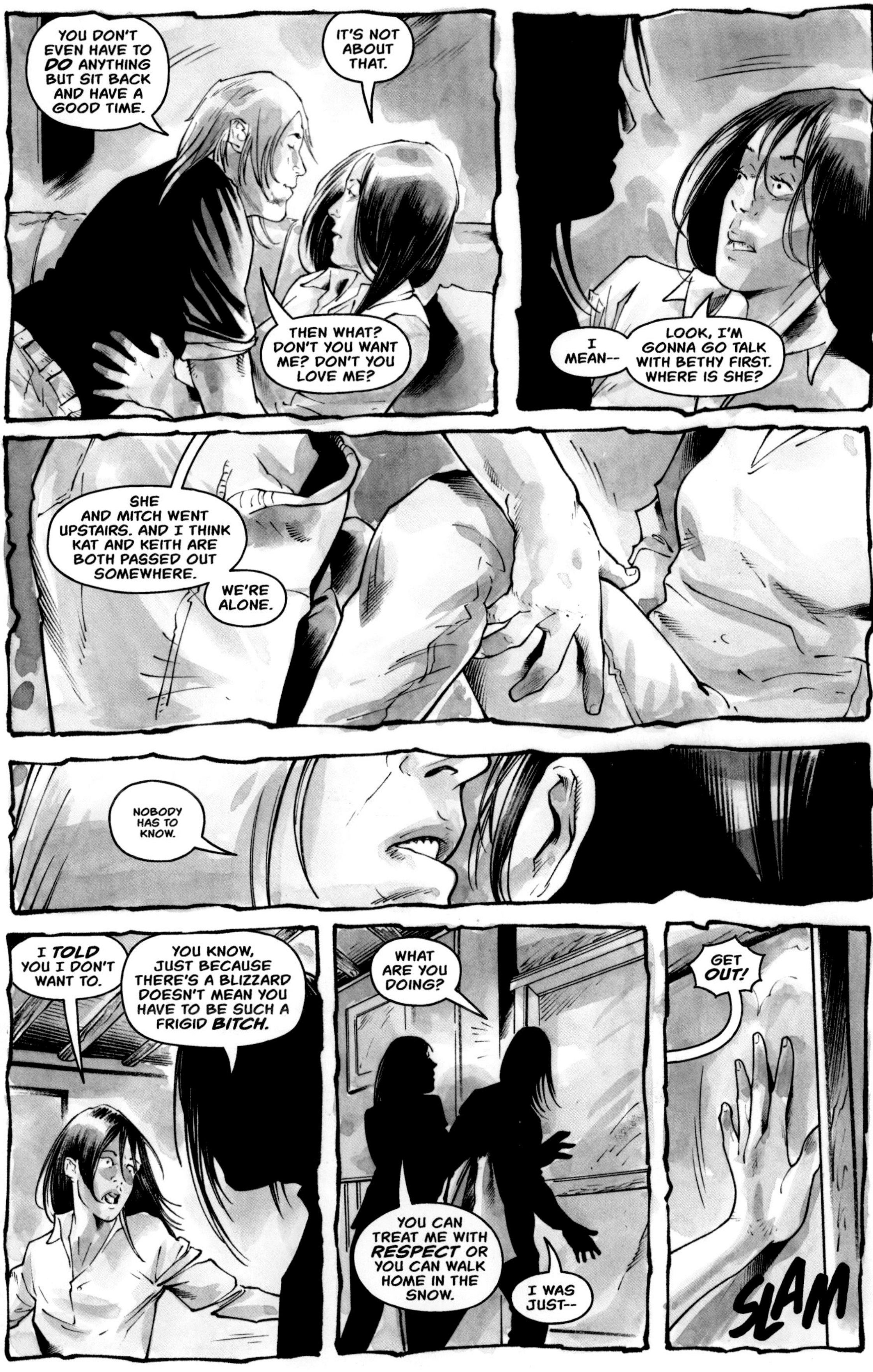
YOU DON'T EVEN HAVE TO **DO** ANYTHING BUT SIT BACK AND HAVE A GOOD TIME.
IT'S NOT ABOUT THAT.
THEN WHAT? DON'T YOU WANT ME? DON'T YOU LOVE ME?
I MEAN--
LOOK, I'M GONNA GO TALK WITH BETHY FIRST. WHERE IS SHE?
SHE AND MITCH WENT UPSTAIRS. AND I THINK KAT AND KEITH ARE BOTH PASSED OUT SOMEWHERE.
WE'RE ALONE.
NOBODY HAS TO KNOW.
I **TOLD** YOU I DON'T WANT TO.
YOU KNOW, JUST BECAUSE THERE'S A BLIZZARD DOESN'T MEAN YOU HAVE TO BE SUCH A FRIGID **BITCH.**
WHAT ARE YOU DOING?
YOU CAN TREAT ME WITH **RESPECT** OR YOU CAN WALK HOME IN THE SNOW.
I WAS JUST--
GET **OUT!**
SLAM

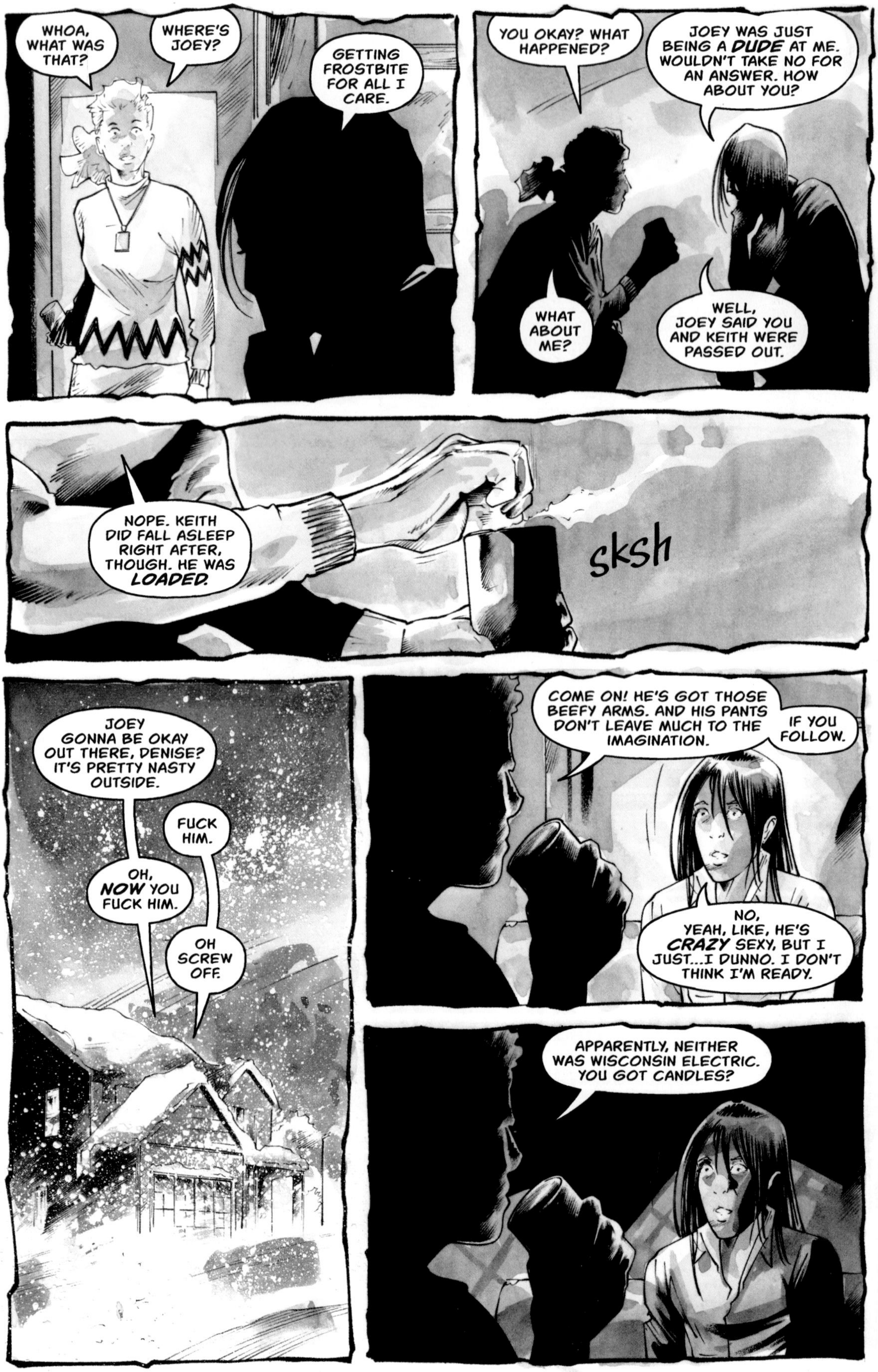
WHOA, WHAT WAS THAT?
WHERE'S JOEY?
GETTING FROSTBITE FOR ALL I CARE.
YOU OKAY? WHAT HAPPENED?
JOEY WAS JUST BEING A DUDE AT ME. WOULDN'T TAKE NO FOR AN ANSWER. HOW ABOUT YOU?
WHAT ABOUT ME?
WELL, JOEY SAID YOU AND KEITH WERE PASSED OUT.
NOPE. KEITH DID FALL ASLEEP RIGHT AFTER, THOUGH. HE WAS LOADED.
sksh
JOEY GONNA BE OKAY OUT THERE, DENISE? IT'S PRETTY NASTY OUTSIDE.
FUCK HIM.
OH, NOW YOU FUCK HIM.
OH SCREW OFF.
COME ON! HE'S GOT THOSE BEEFY ARMS. AND HIS PANTS DON'T LEAVE MUCH TO THE IMAGINATION.
IF YOU FOLLOW.
NO, YEAH, LIKE, HE'S CRAZY SEXY, BUT I JUST...I DUNNO. I DON'T THINK I'M READY.
APPARENTLY, NEITHER WAS WISCONSIN ELECTRIC. YOU GOT CANDLES?

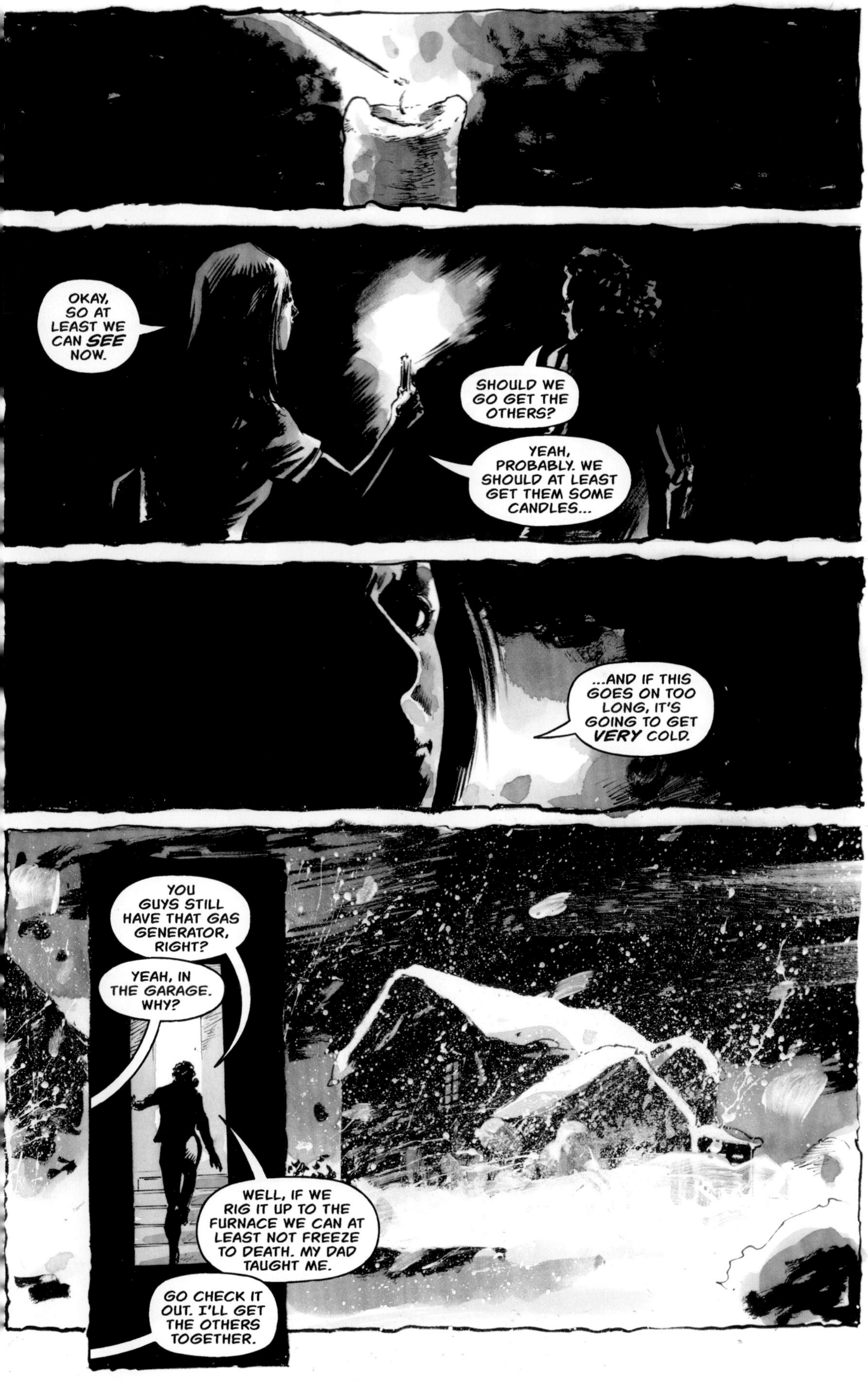
OKAY, SO AT LEAST WE CAN SEE NOW.
SHOULD WE GO GET THE OTHERS?
YEAH, PROBABLY. WE SHOULD AT LEAST GET THEM SOME CANDLES...
...AND IF THIS GOES ON TOO LONG, IT'S GOING TO GET VERY COLD.
YOU GUYS STILL HAVE THAT GAS GENERATOR, RIGHT?
YEAH, IN THE GARAGE. WHY?
WELL, IF WE RIG IT UP TO THE FURNACE WE CAN AT LEAST NOT FREEZE TO DEATH. MY DAD TAUGHT ME.
GO CHECK IT OUT. I'LL GET THE OTHERS TOGETHER.

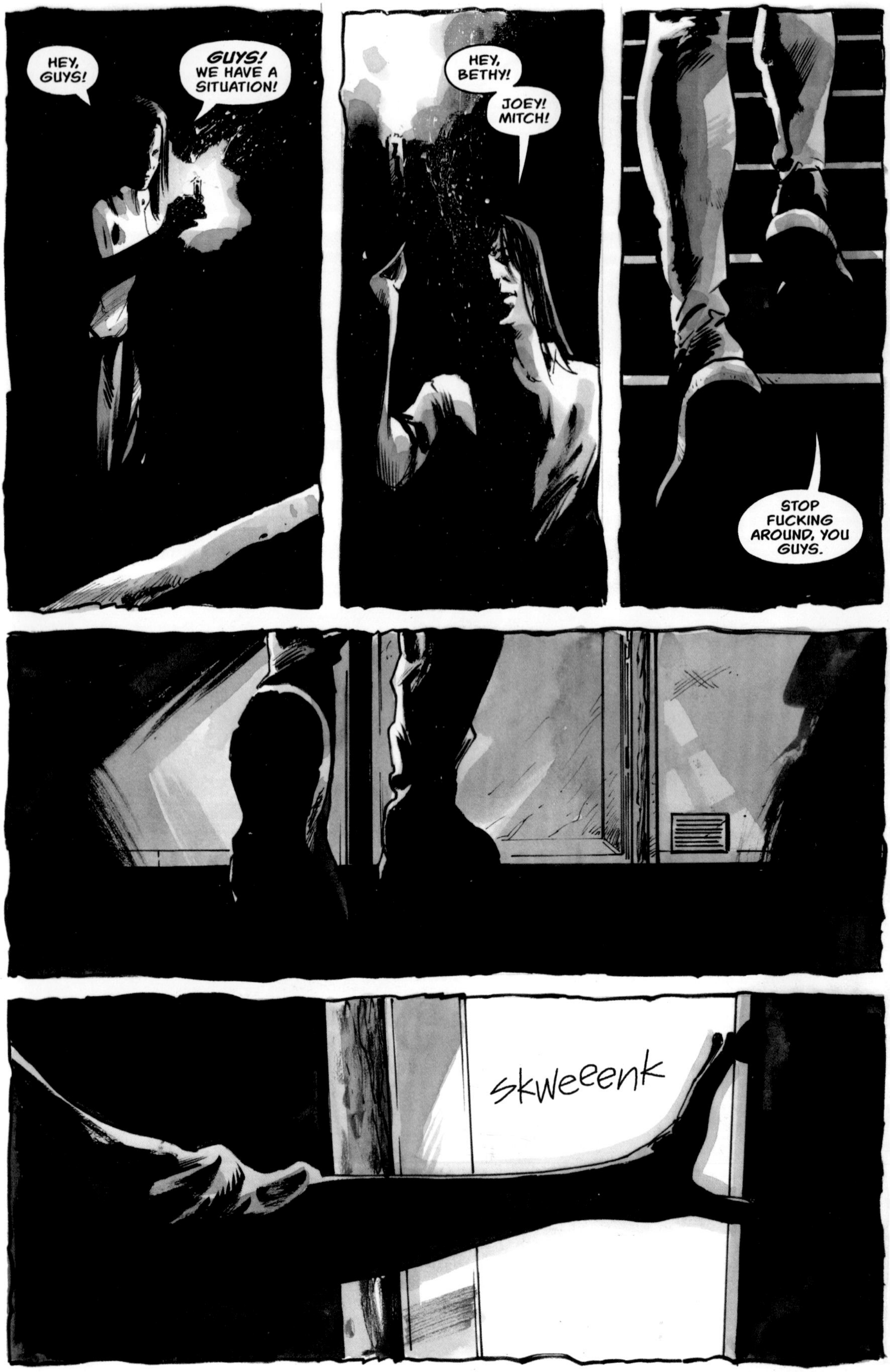
HEY, GUYS!
GUYS! WE HAVE A SITUATION!
HEY, BETHY!
JOEY! MITCH!
STOP FUCKING AROUND, YOU GUYS.
skweeenk

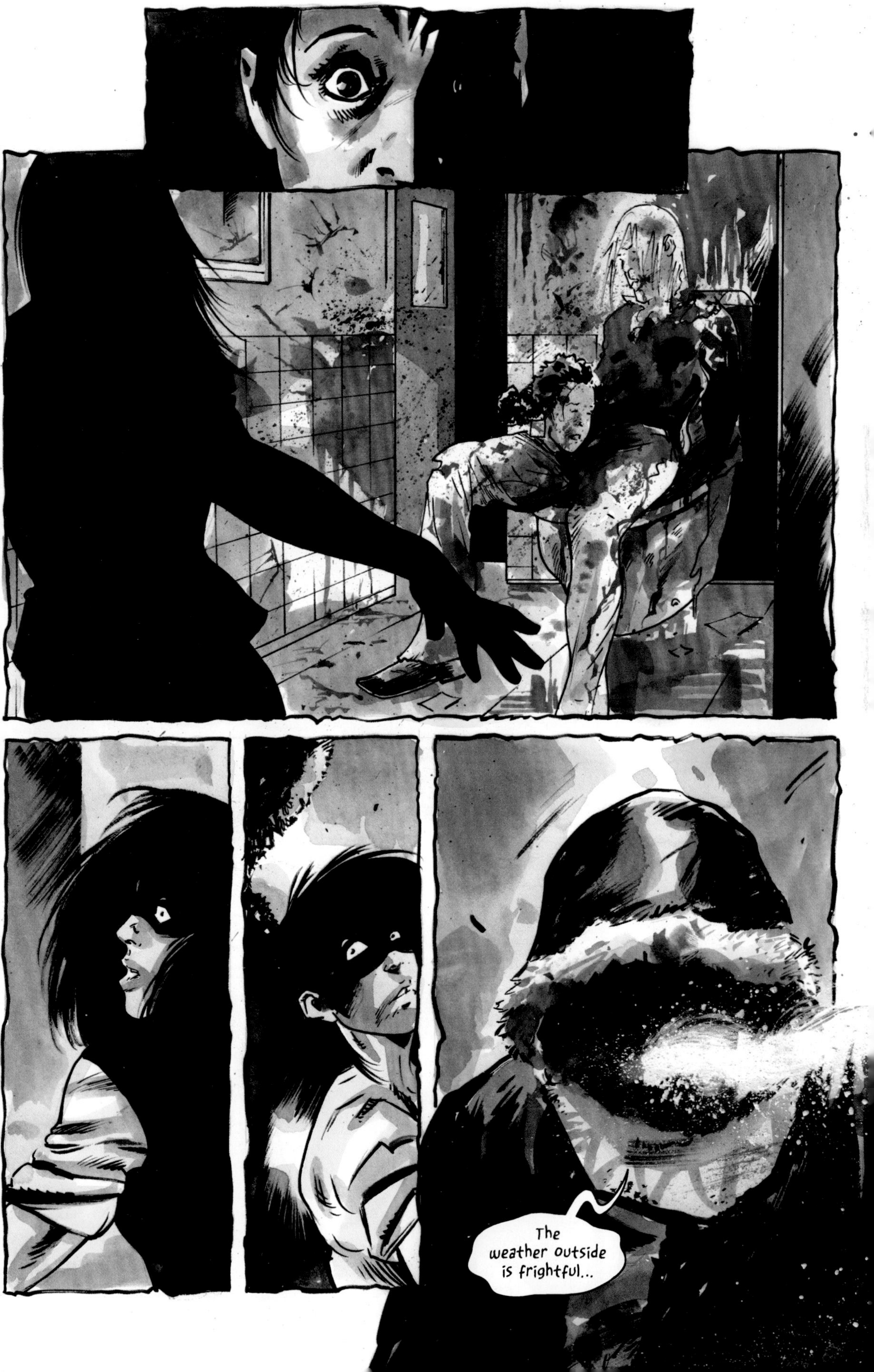
The weather outside is frightful...

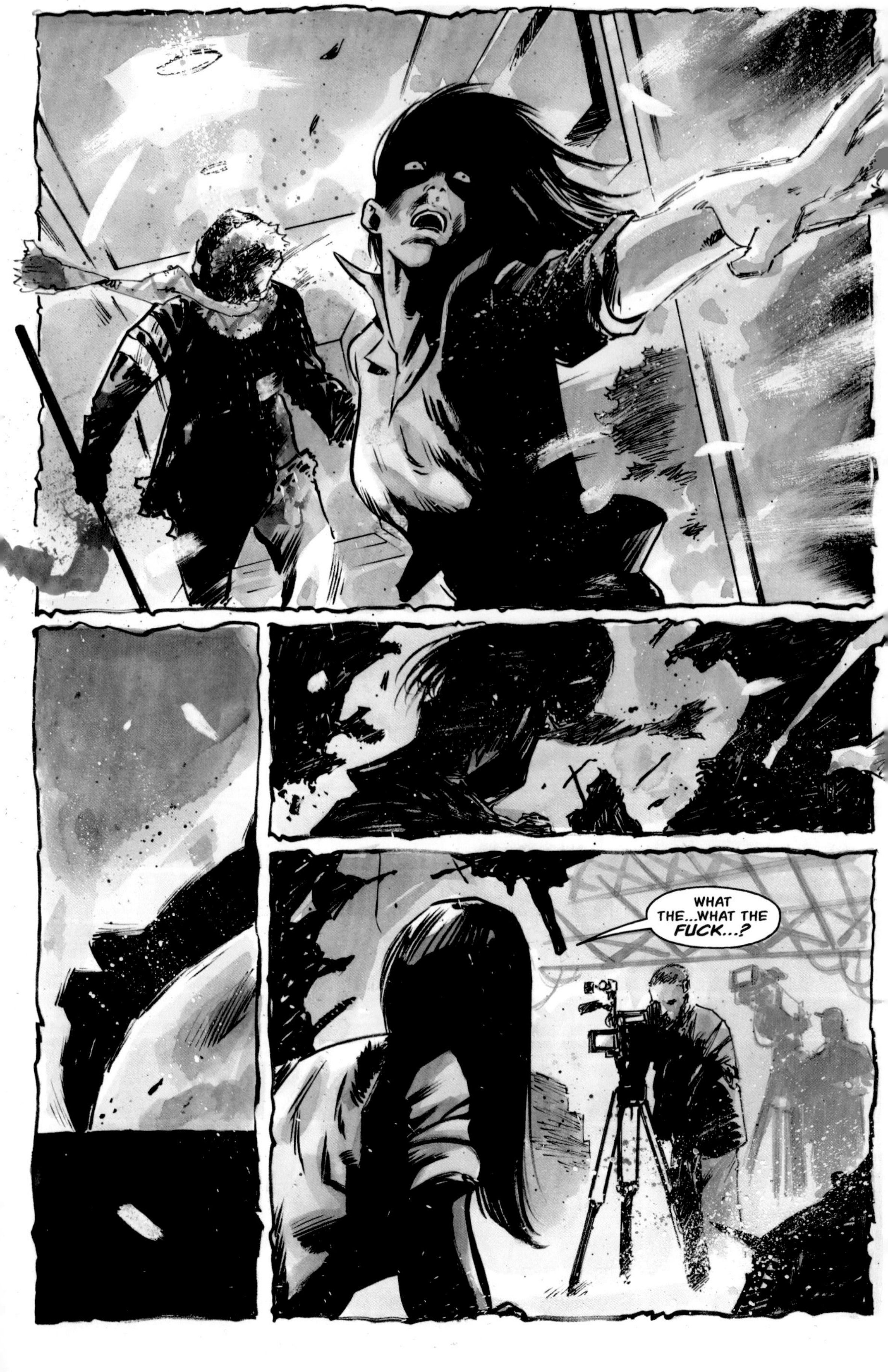
WHAT THE...WHAT THE FUCK...?

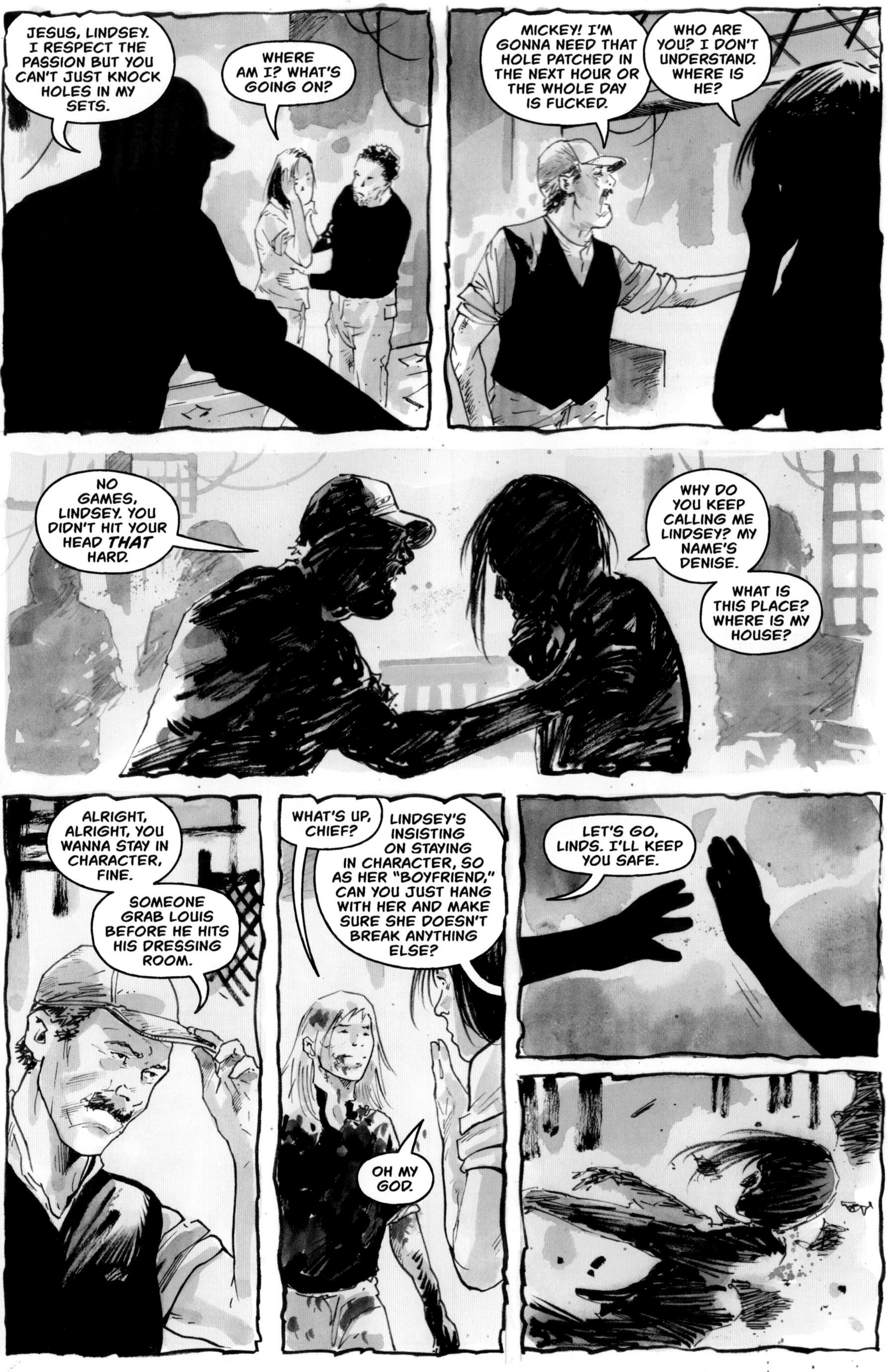
JESUS, LINDSEY. I RESPECT THE PASSION BUT YOU CAN'T JUST KNOCK HOLES IN MY SETS.
WHERE AM I? WHAT'S GOING ON?
MICKEY! I'M GONNA NEED THAT HOLE PATCHED IN THE NEXT HOUR OR THE WHOLE DAY IS FUCKED.
WHO ARE YOU? I DON'T UNDERSTAND. WHERE IS HE?
NO GAMES, LINDSEY. YOU DIDN'T HIT YOUR HEAD *THAT* HARD.
WHY DO YOU KEEP CALLING ME LINDSEY? MY NAME'S DENISE.
WHAT IS THIS PLACE? WHERE IS MY HOUSE?
ALRIGHT, ALRIGHT, YOU WANNA STAY IN CHARACTER, FINE.
SOMEONE GRAB LOUIS BEFORE HE HITS HIS DRESSING ROOM.
WHAT'S UP, CHIEF?
LINDSEY'S INSISTING ON STAYING IN CHARACTER, SO AS HER "BOYFRIEND," CAN YOU JUST HANG WITH HER AND MAKE SURE SHE DOESN'T BREAK ANYTHING ELSE?
OH MY GOD.
LET'S GO, LINDS. I'LL KEEP YOU SAFE.

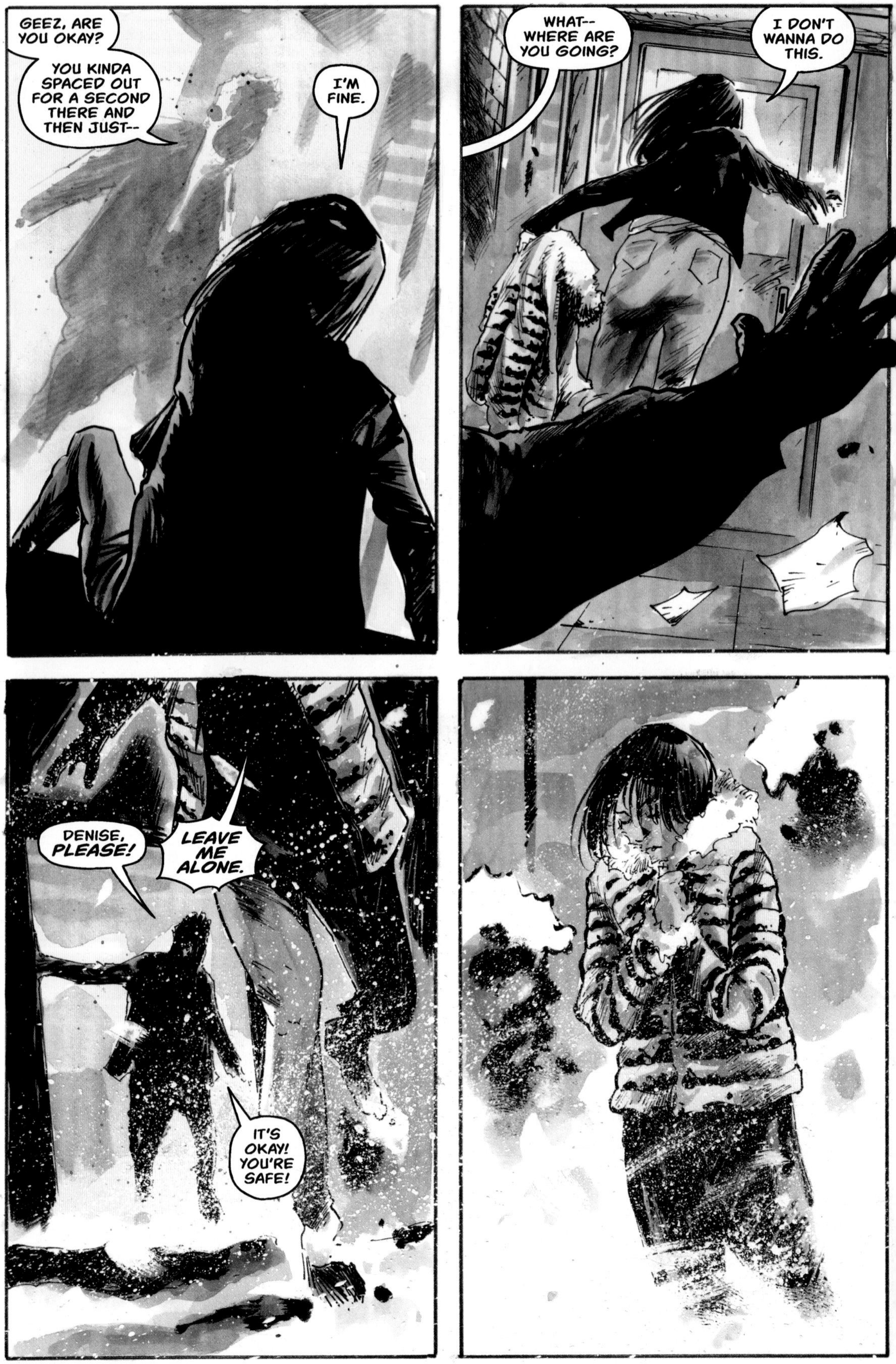
GEEZ, ARE YOU OKAY?
YOU KINDA SPACED OUT FOR A SECOND THERE AND THEN JUST--
I'M FINE.
WHAT-- WHERE ARE YOU GOING?
I DON'T WANNA DO THIS.
DENISE, PLEASE!
LEAVE ME ALONE.
IT'S OKAY! YOU'RE SAFE!

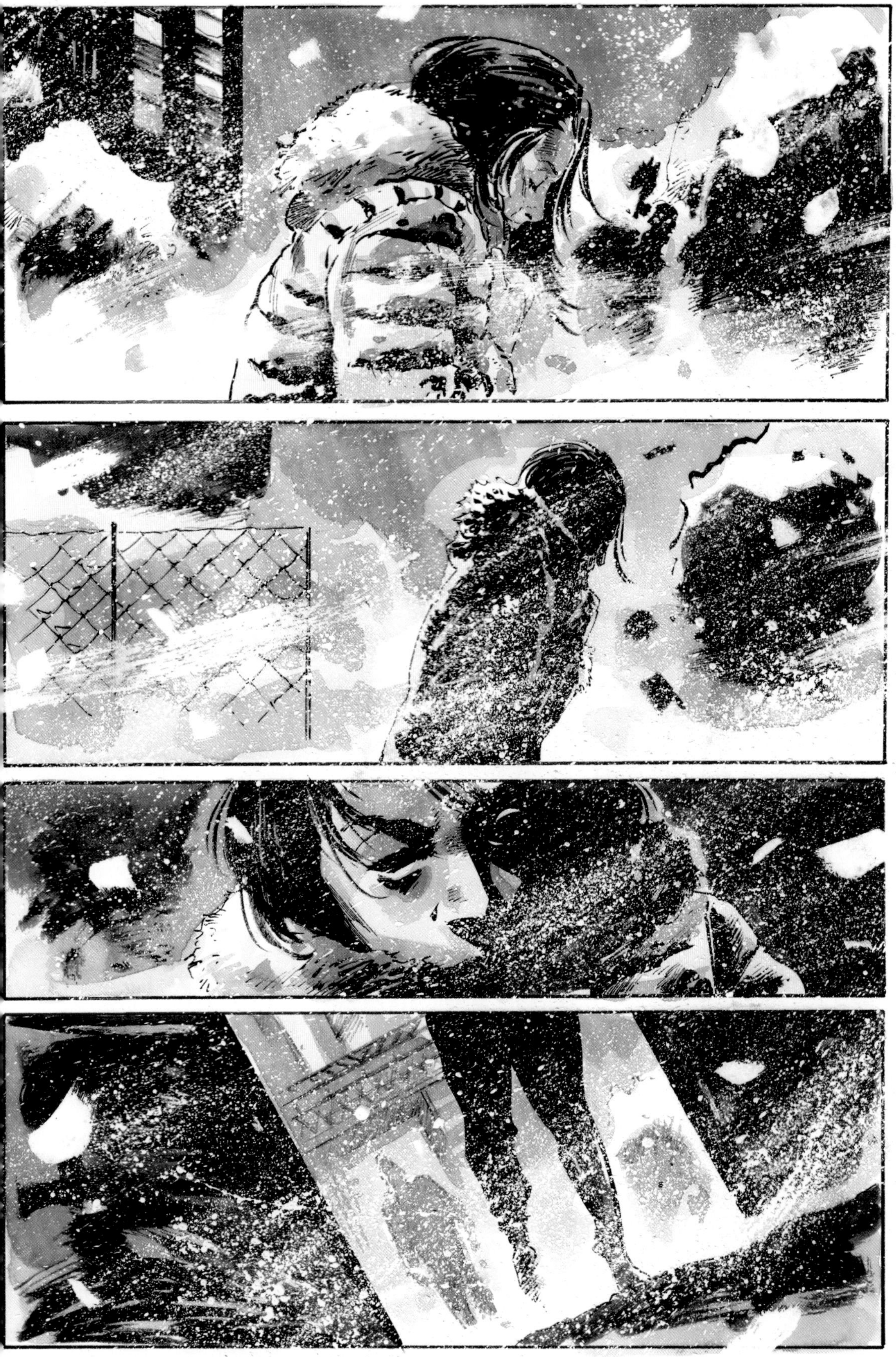

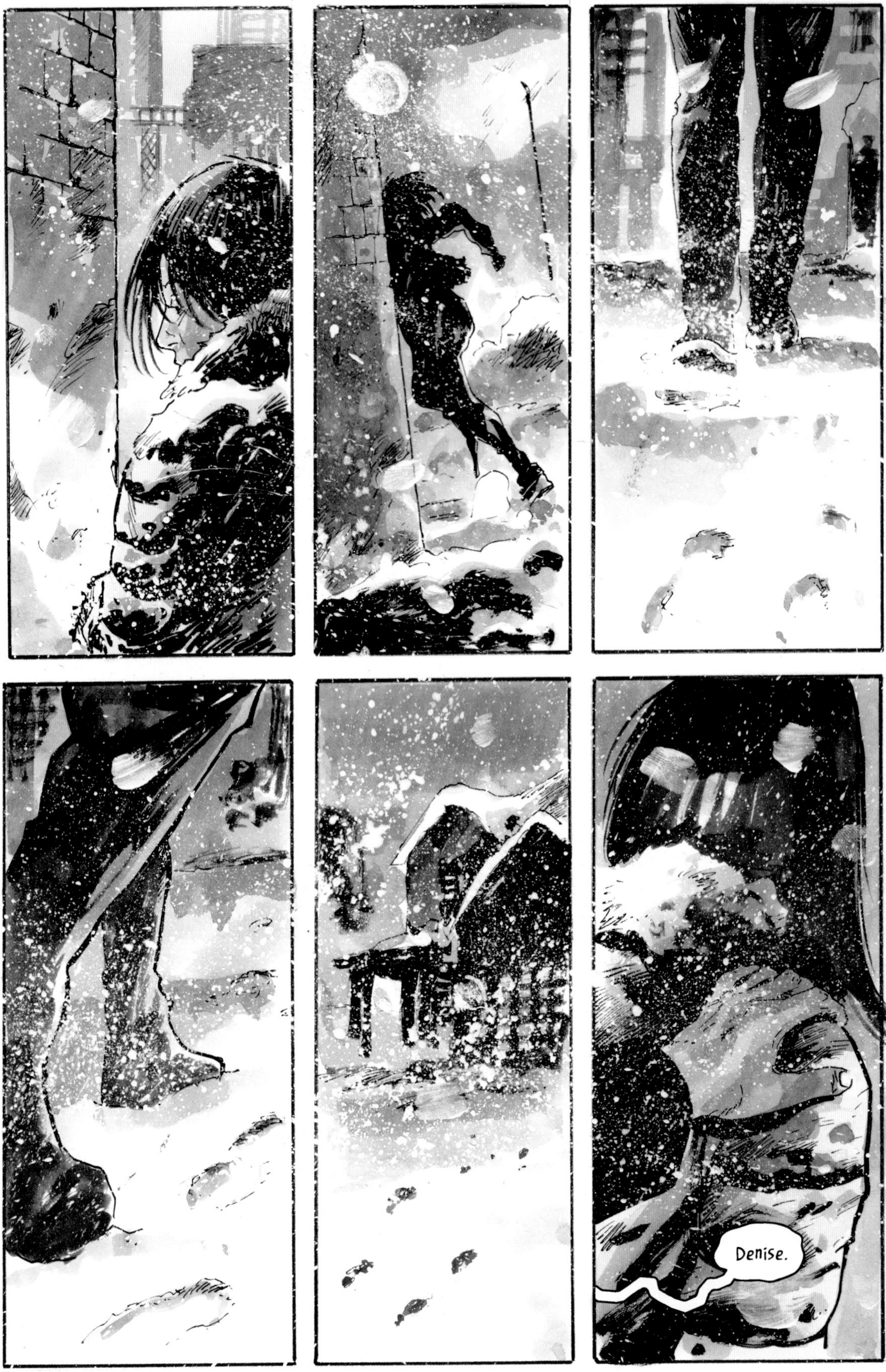
Denise.

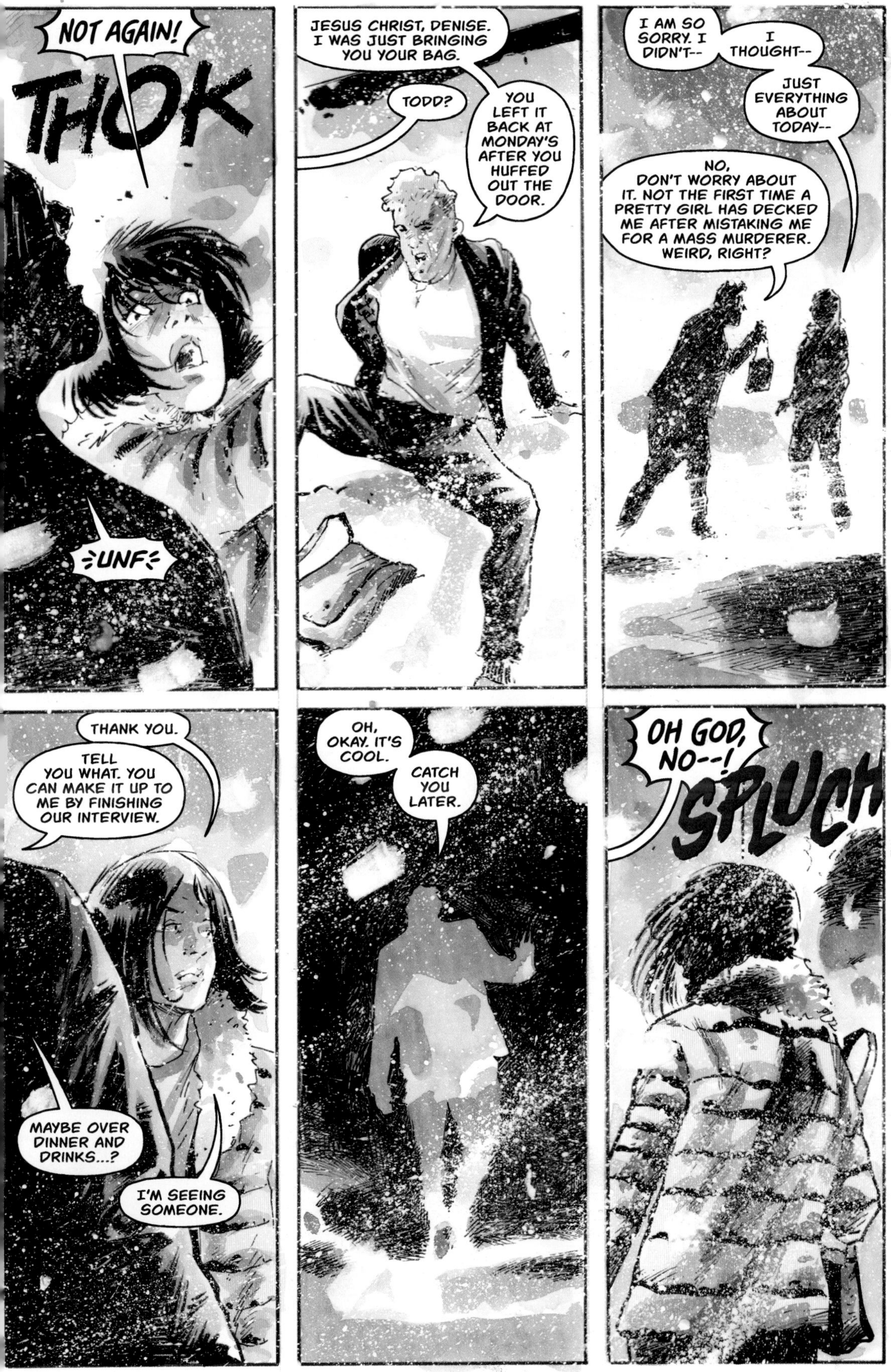
NOT AGAIN!
THOK
UNF
JESUS CHRIST, DENISE. I WAS JUST BRINGING YOU YOUR BAG.
TODD?
YOU LEFT IT BACK AT MONDAY'S AFTER YOU HUFFED OUT THE DOOR.
I AM SO SORRY. I DIDN'T--
I THOUGHT--
JUST EVERYTHING ABOUT TODAY--
NO, DON'T WORRY ABOUT IT. NOT THE FIRST TIME A PRETTY GIRL HAS DECKED ME AFTER MISTAKING ME FOR A MASS MURDERER. WEIRD, RIGHT?
THANK YOU.
TELL YOU WHAT. YOU CAN MAKE IT UP TO ME BY FINISHING OUR INTERVIEW.
MAYBE OVER DINNER AND DRINKS...?
I'M SEEING SOMEONE.
OH, OKAY. IT'S COOL.
CATCH YOU LATER.
OH GOD, NO--!
SPLUCH

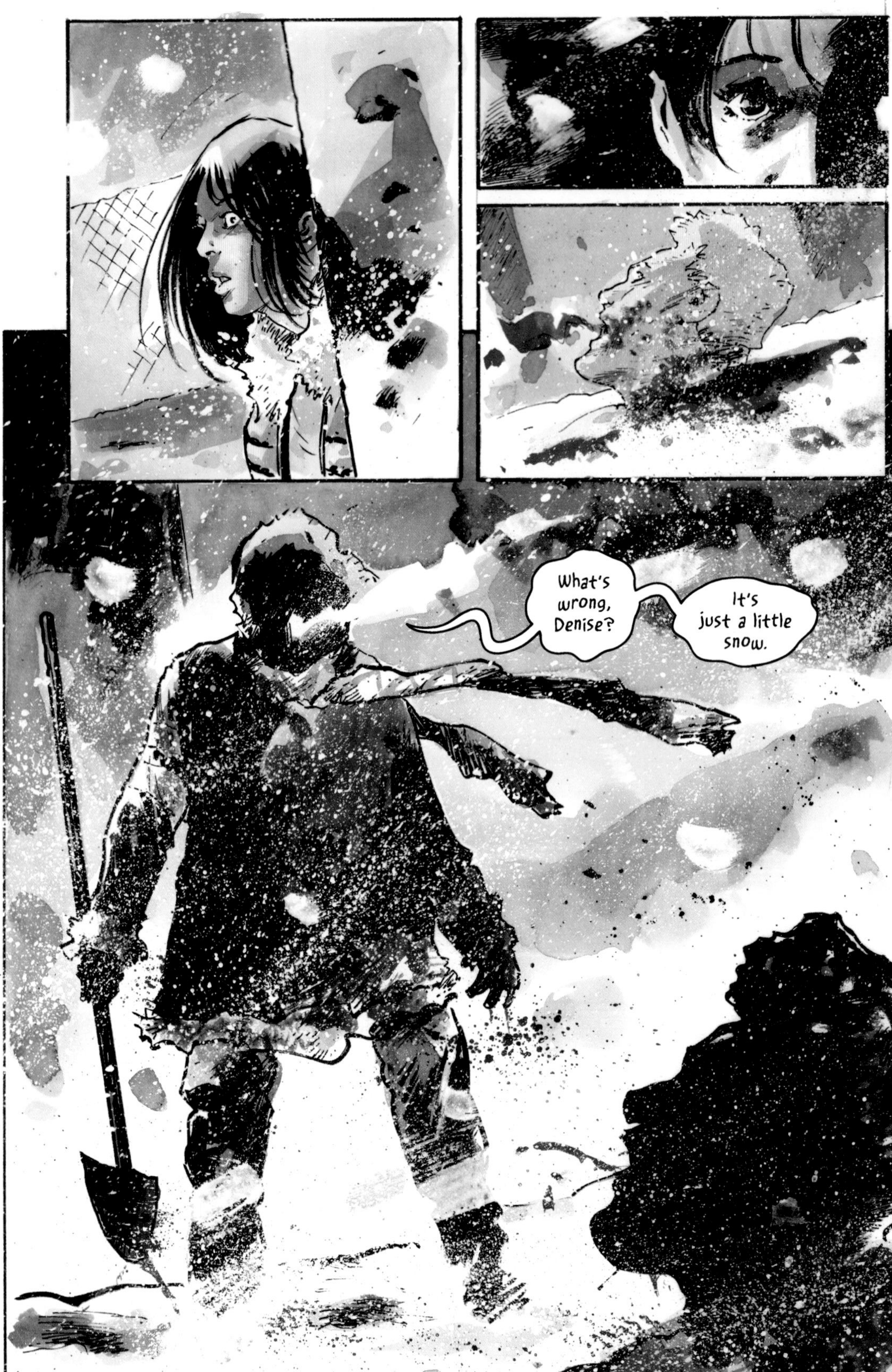
What's wrong, Denise?
It's just a little snow.

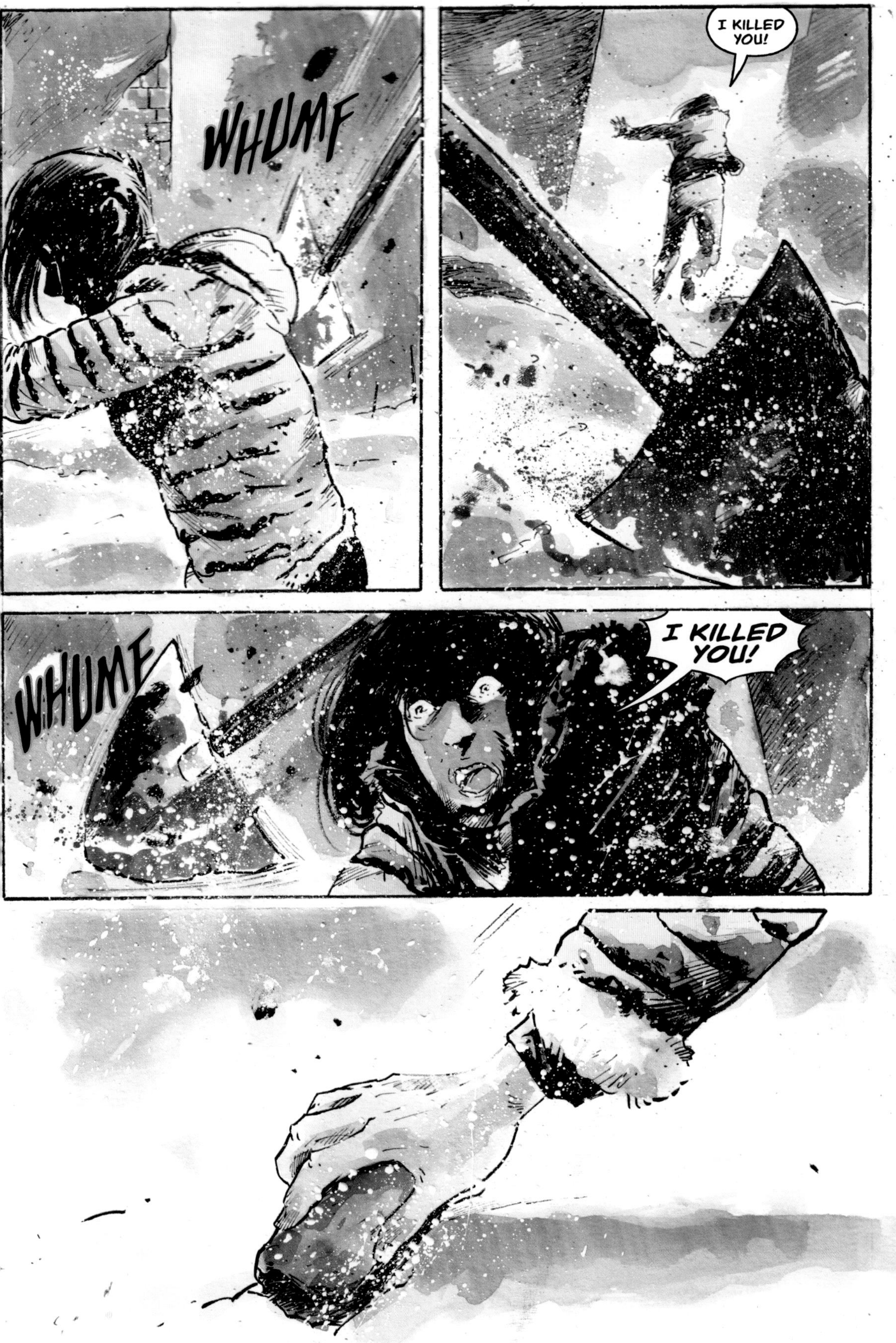
WHUMF
I KILLED YOU!
WHUMF
I KILLED YOU!

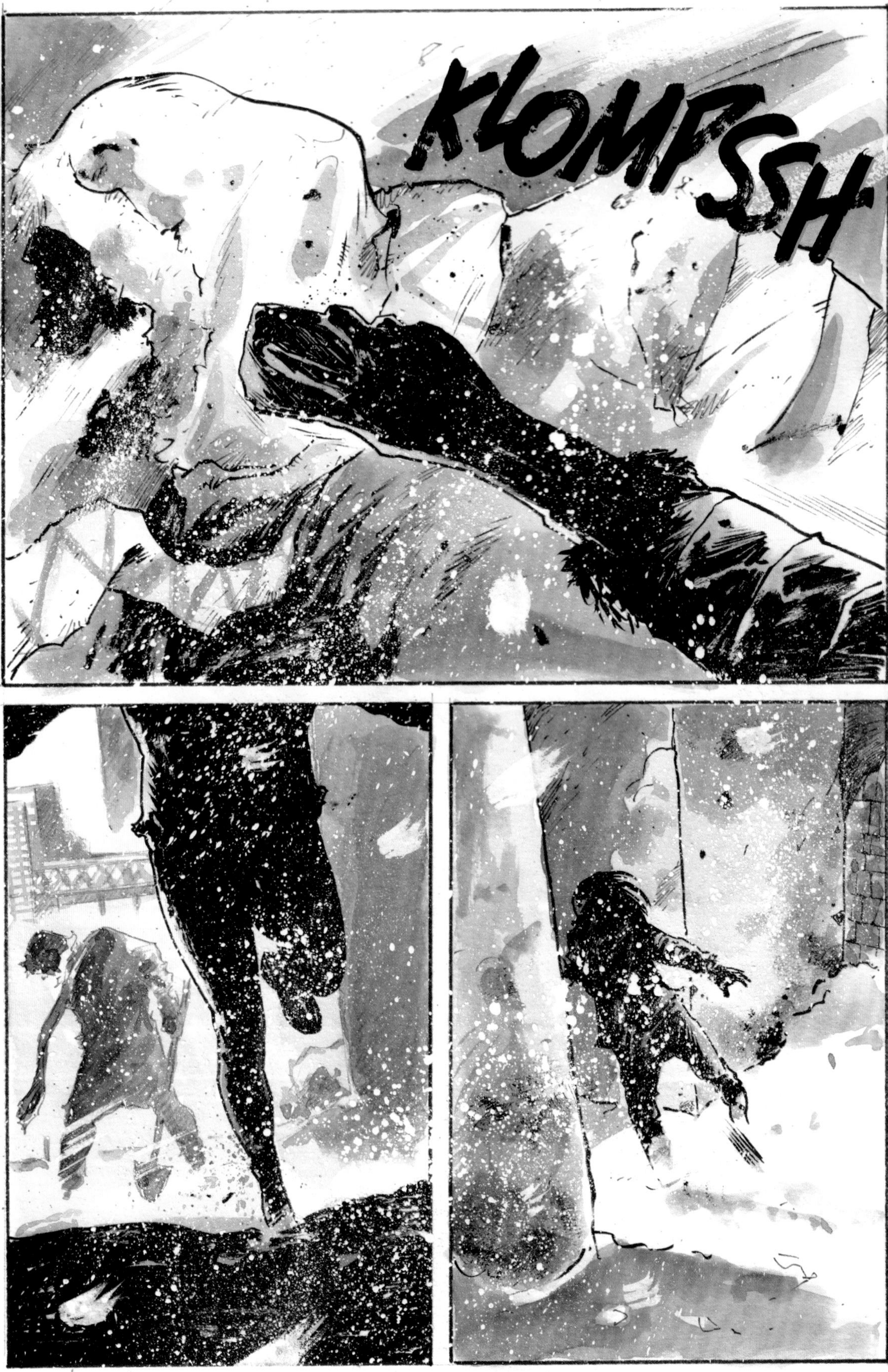
KLOMPSSH

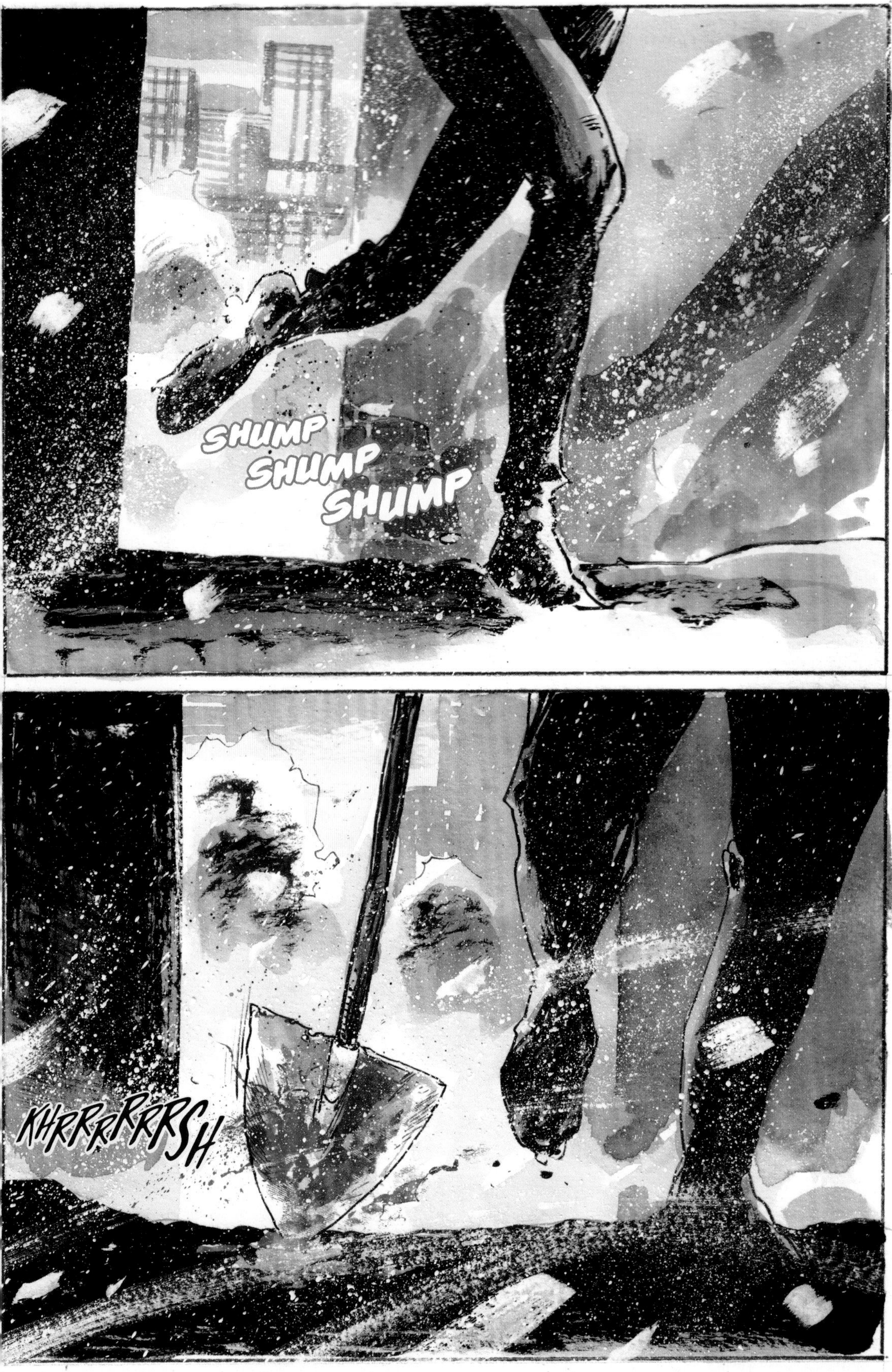
SHUMP
SHUMP
SHUMP
KHRRRRRRSH

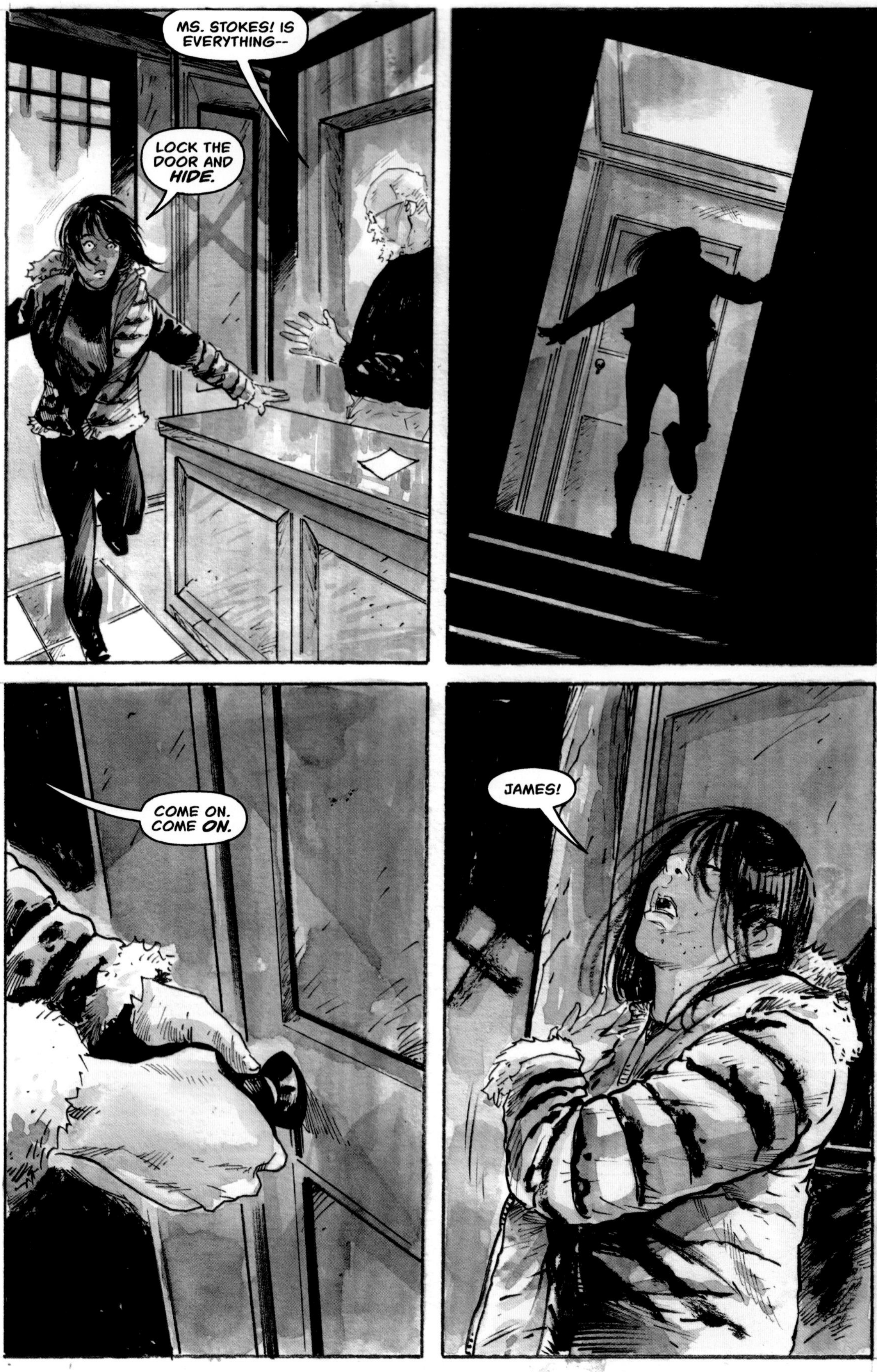
MS. STOKES! IS EVERYTHING--
LOCK THE DOOR AND HIDE.
COME ON. COME ON.
JAMES!

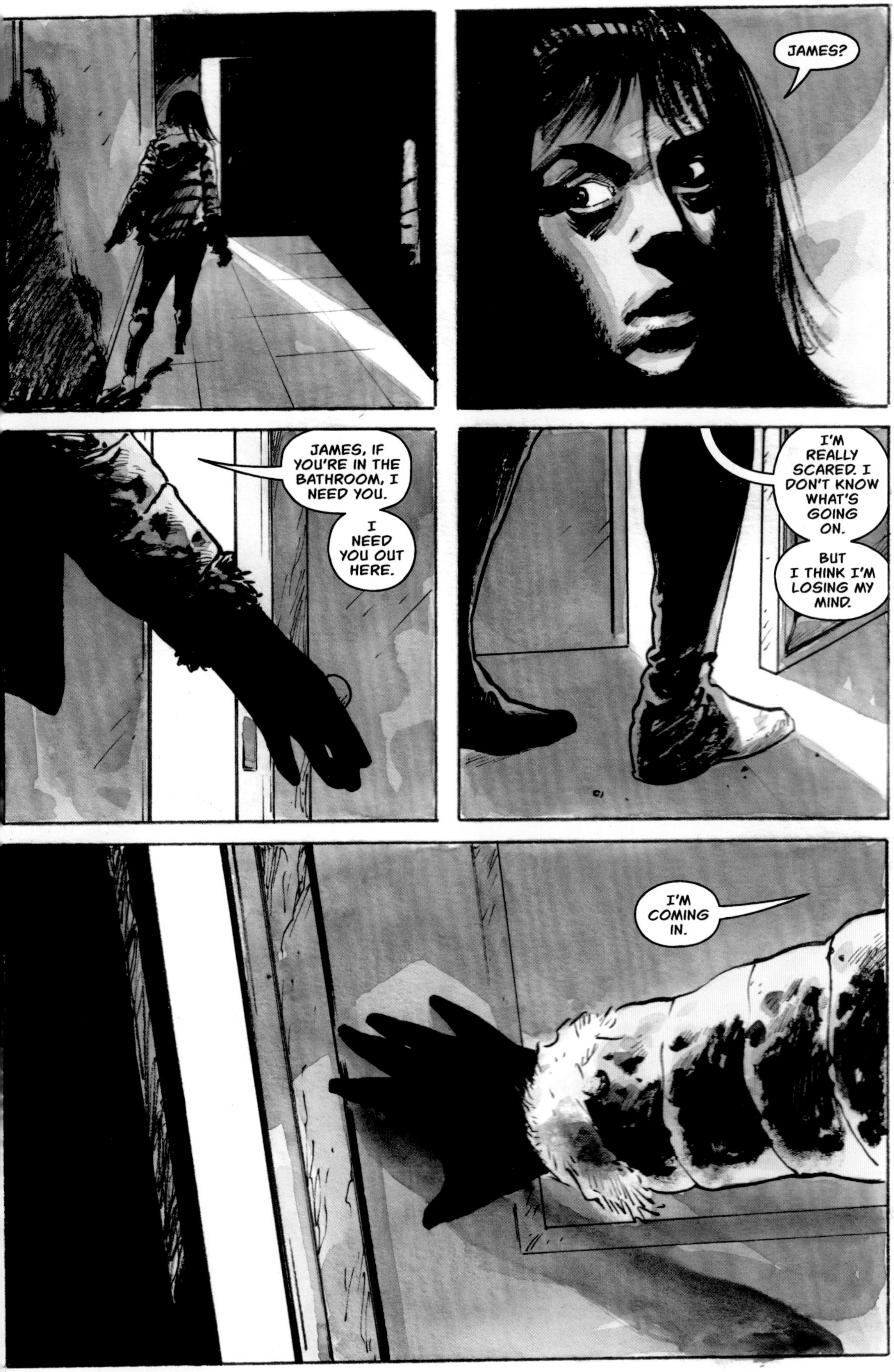
JAMES?
JAMES, IF YOU'RE IN THE BATHROOM, I NEED YOU.
I NEED YOU OUT HERE.
I'M REALLY SCARED. I DON'T KNOW WHAT'S GOING ON.
BUT I THINK I'M LOSING MY MIND.
I'M COMING IN.

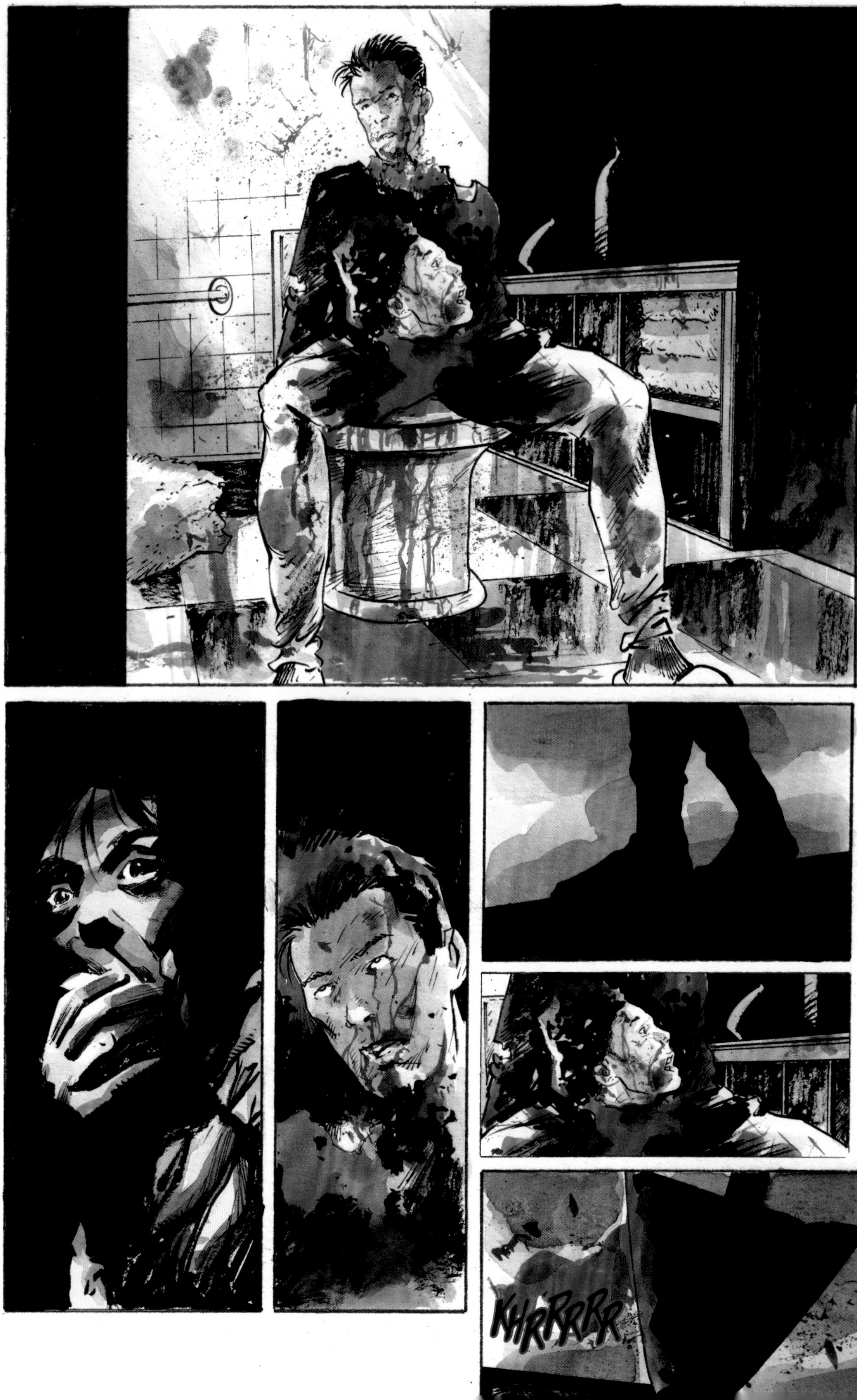
KHRRRRR

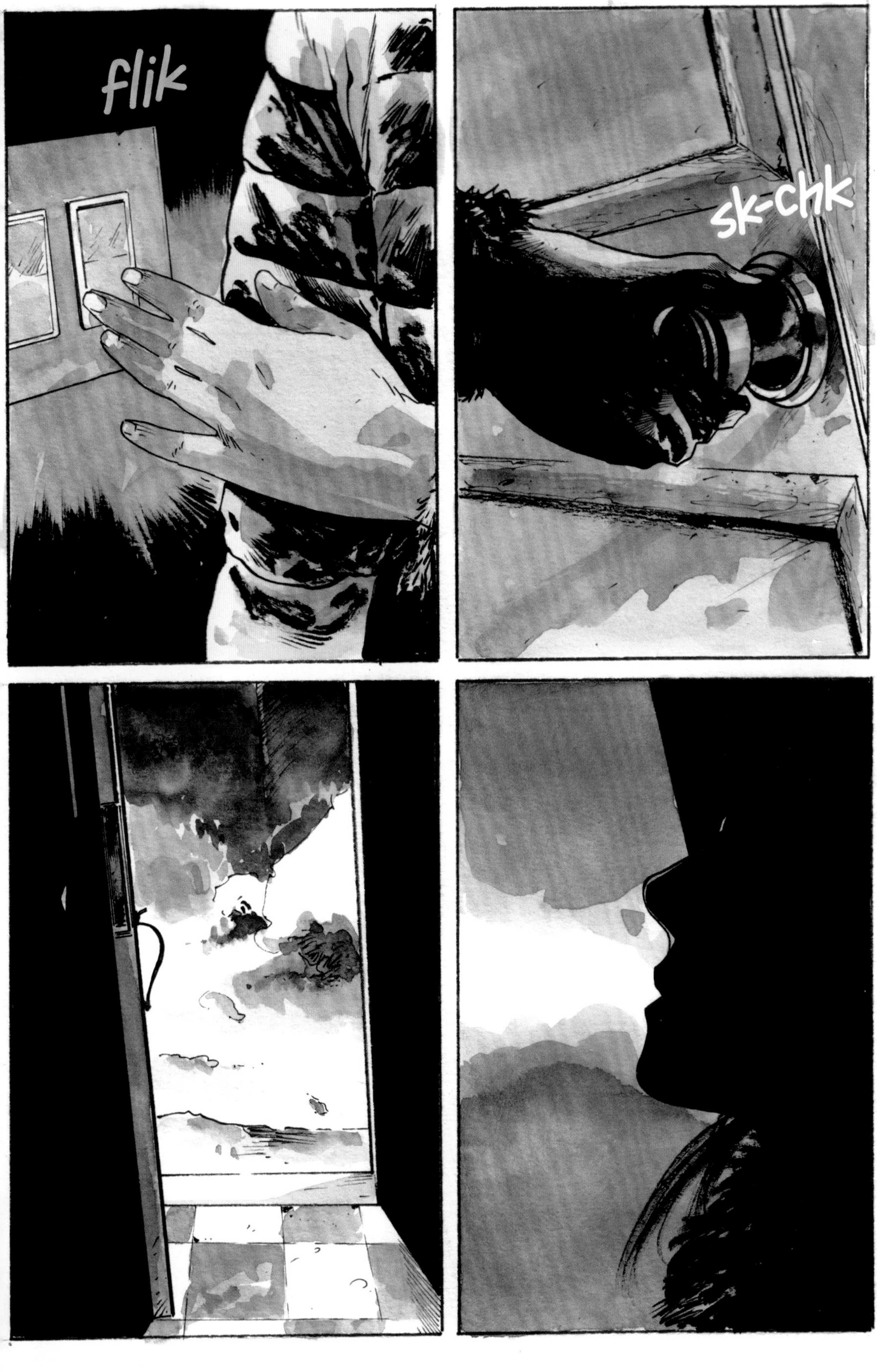
flik
sk-chk

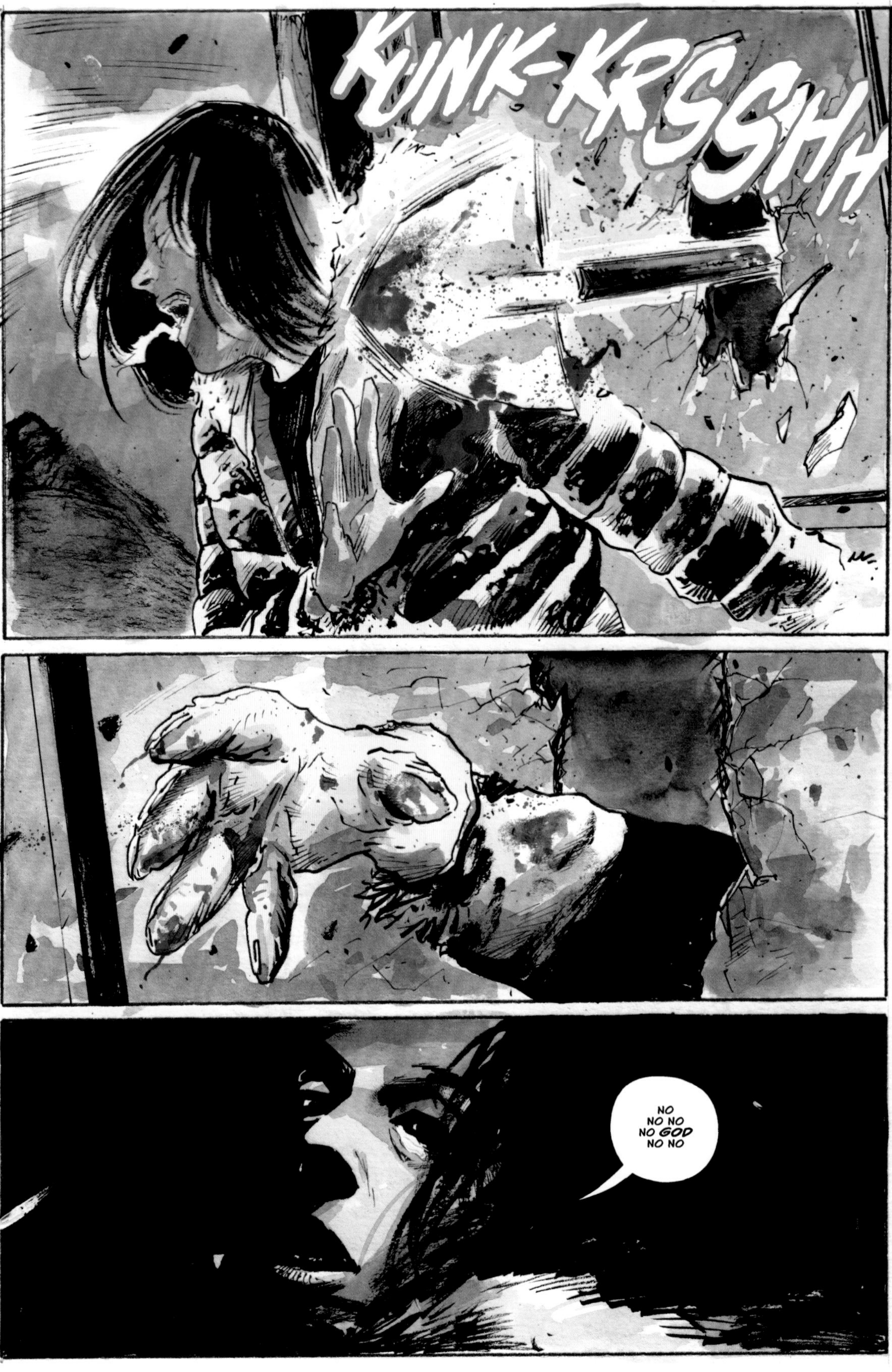
KLUNK-KRSSHH
NO NO NO NO *GOD* NO NO

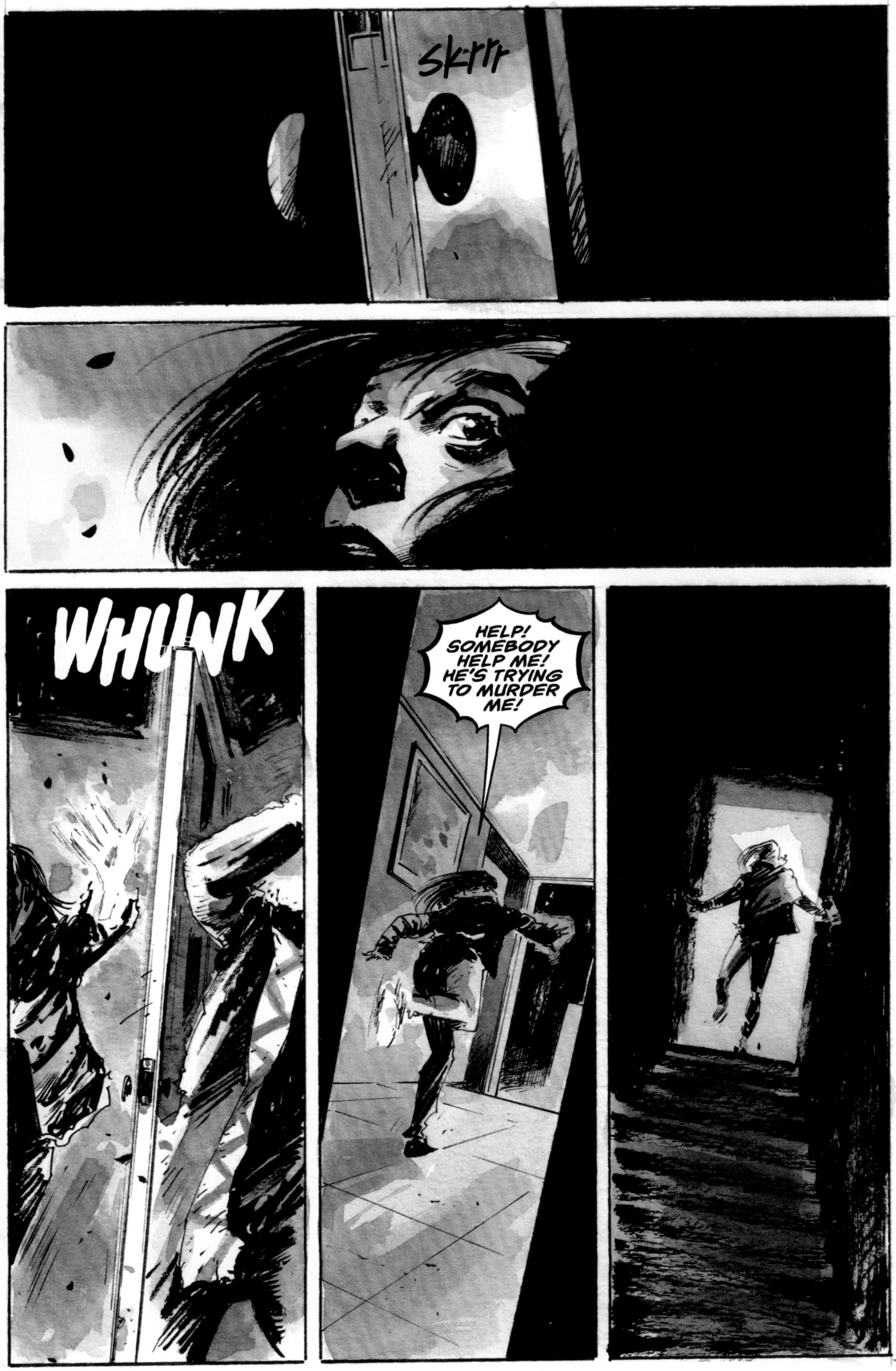
SKRRR
WHUNK
HELP! SOMEBODY HELP ME! HE'S TRYING TO MURDER ME!

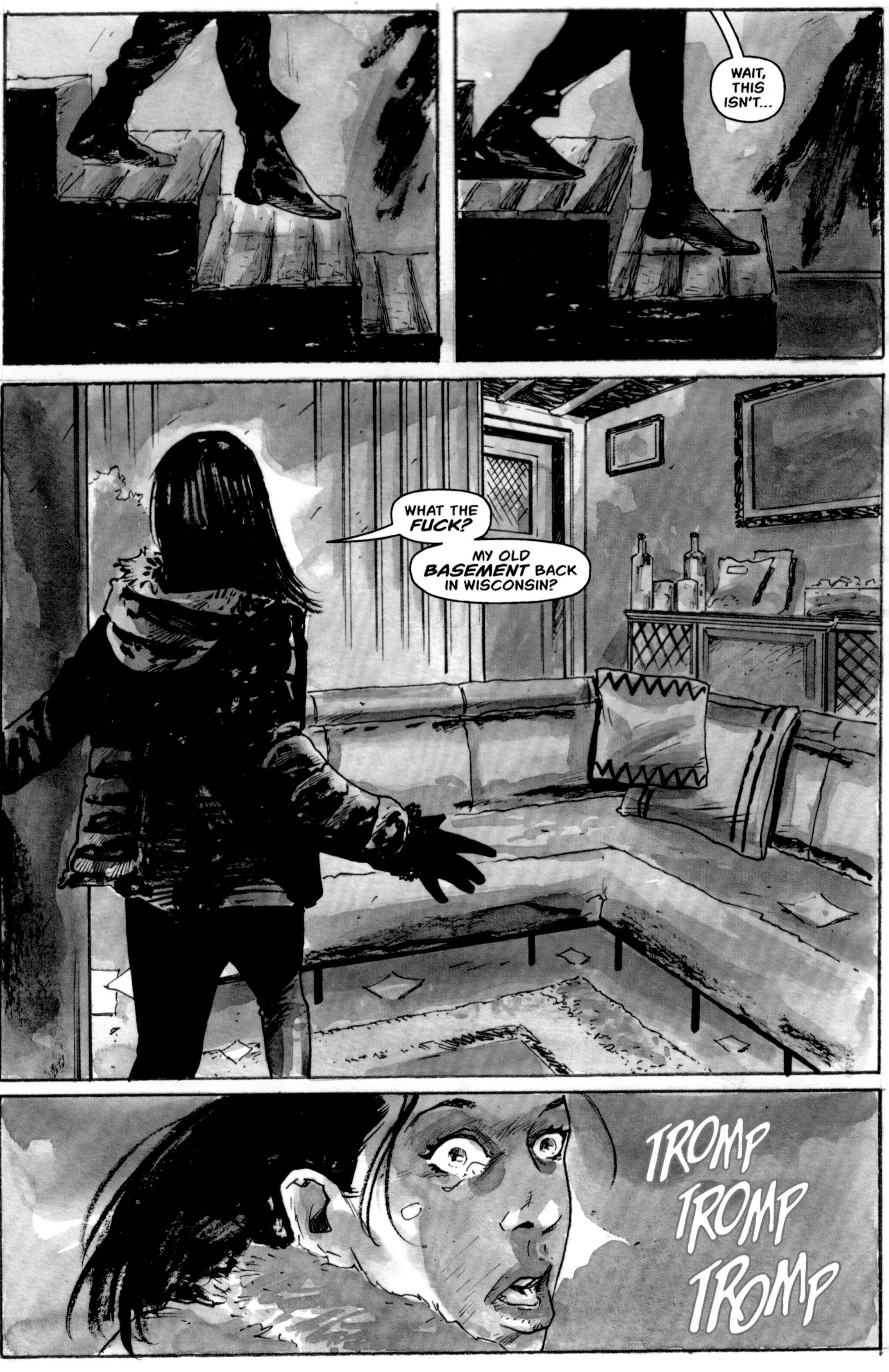
WAIT, THIS ISN'T...
WHAT THE FUCK?
MY OLD BASEMENT BACK IN WISCONSIN?
TROMP TROMP TROMP

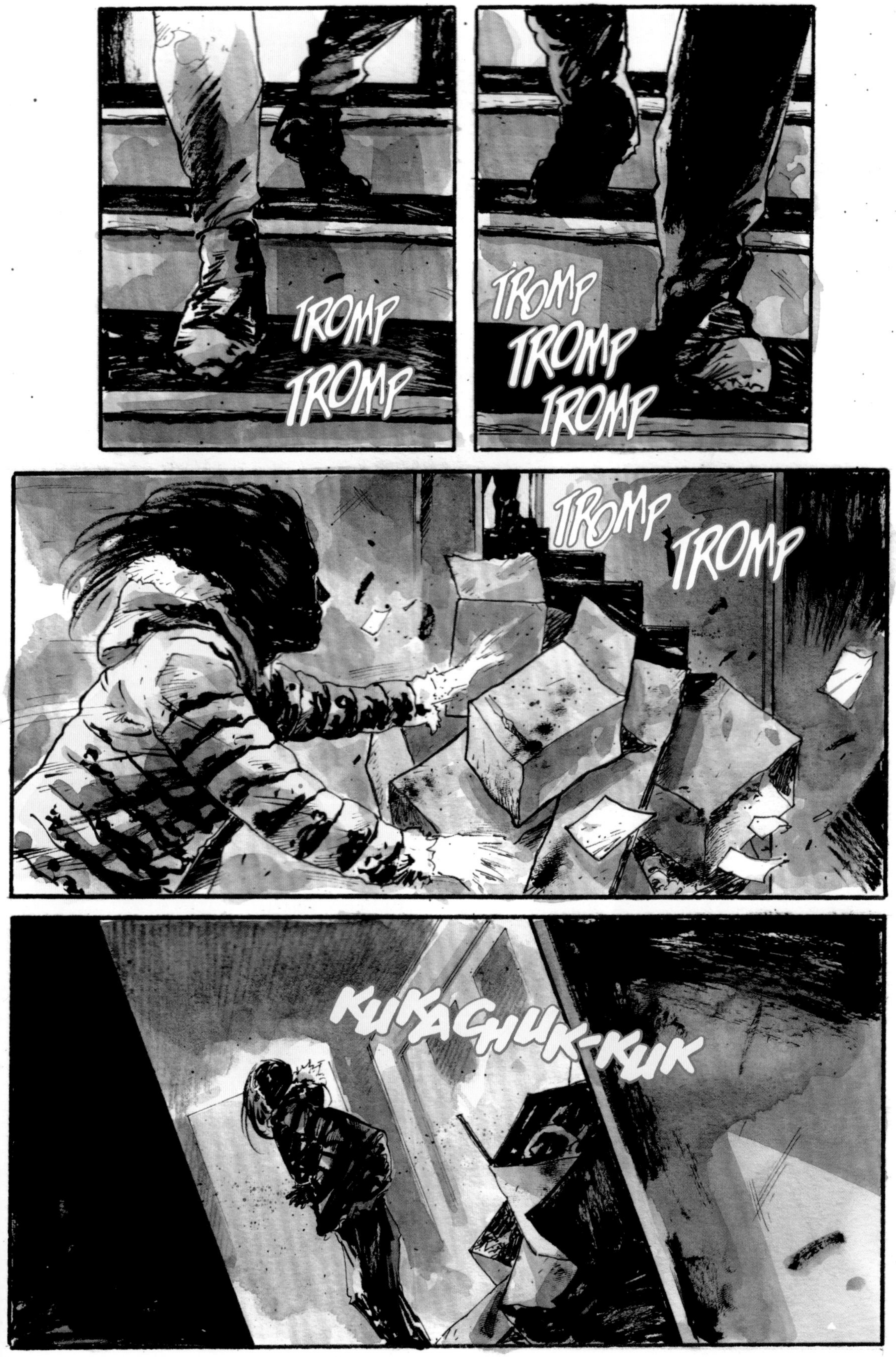
TROMP
TROMP
TROMP
TROMP
TROMP
TROMP
TROMP
KUKACHUK-KUK

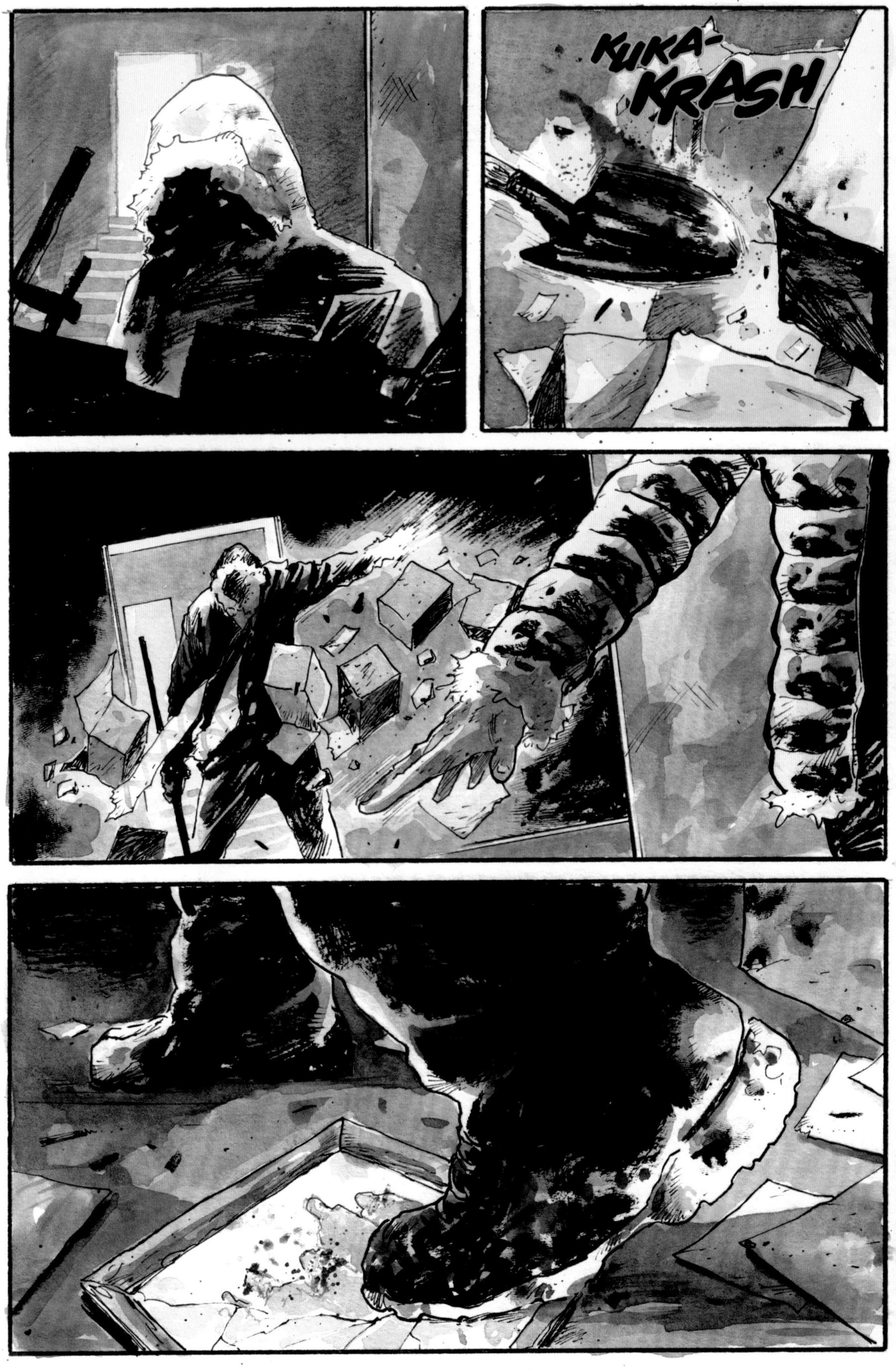
KUKA-
KRASH

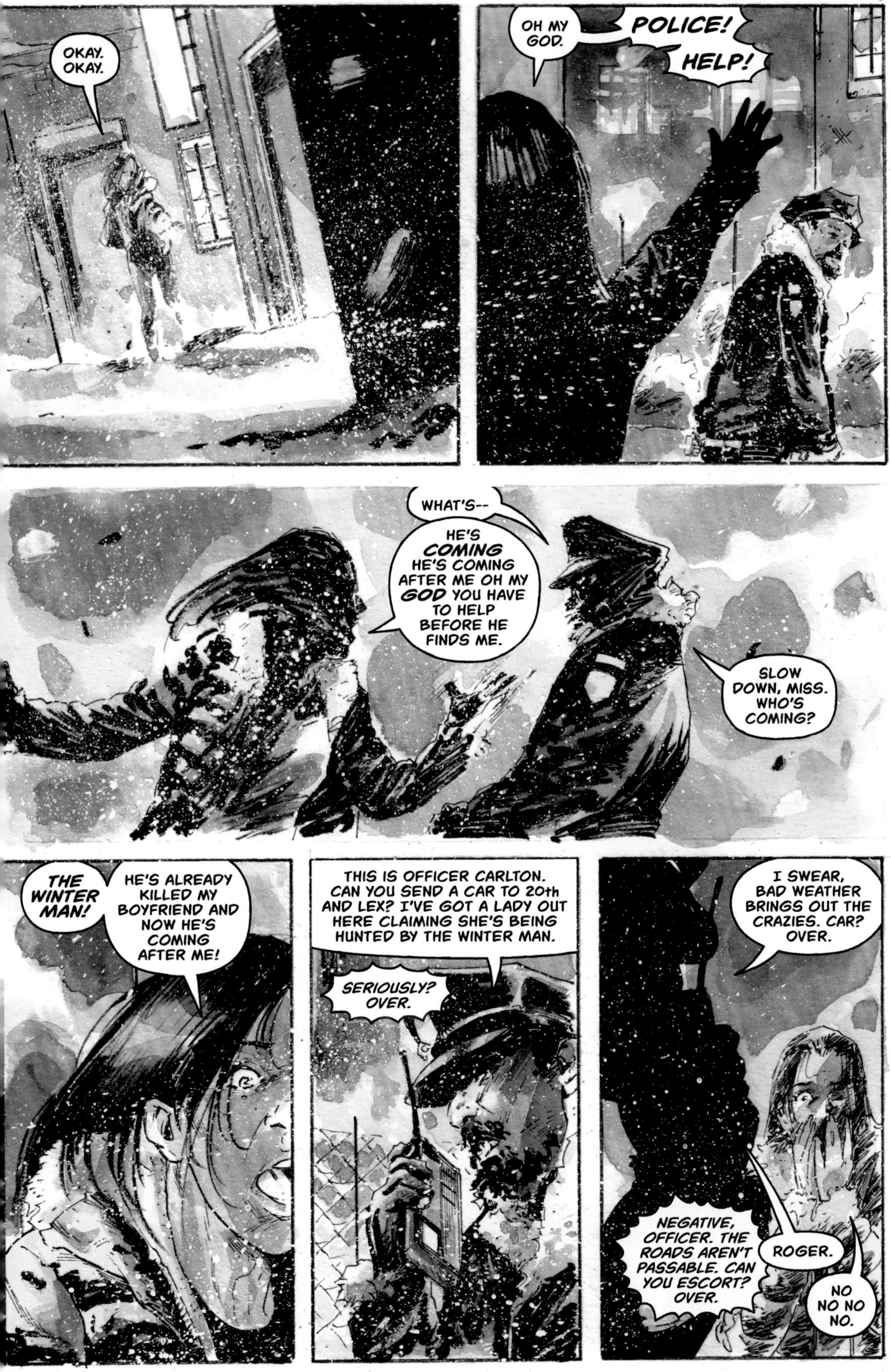
OKAY. OKAY.
OH MY GOD.
POLICE!
HELP!
WHAT'S--
HE'S COMING HE'S COMING AFTER ME OH MY GOD YOU HAVE TO HELP BEFORE HE FINDS ME.
SLOW DOWN, MISS. WHO'S COMING?
THE WINTER MAN!
HE'S ALREADY KILLED MY BOYFRIEND AND NOW HE'S COMING AFTER ME!
THIS IS OFFICER CARLTON. CAN YOU SEND A CAR TO 20th AND LEX? I'VE GOT A LADY OUT HERE CLAIMING SHE'S BEING HUNTED BY THE WINTER MAN.
SERIOUSLY? OVER.
I SWEAR, BAD WEATHER BRINGS OUT THE CRAZIES. CAR? OVER.
NEGATIVE, OFFICER. THE ROADS AREN'T PASSABLE. CAN YOU ESCORT? OVER.
ROGER.
NO NO NO NO.

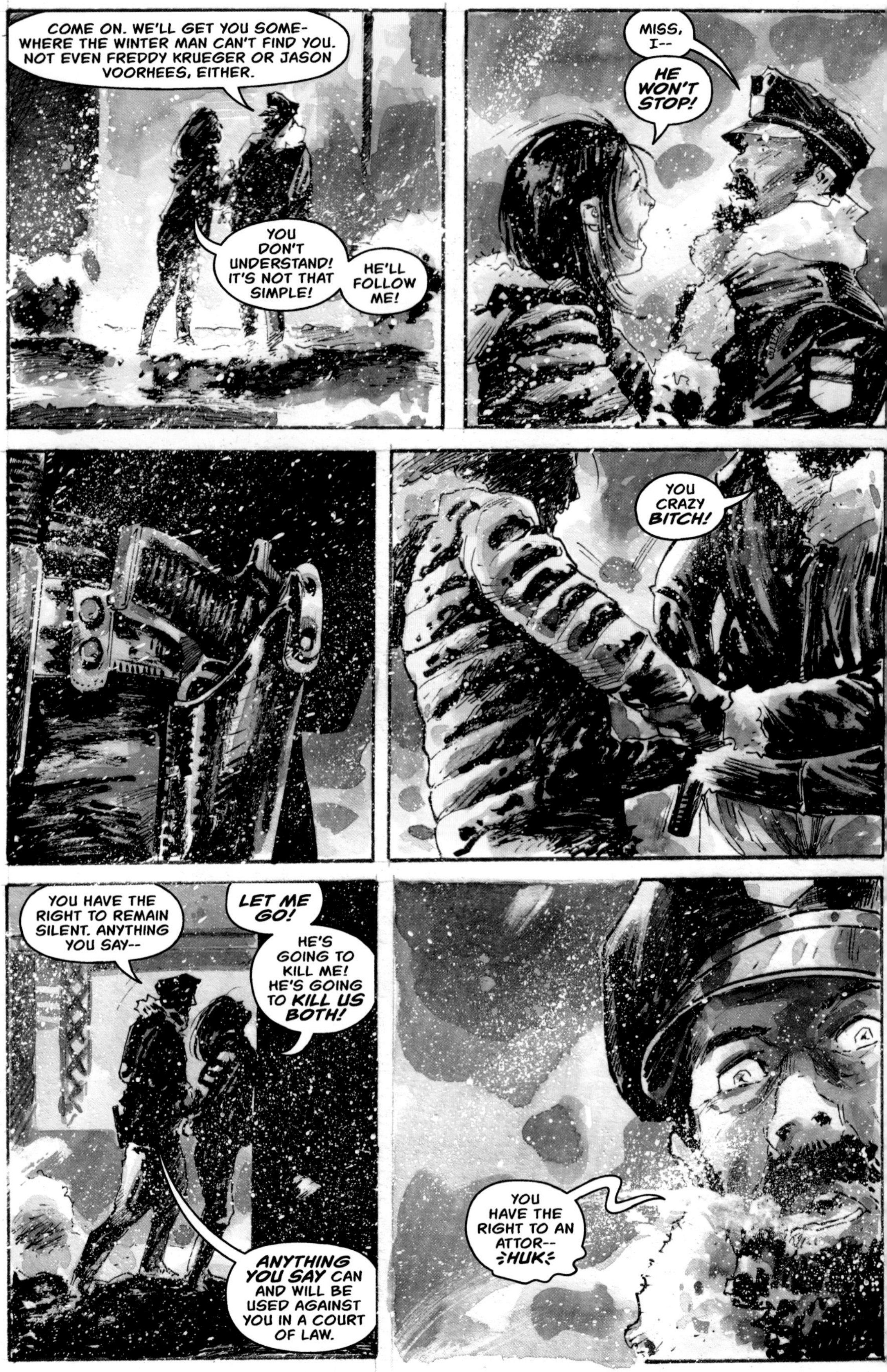
COME ON. WE'LL GET YOU SOME-WHERE THE WINTER MAN CAN'T FIND YOU. NOT EVEN FREDDY KRUEGER OR JASON VOORHEES, EITHER.
YOU DON'T UNDERSTAND! IT'S NOT THAT SIMPLE!
HE'LL FOLLOW ME!
MISS, I--
HE WON'T STOP!
YOU CRAZY BITCH!
YOU HAVE THE RIGHT TO REMAIN SILENT. ANYTHING YOU SAY--
LET ME GO!
HE'S GOING TO KILL ME! HE'S GOING TO KILL US BOTH!
ANYTHING YOU SAY CAN AND WILL BE USED AGAINST YOU IN A COURT OF LAW.
YOU HAVE THE RIGHT TO AN ATTOR-- HUK

ATT...
ATTOR...

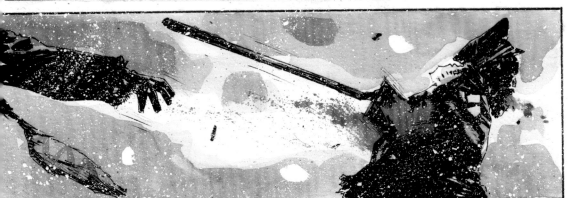

SPLURCH

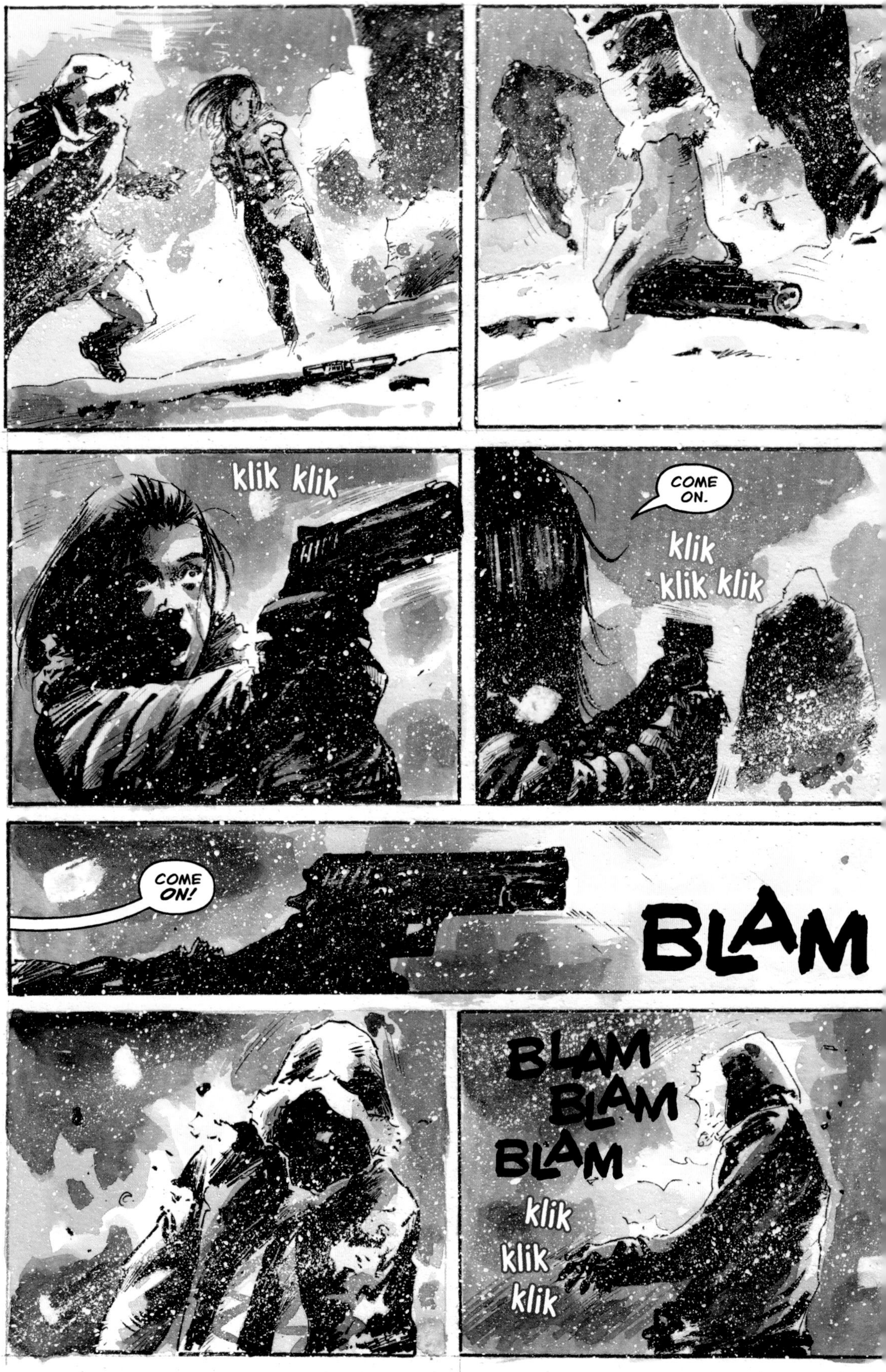
klik klik
COME ON.
klik
klik klik
COME ON!
BLAM
BLAM
BLAM
BLAM
klik
klik
klik

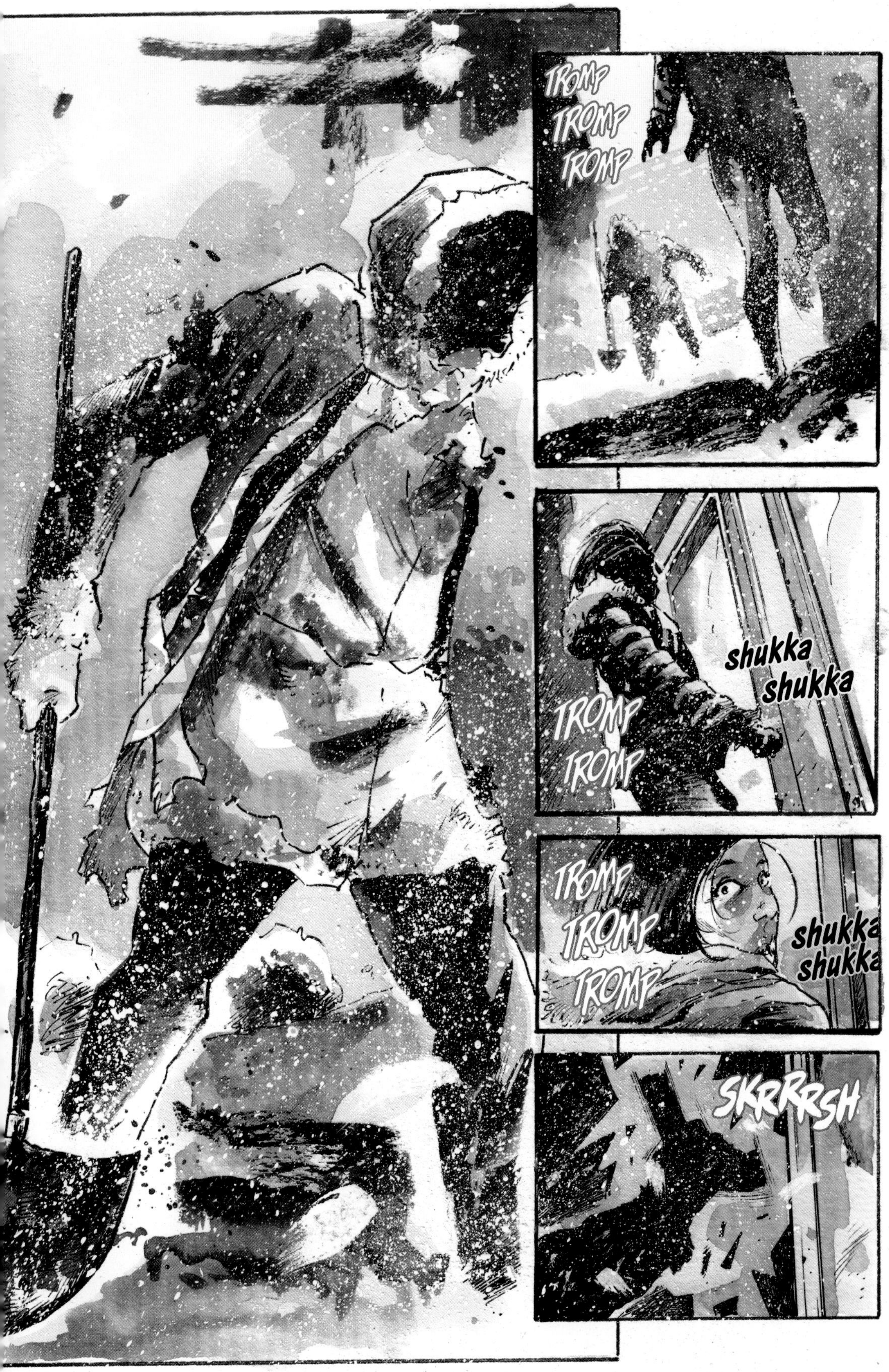
TROMP
TROMP
TROMP
shukka
shukka
TROMP
TROMP
TROMP
TROMP
TROMP
shukka
shukka
SKRRRSH

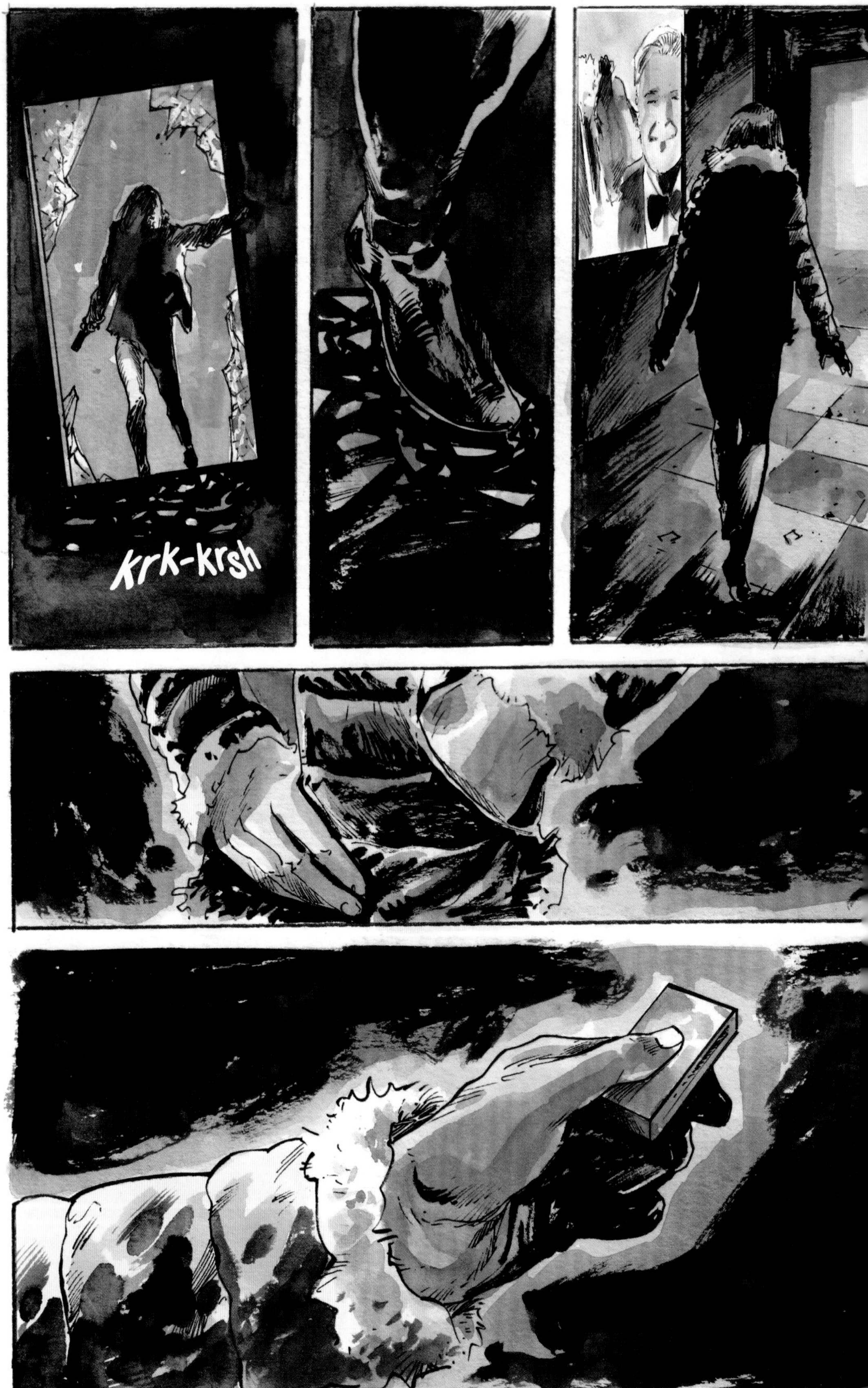
krk-krsh

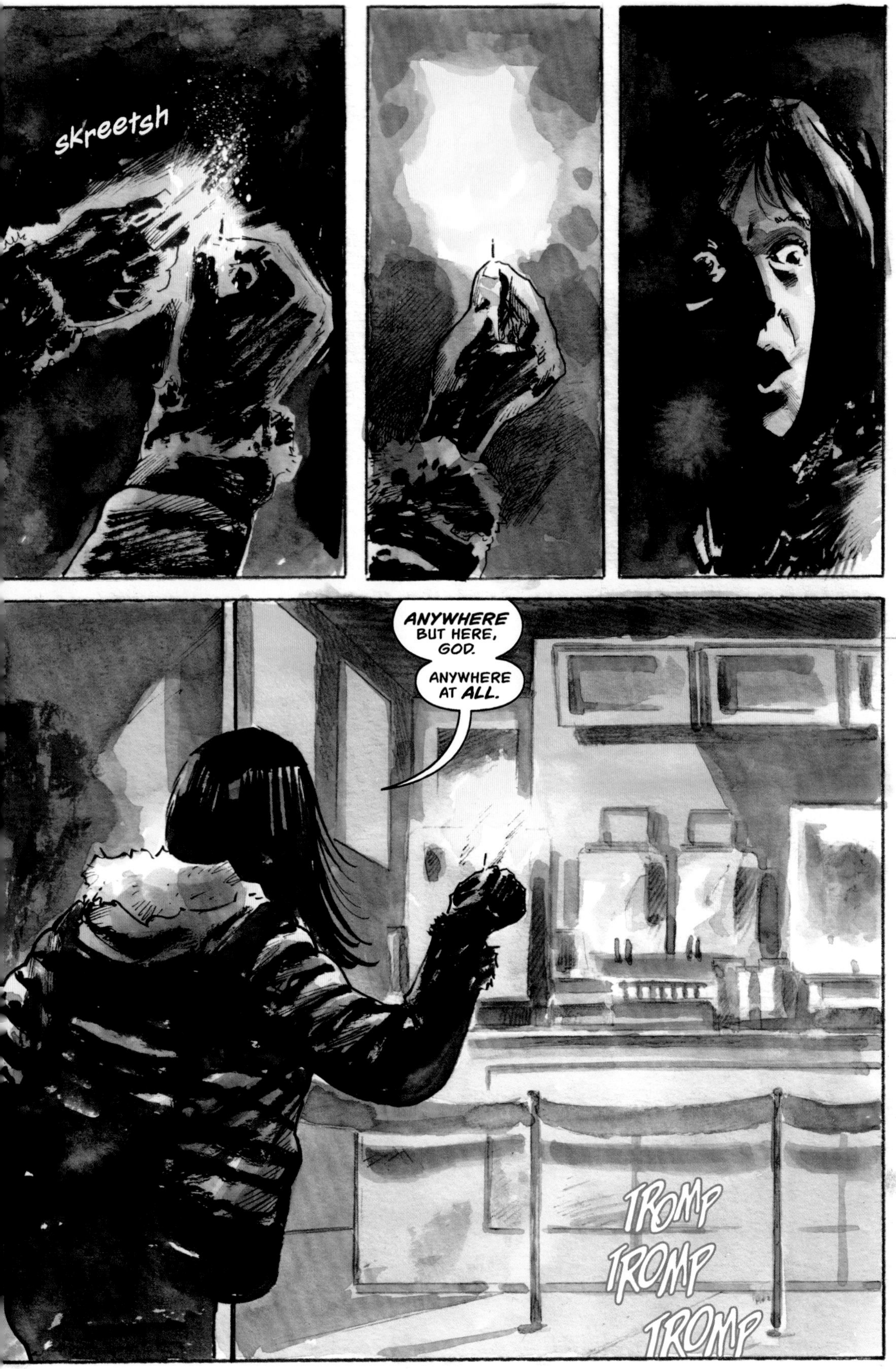
skreetsh
ANYWHERE BUT HERE, GOD.
ANYWHERE AT ALL.
TROMP
TROMP
TROMP

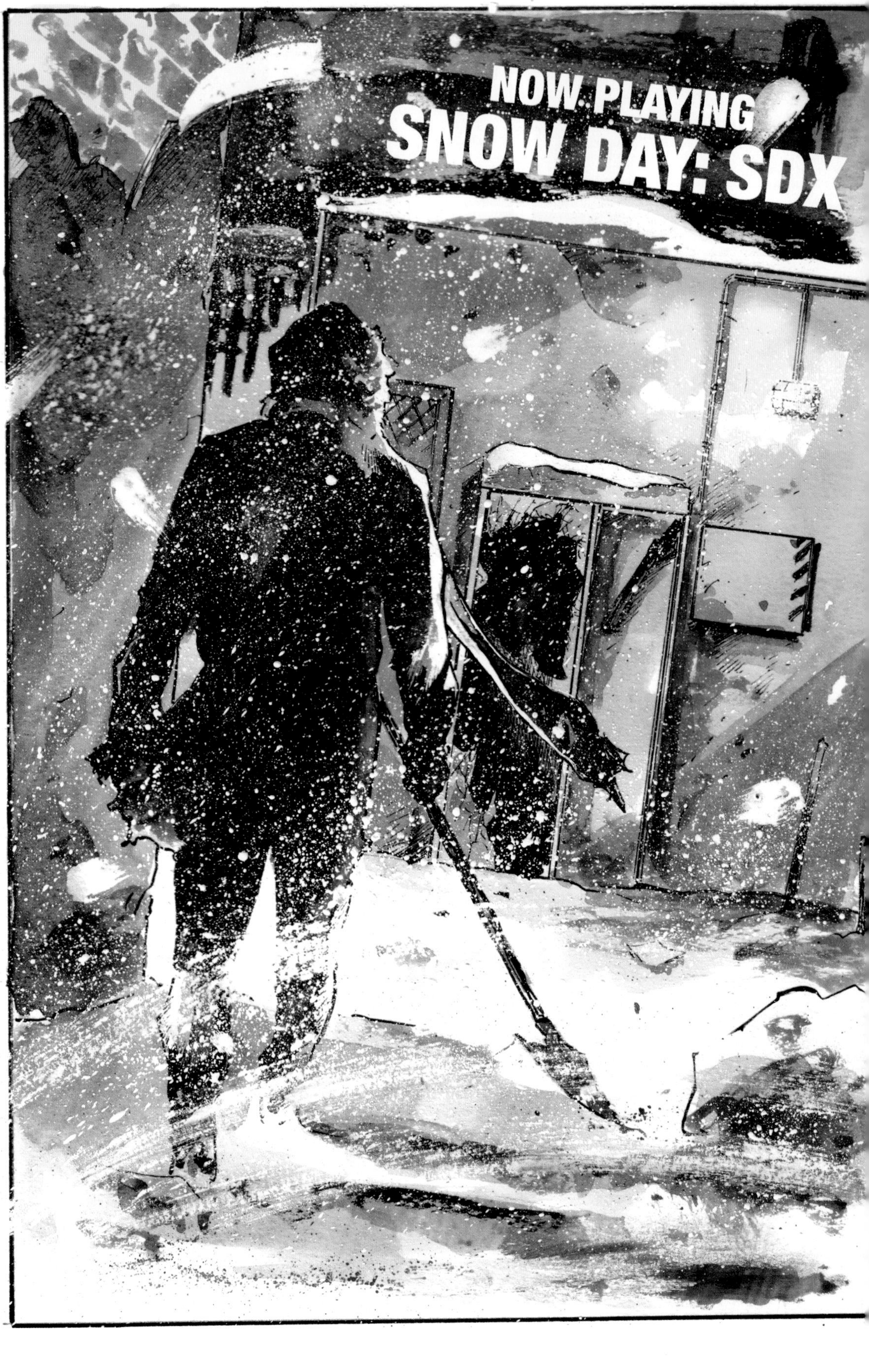
NOW PLAYING
SNOW DAY: SDX

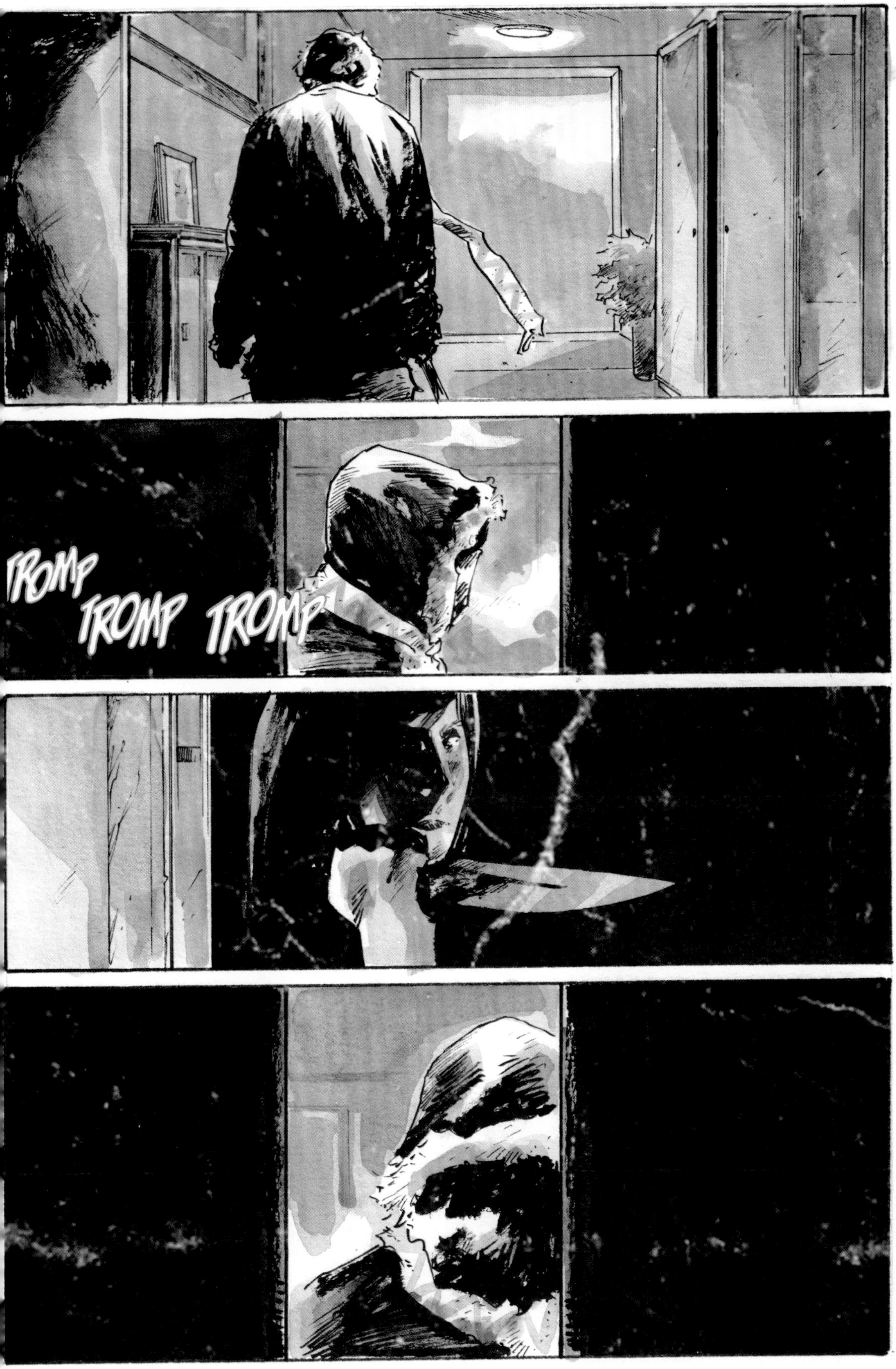
TROMP TROMP TROMP

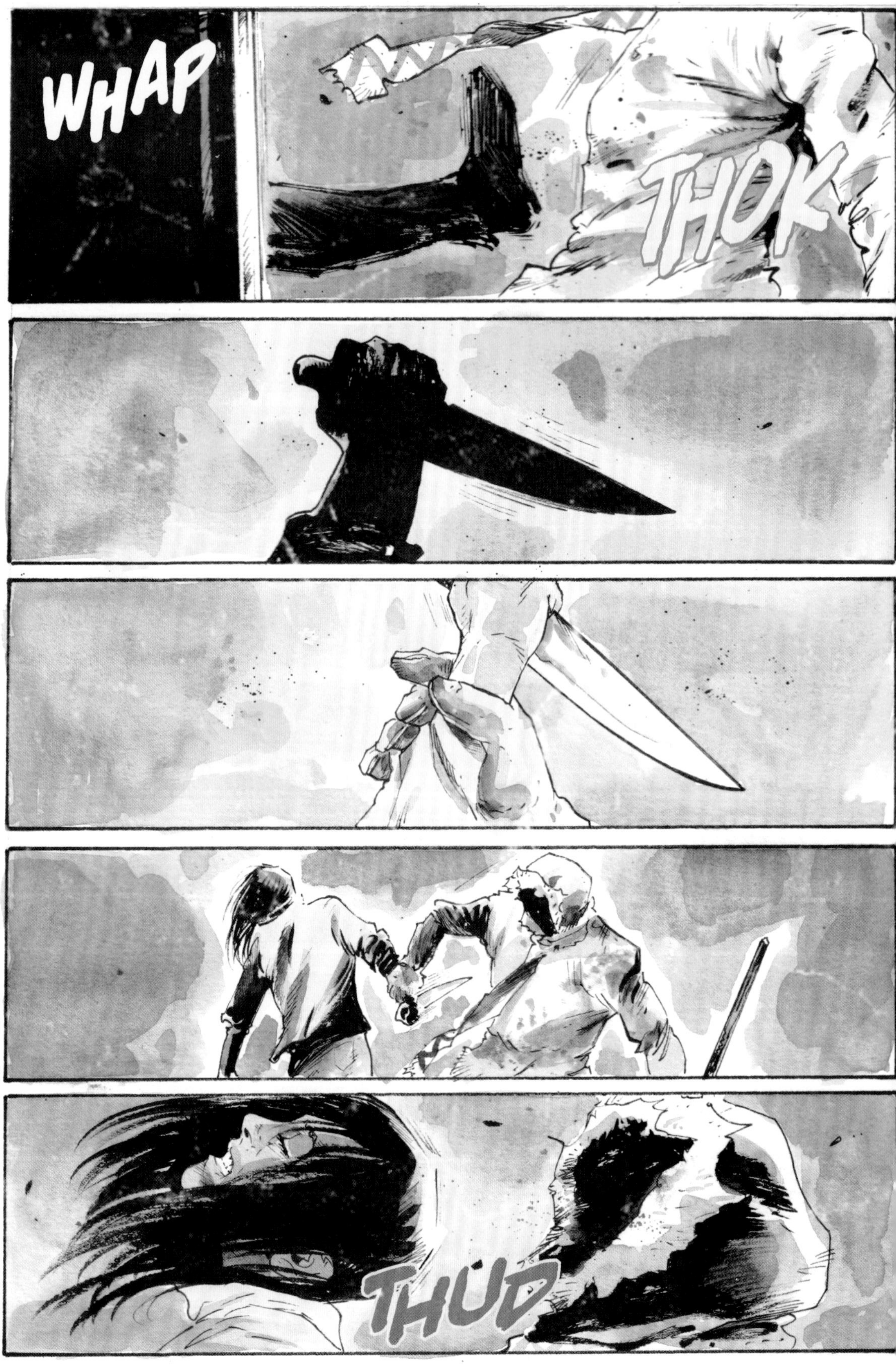
WHAP
THOK
THUD

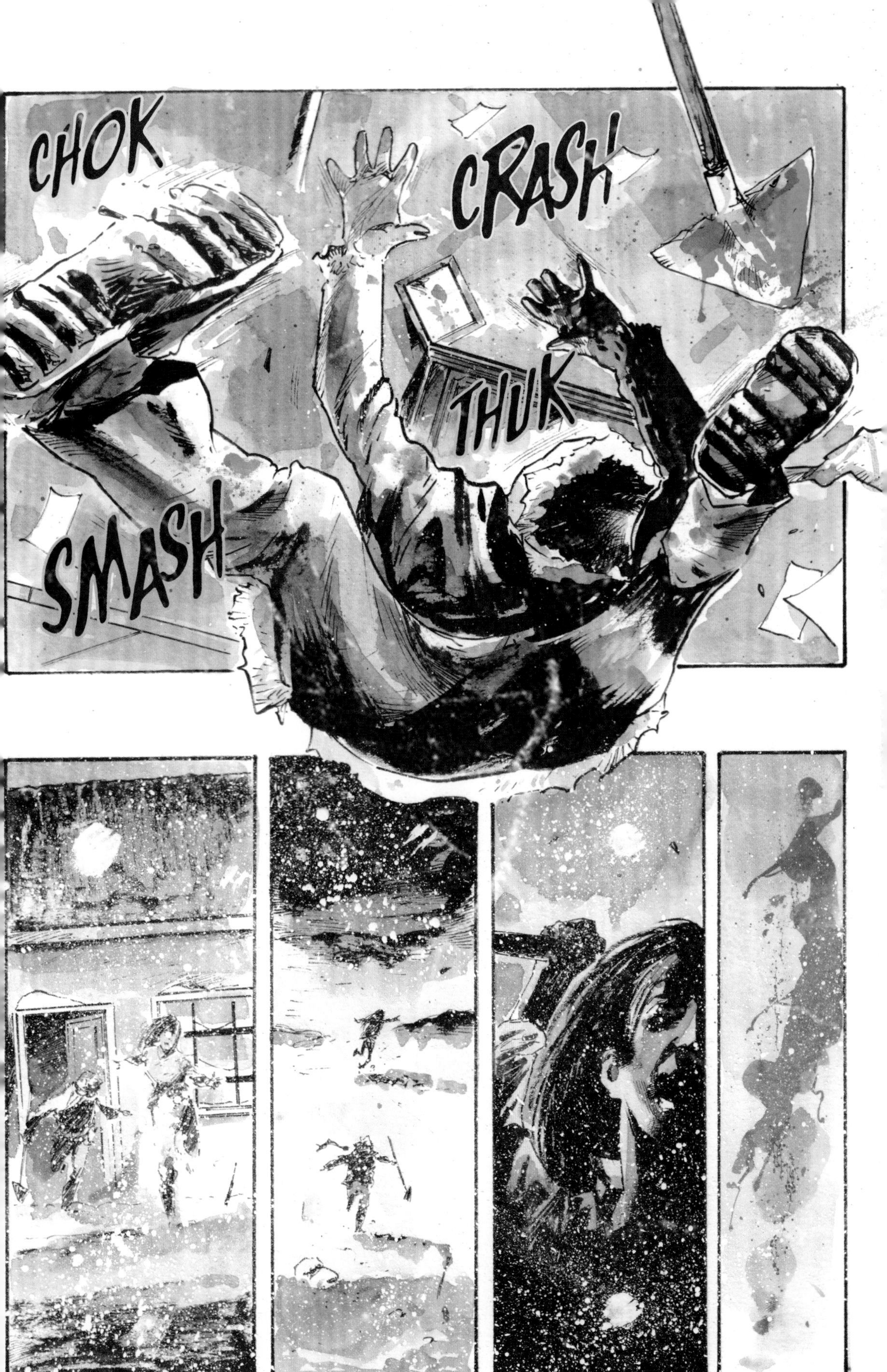
CHOK
CRASH
THUK
SMASH

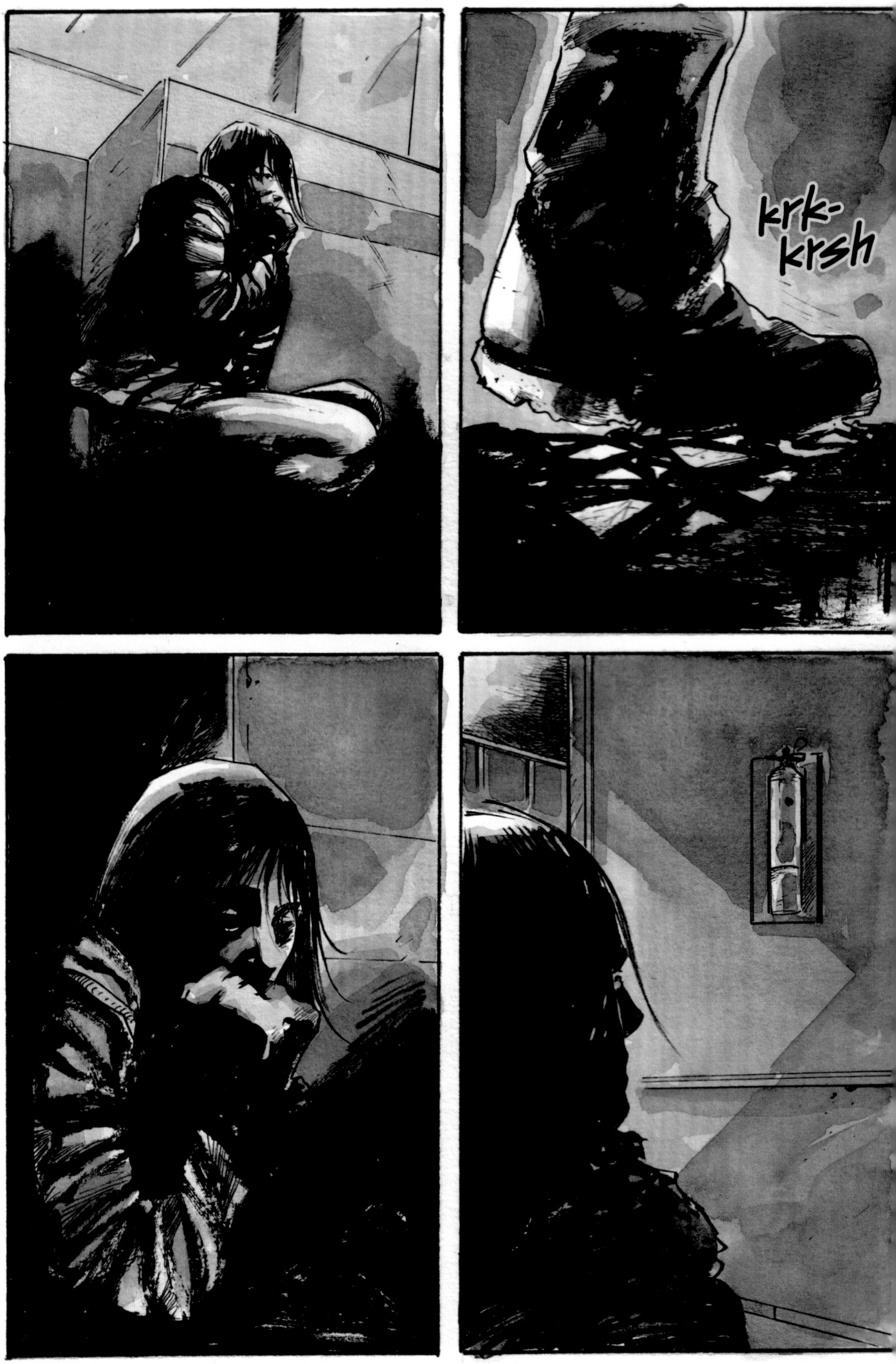
krk-
krsh

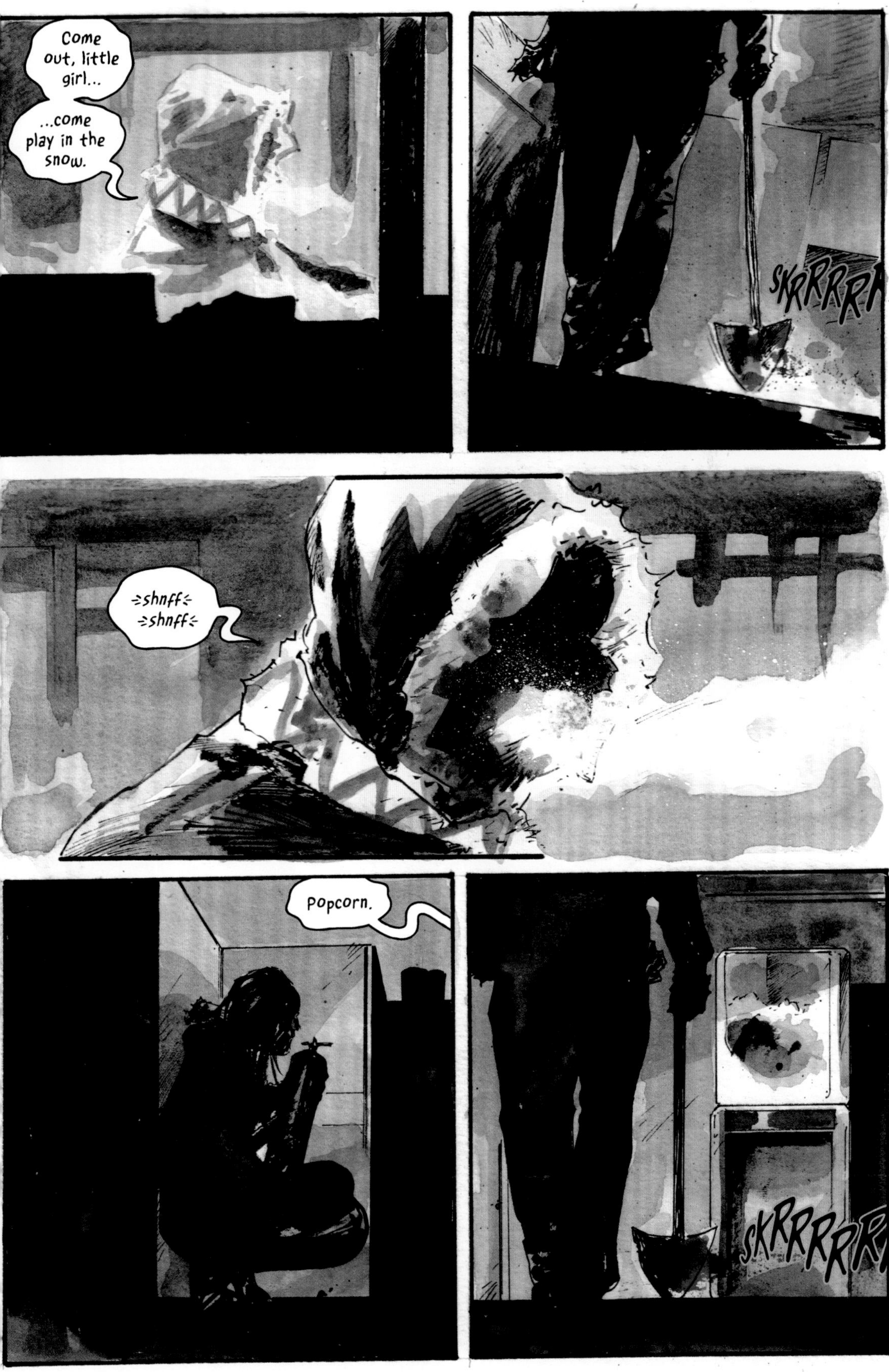

Come out, little girl...
...come play in the snow.
SKRRRRR
=shnff=
=shnff=
Popcorn.
SKRRRRR

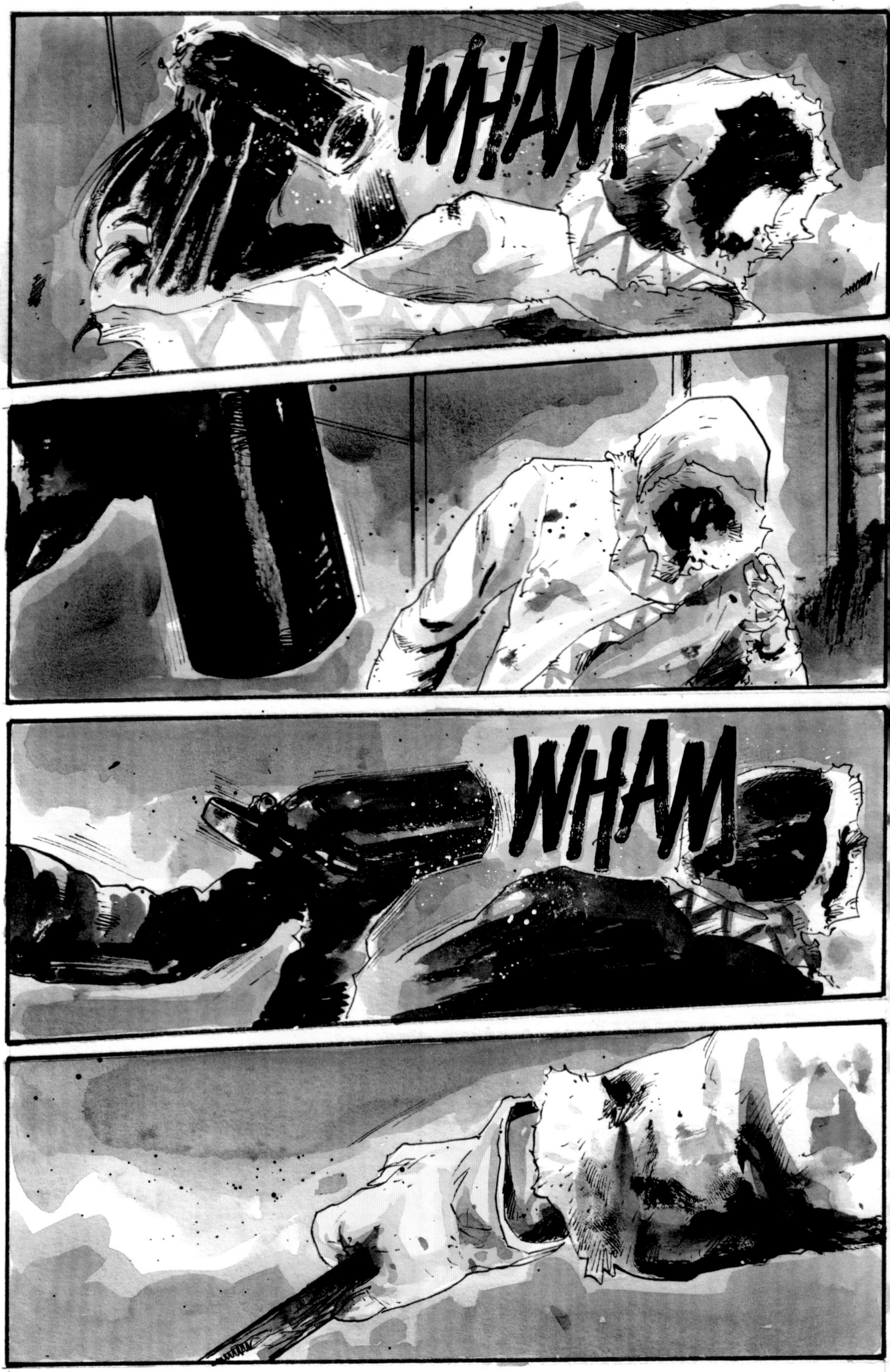
WHAM
WHAM

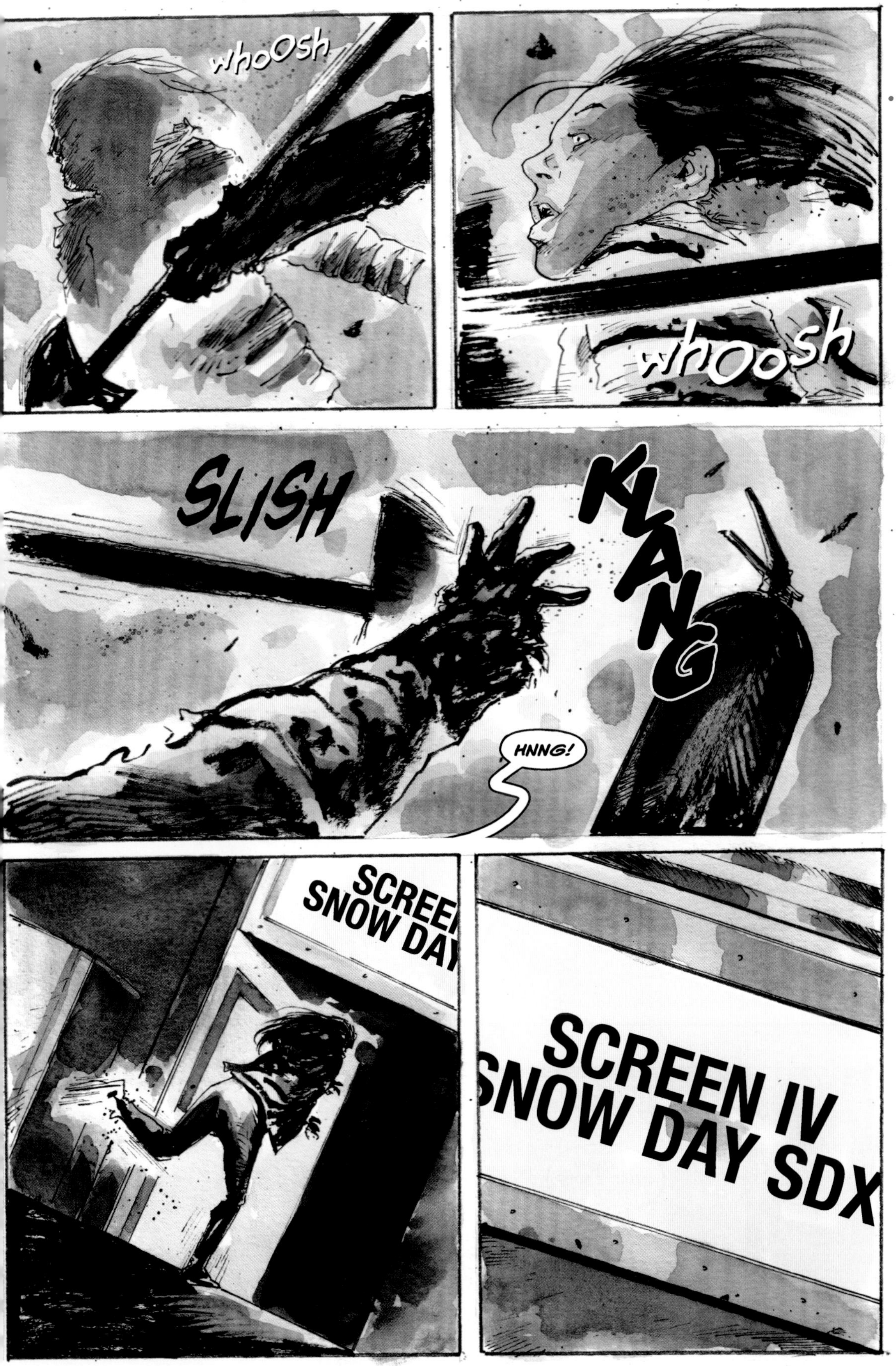
whoOsh
whOosh
SLISH
KLANG
HNNG!
SCREEN
SNOW DAY
SCREEN IV
SNOW DAY SDX

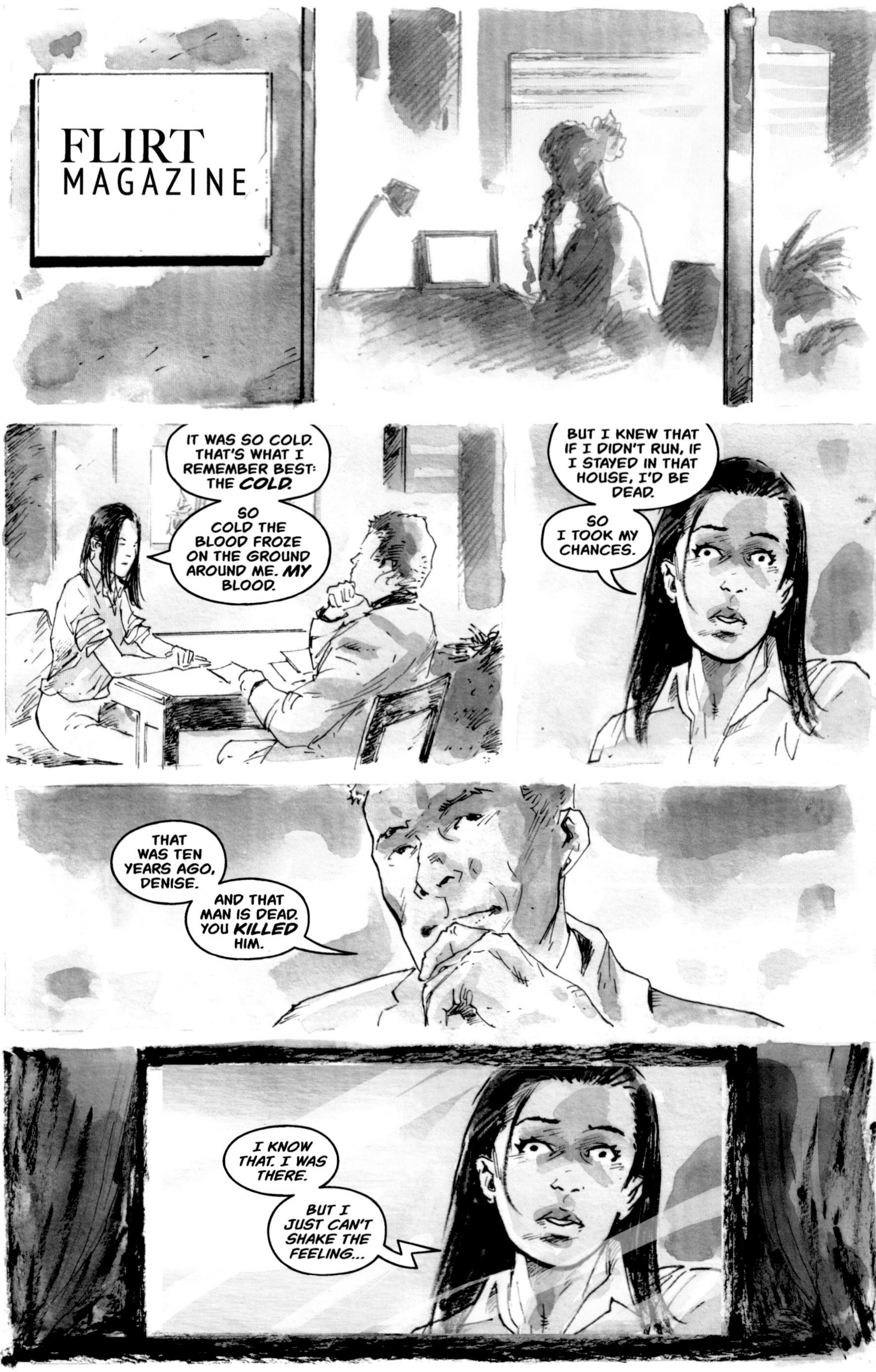
FLIRT
MAGAZINE
IT WAS SO COLD. THAT'S WHAT I REMEMBER BEST: THE COLD.
SO COLD THE BLOOD FROZE ON THE GROUND AROUND ME. MY BLOOD.
BUT I KNEW THAT IF I DIDN'T RUN, IF I STAYED IN THAT HOUSE, I'D BE DEAD.
SO I TOOK MY CHANCES.
THAT WAS TEN YEARS AGO, DENISE.
AND THAT MAN IS DEAD. YOU KILLED HIM.
I KNOW THAT. I WAS THERE.
BUT I JUST CAN'T SHAKE THE FEELING...

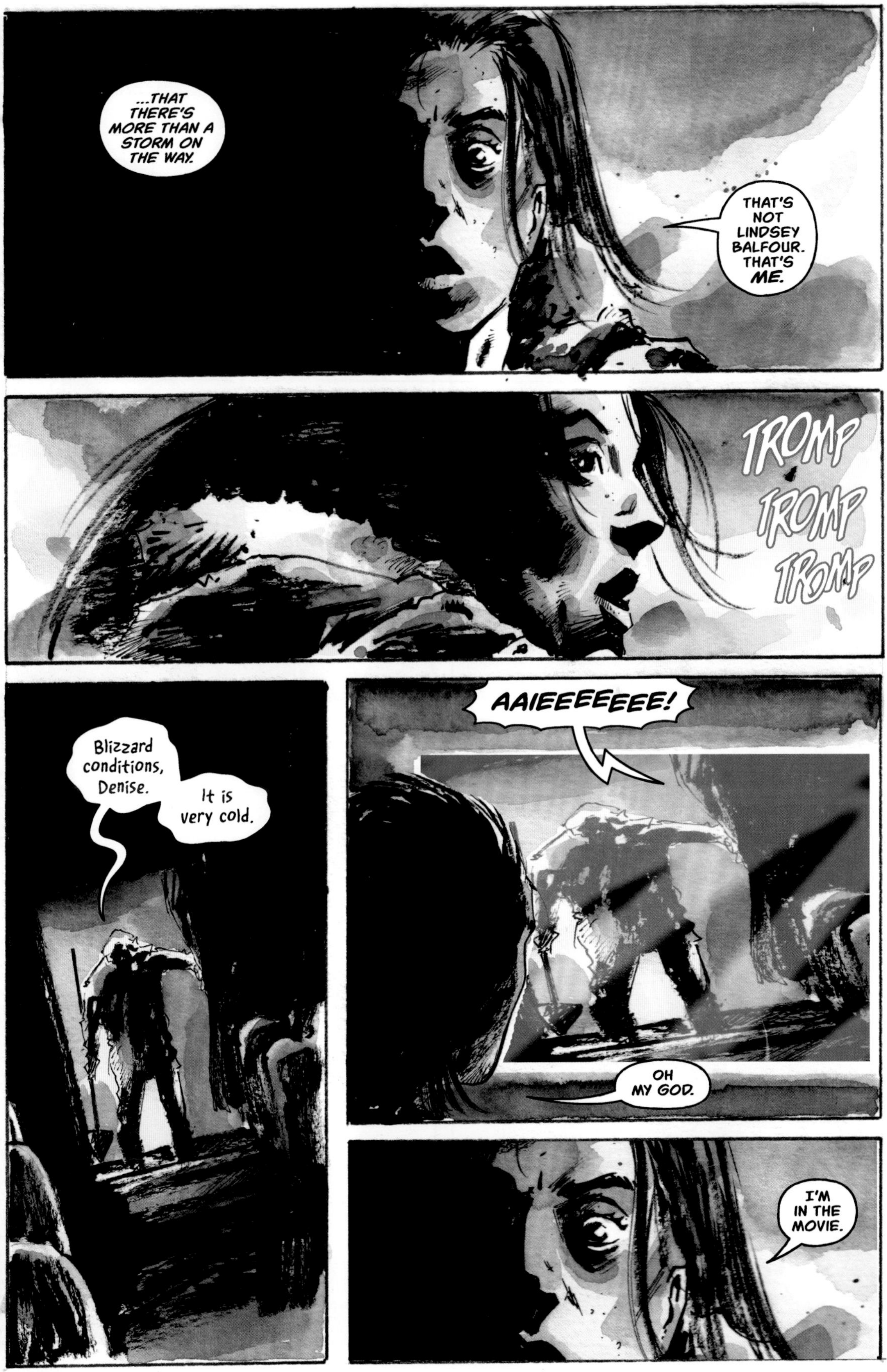
...THAT THERE'S MORE THAN A STORM ON THE WAY.
THAT'S NOT LINDSEY BALFOUR. THAT'S *ME.*
TROMP TROMP TROMP
Blizzard conditions, Denise.
It is very cold.
AAIEEEEEEE!
OH MY GOD.
I'M IN THE MOVIE.

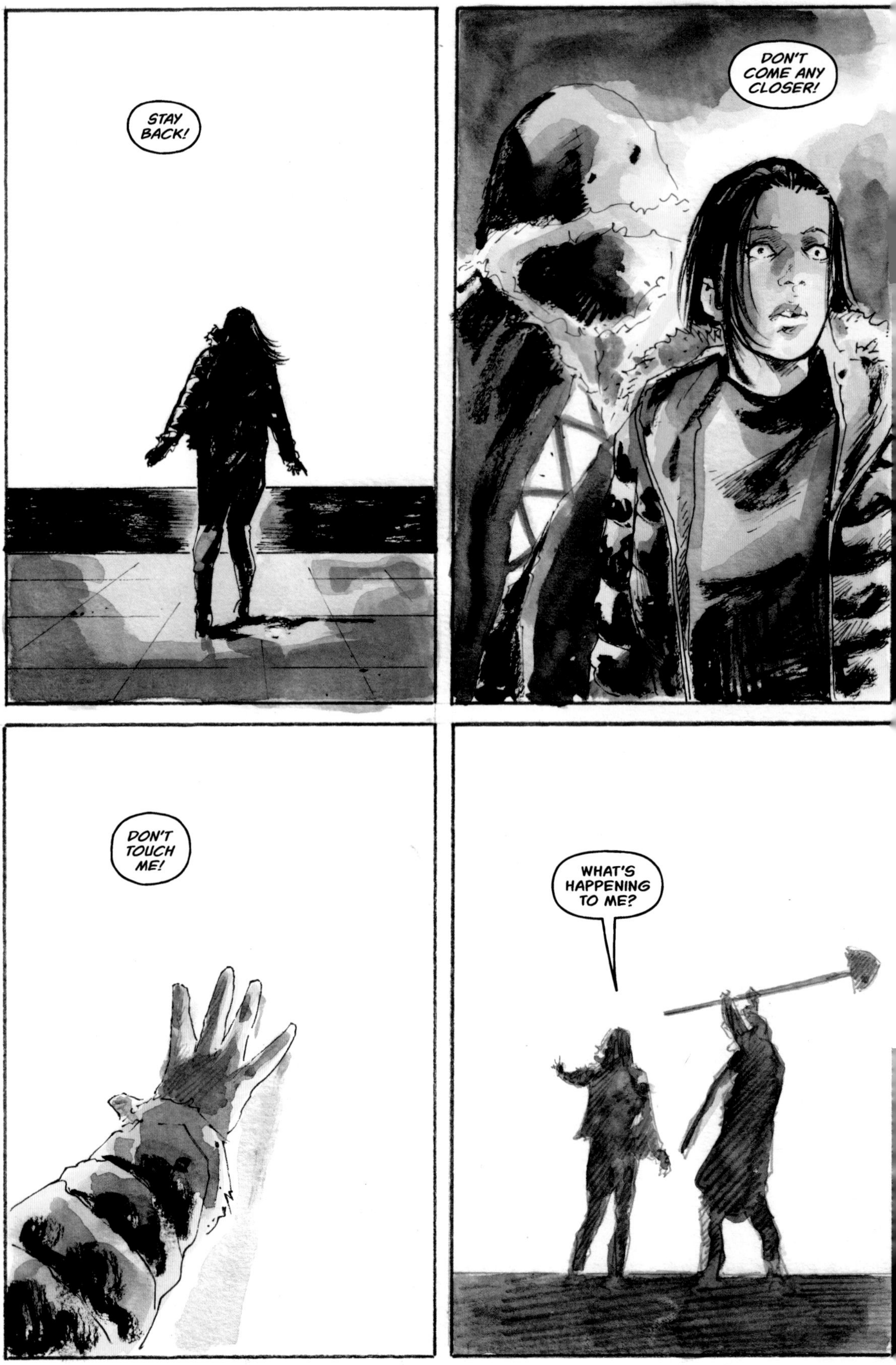
STAY BACK!
DON'T COME ANY CLOSER!
DON'T TOUCH ME!
WHAT'S HAPPENING TO ME?

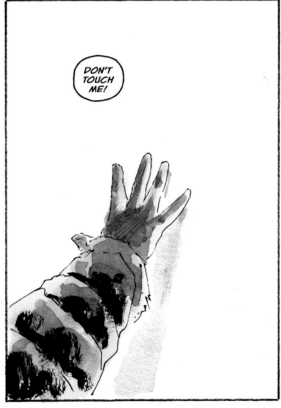

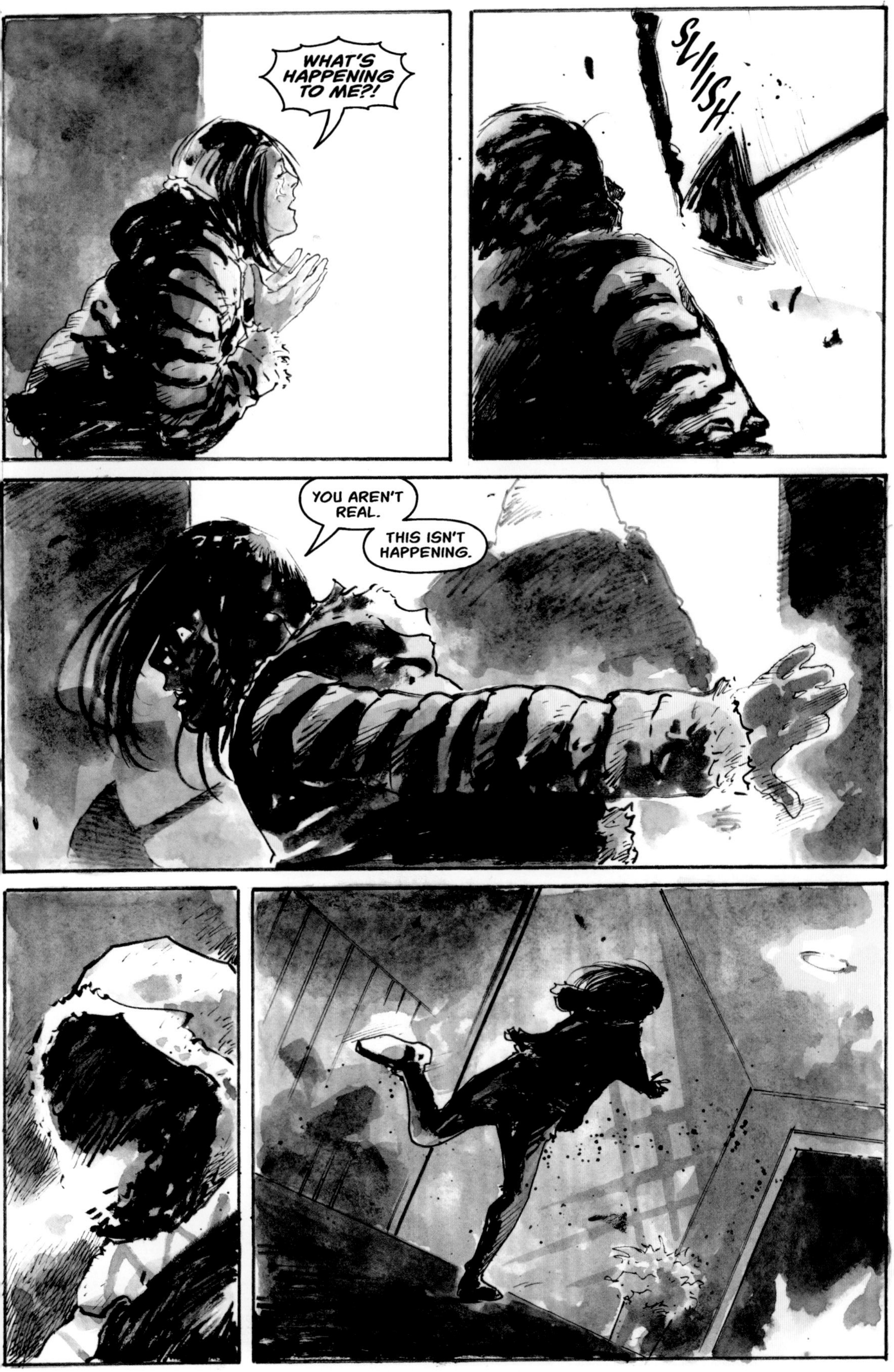
WHAT'S HAPPENING TO ME?!
SWISH
YOU AREN'T REAL.
THIS ISN'T HAPPENING.

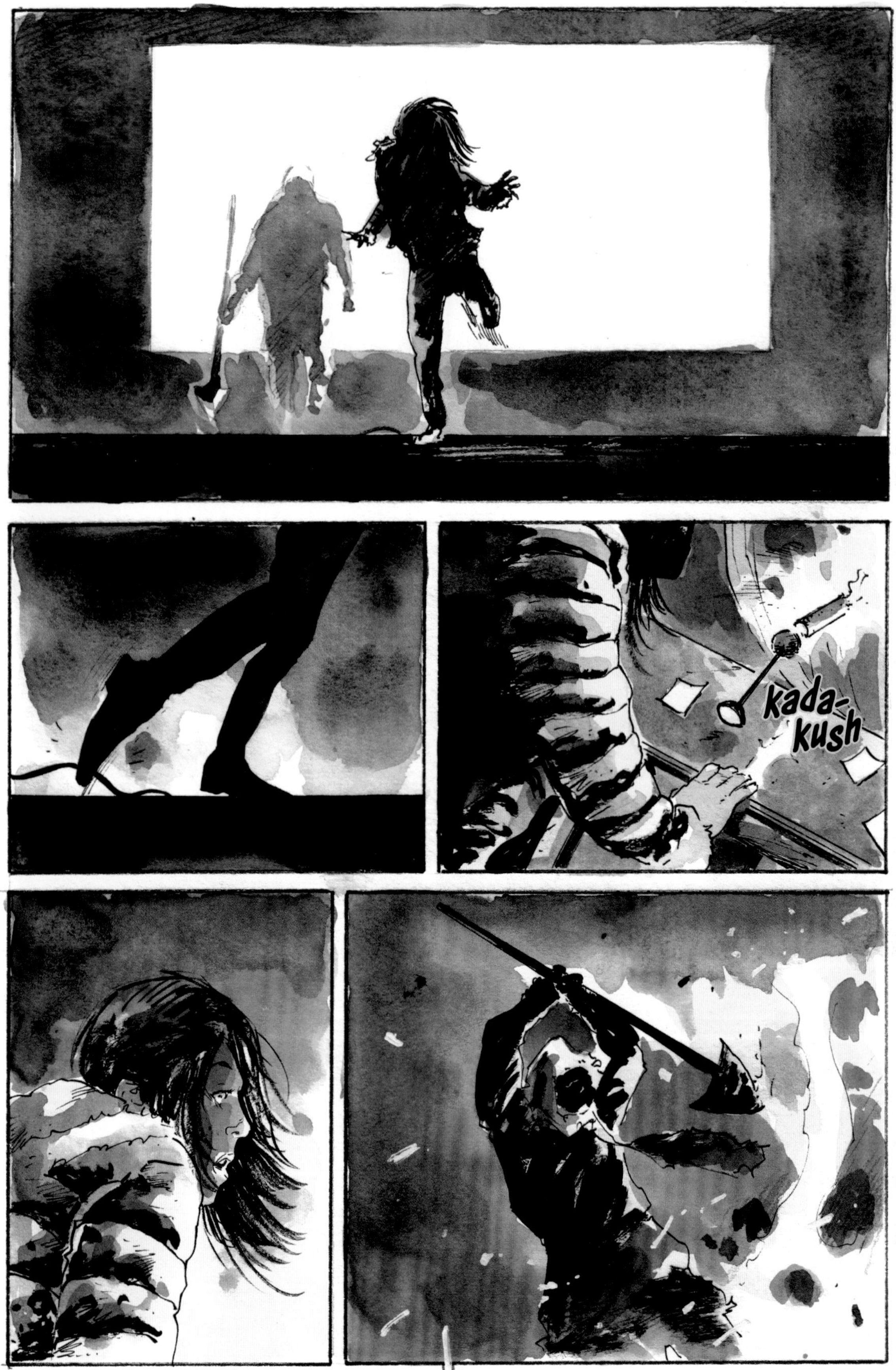
kada-
kush

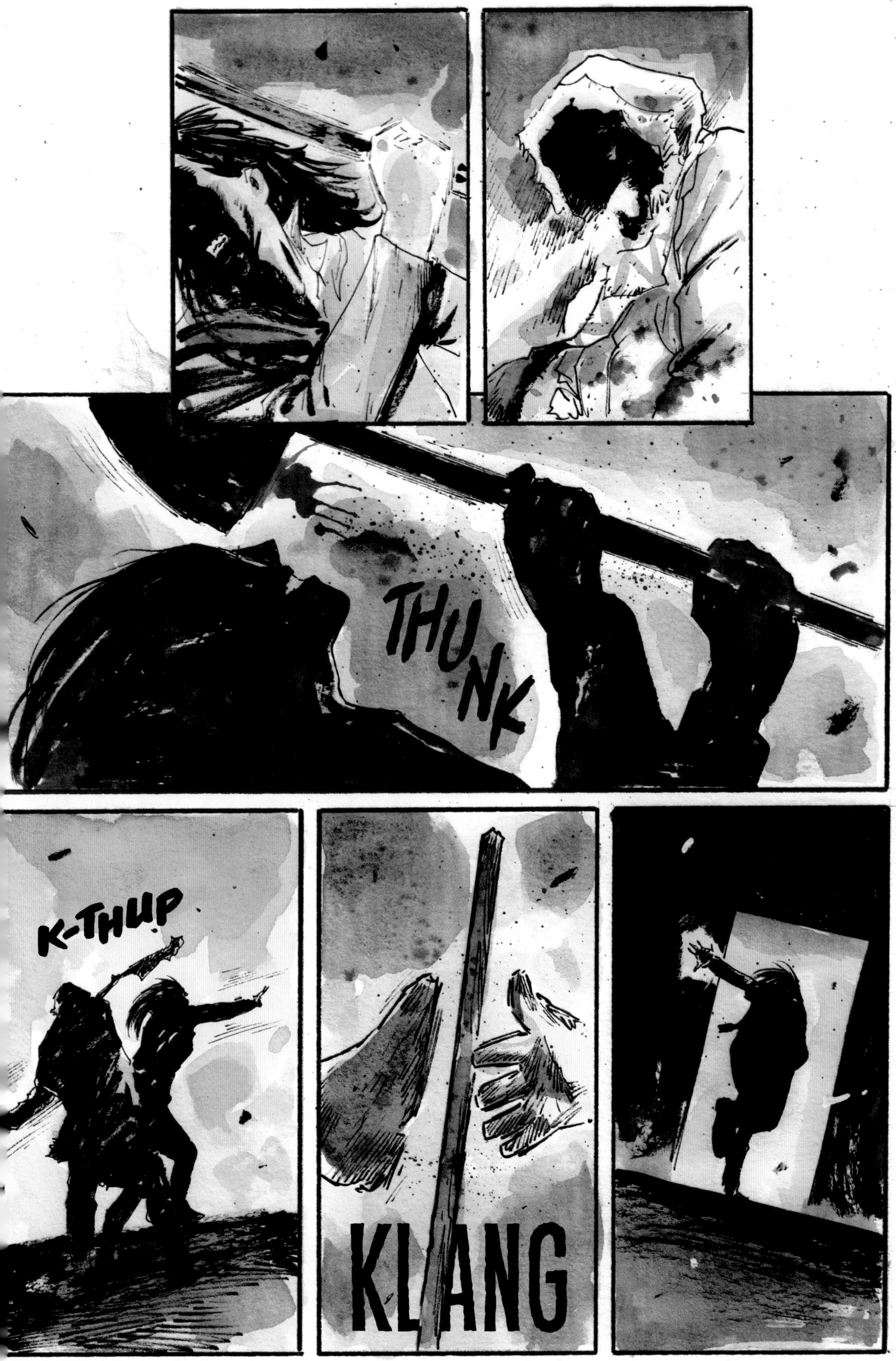
THUNK
K-THUP
KLANG

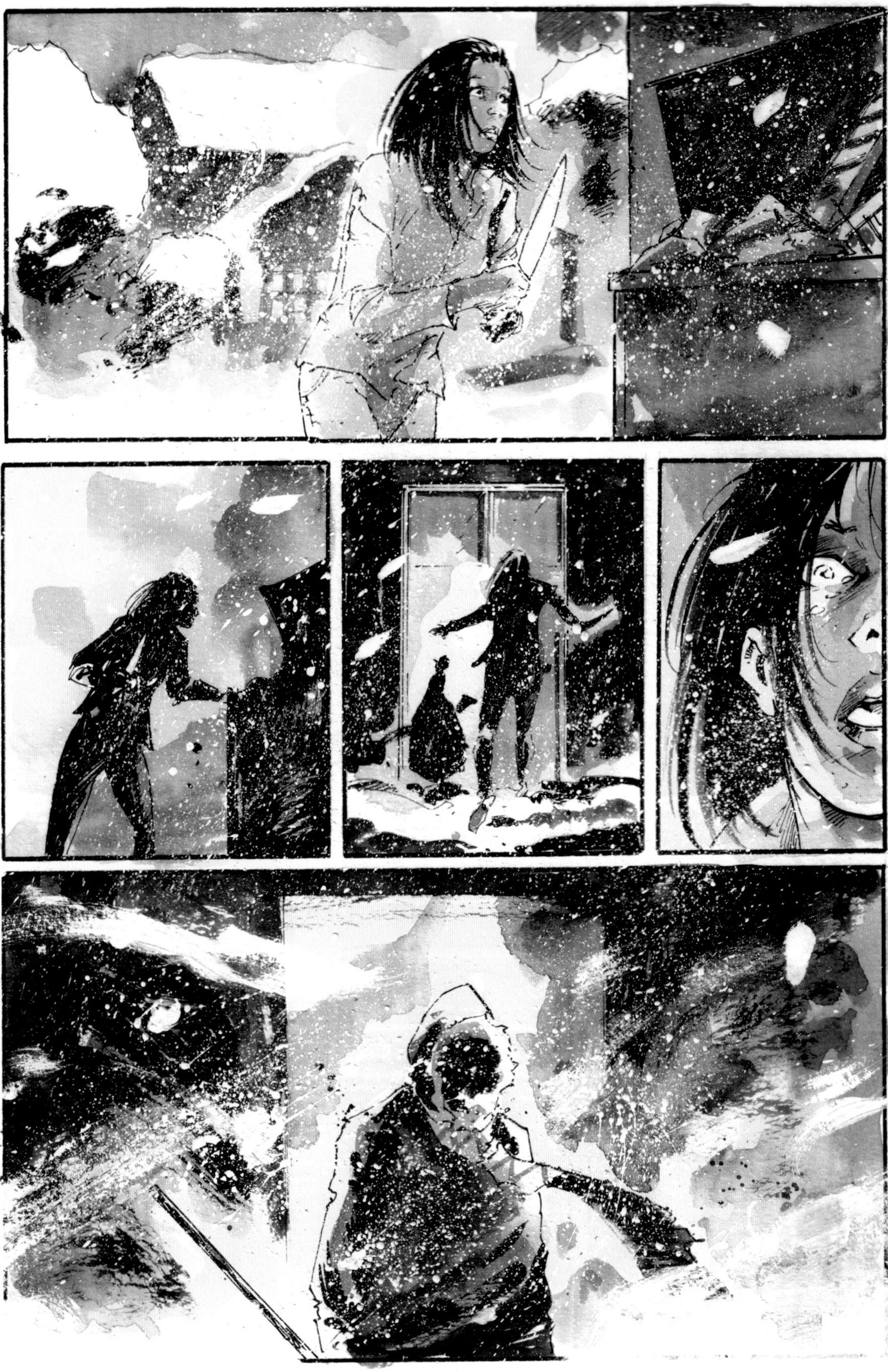

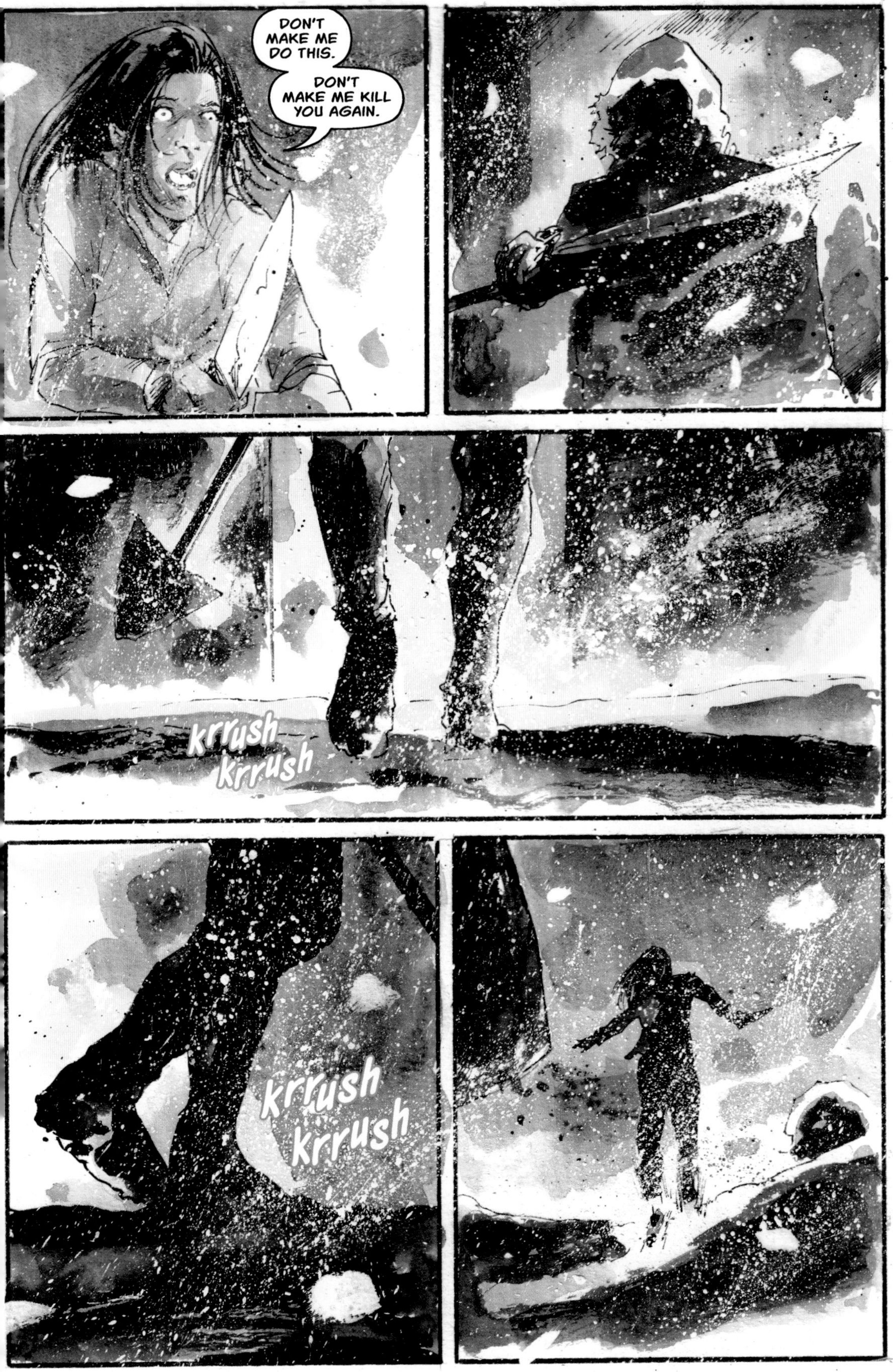
DON'T MAKE ME DO THIS.
DON'T MAKE ME KILL YOU AGAIN.
krrush
krrush
krrush
krrush

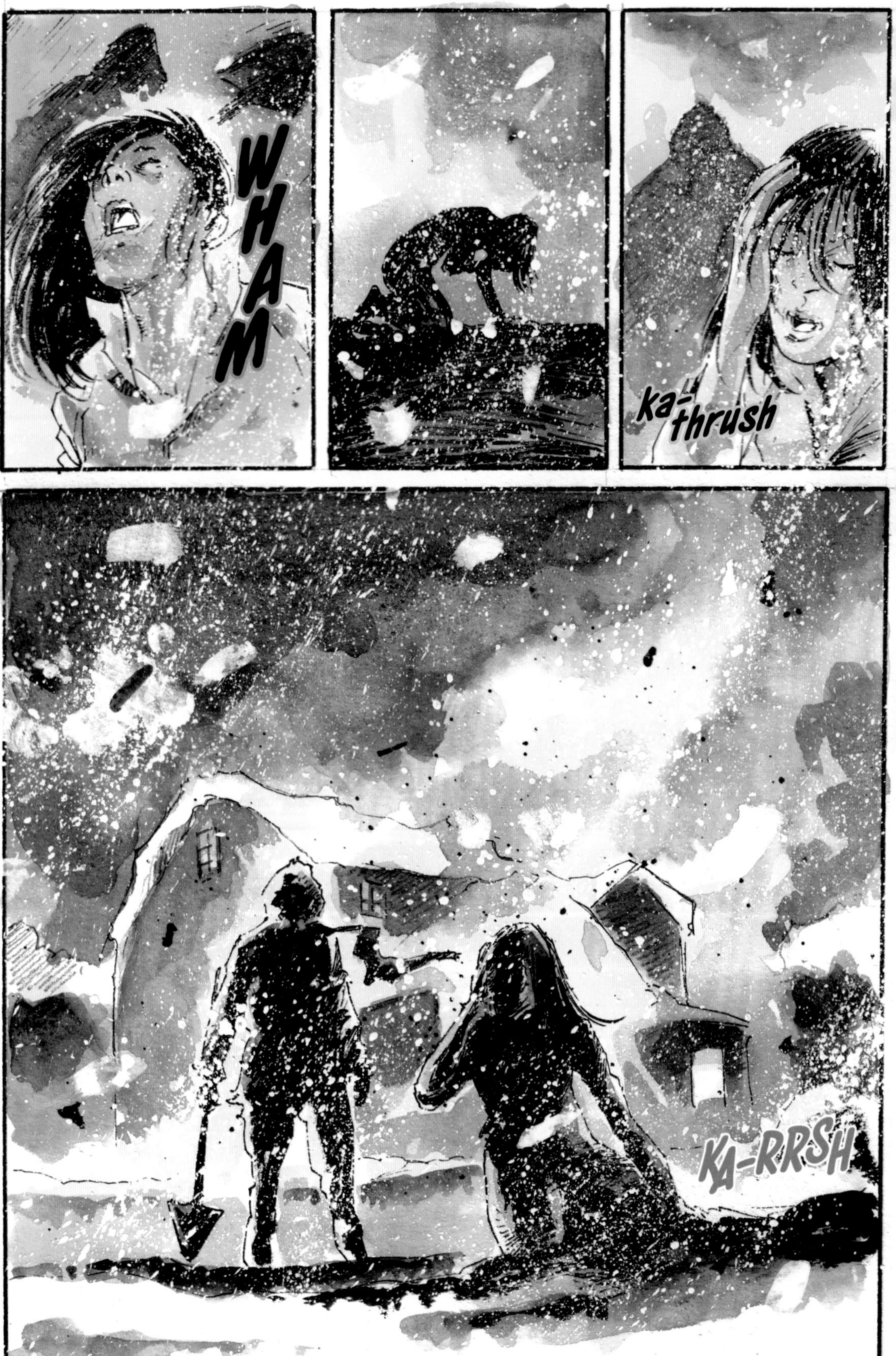
WHAM
ka-thrush
KA-RRSH

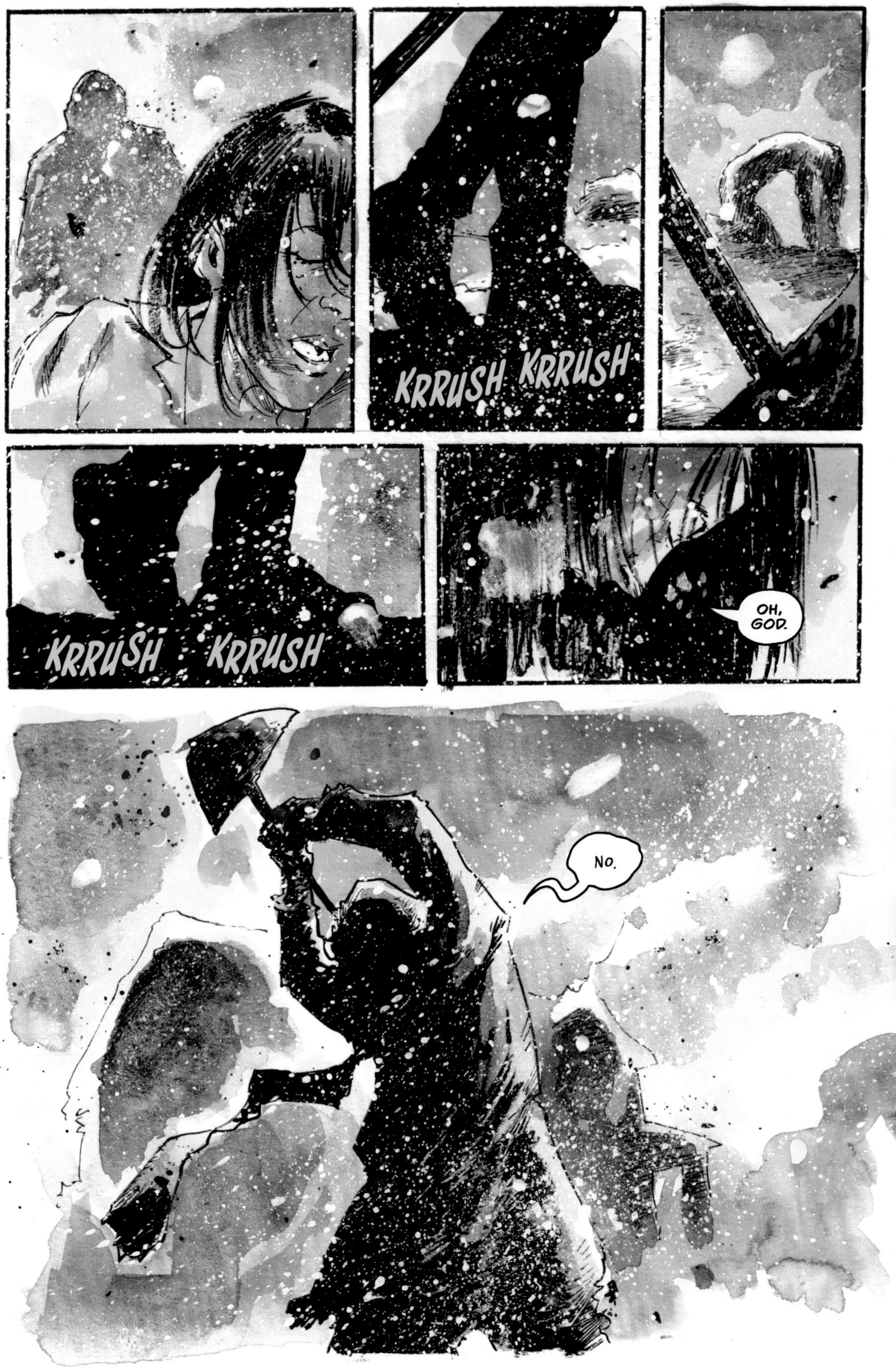
KRRUSH KRRUSH
KRRUSH KRRUSH
OH, GOD.
NO.

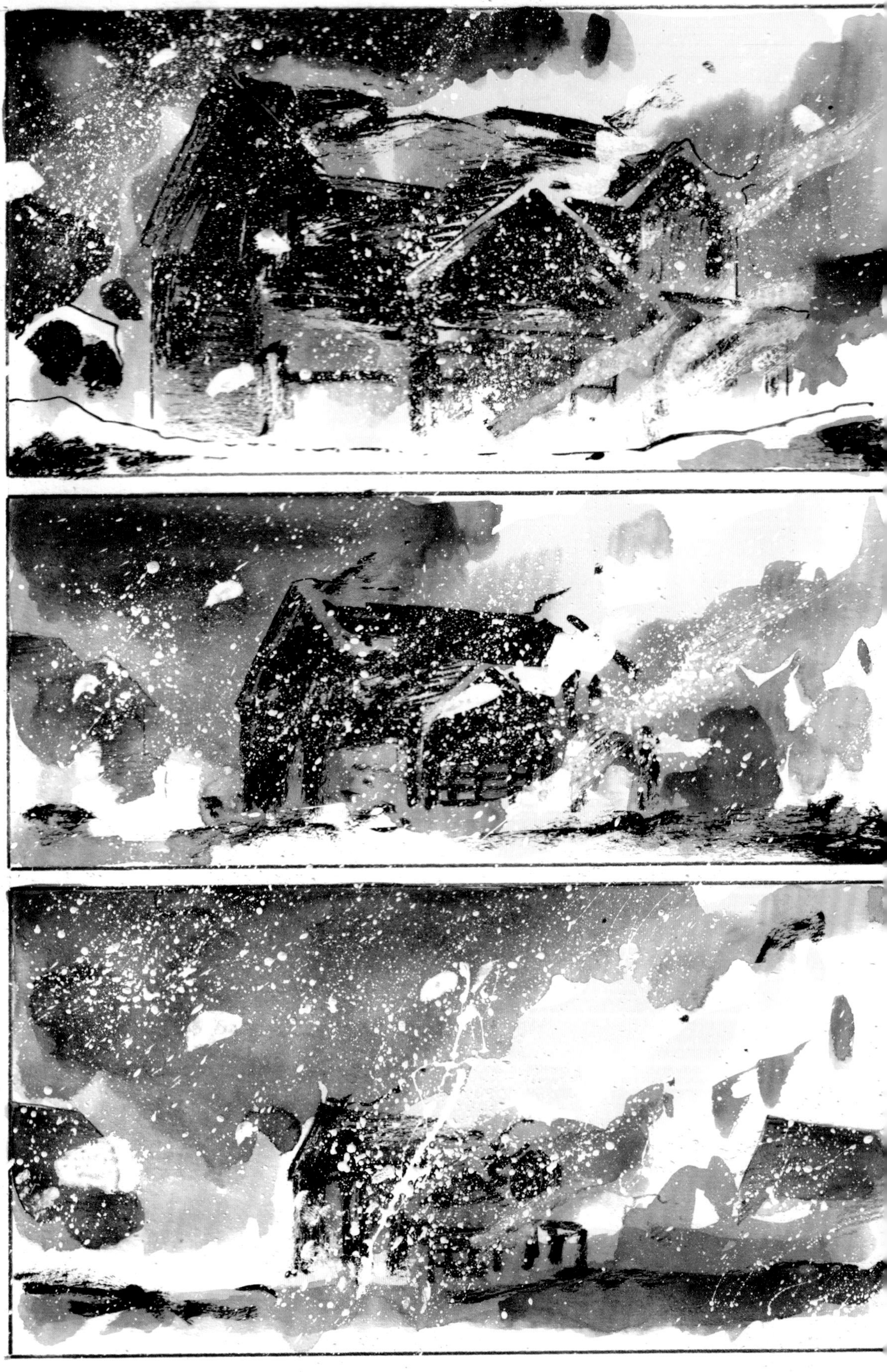

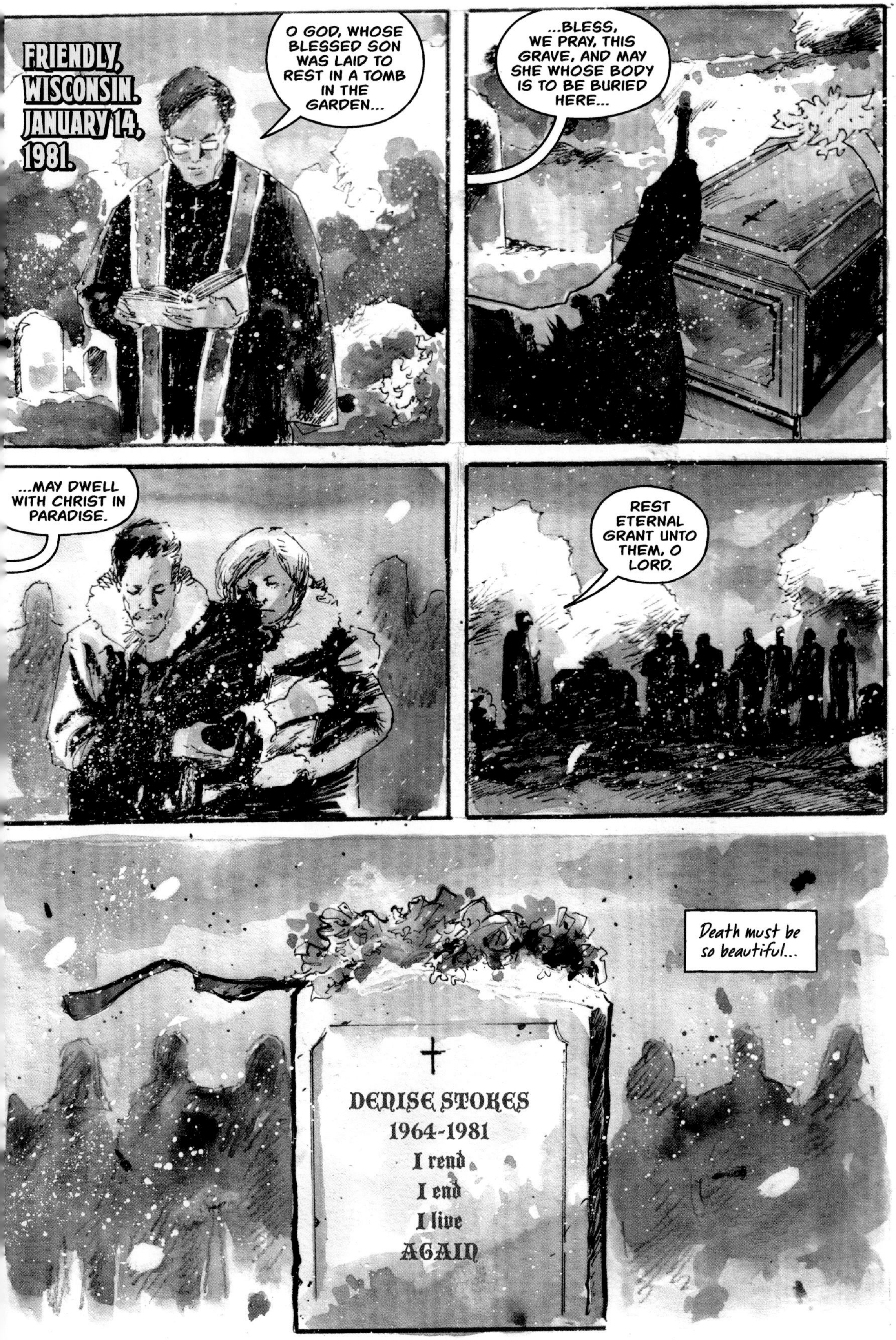
FRIENDLY, WISCONSIN. JANUARY 14, 1981.
O GOD, WHOSE BLESSED SON WAS LAID TO REST IN A TOMB IN THE GARDEN...
...BLESS, WE PRAY, THIS GRAVE, AND MAY SHE WHOSE BODY IS TO BE BURIED HERE...
...MAY DWELL WITH CHRIST IN PARADISE.
REST ETERNAL GRANT UNTO THEM, O LORD.
Death must be so beautiful...
DENISE STOKES
1964-1981
I rend
I end
I live
AGAIN

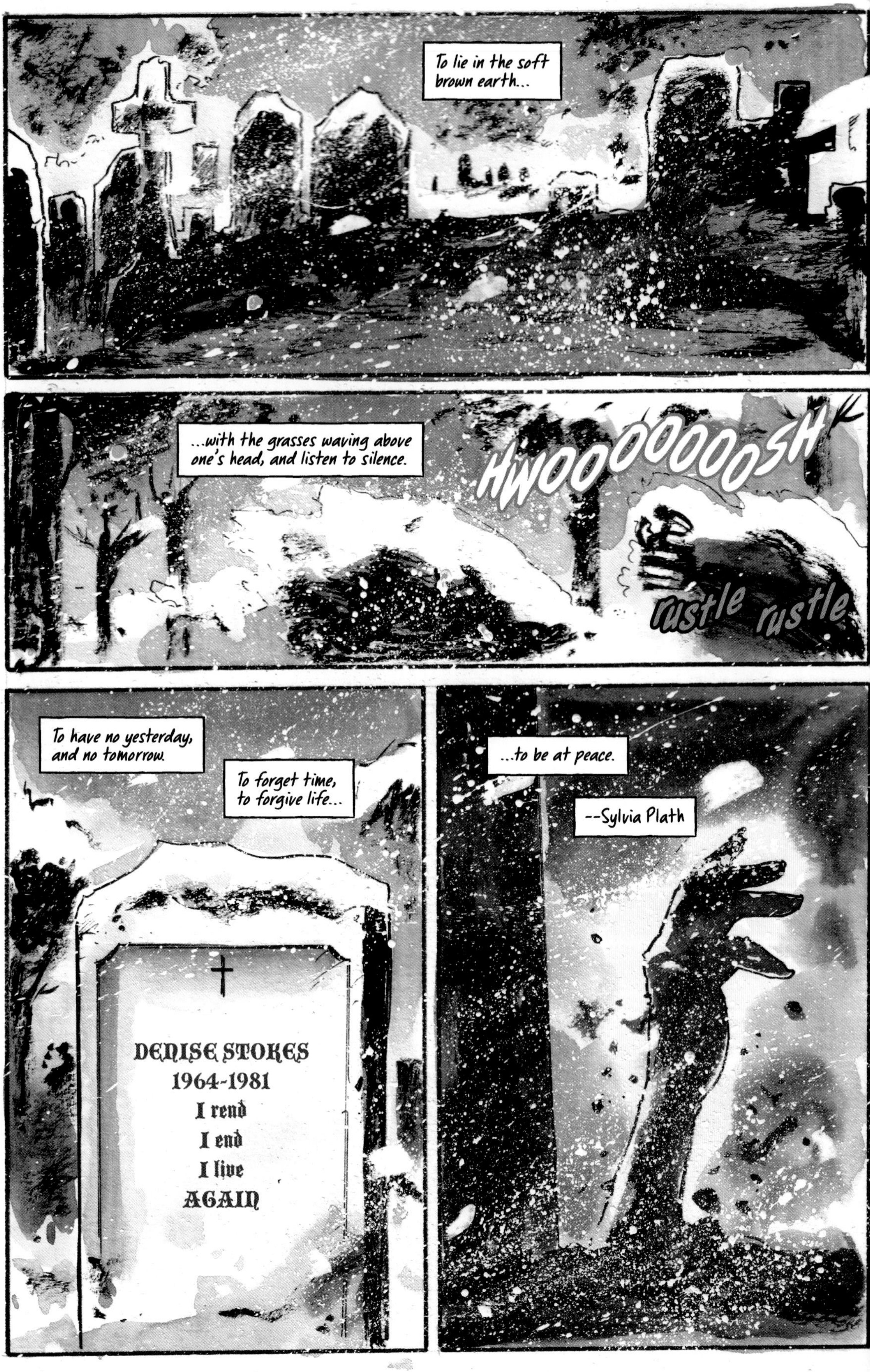
To lie in the soft brown earth...
...with the grasses waving above one's head, and listen to silence.
HWOOOOOOOOSH
rustle rustle
To have no yesterday, and no tomorrow.
To forget time, to forgive life...
DENISE STOKES
1964-1981
I rend
I end
I live
AGAIN
...to be at peace.
--Sylvia Plath

## SKETCHBOOK

# COLD BODIES™

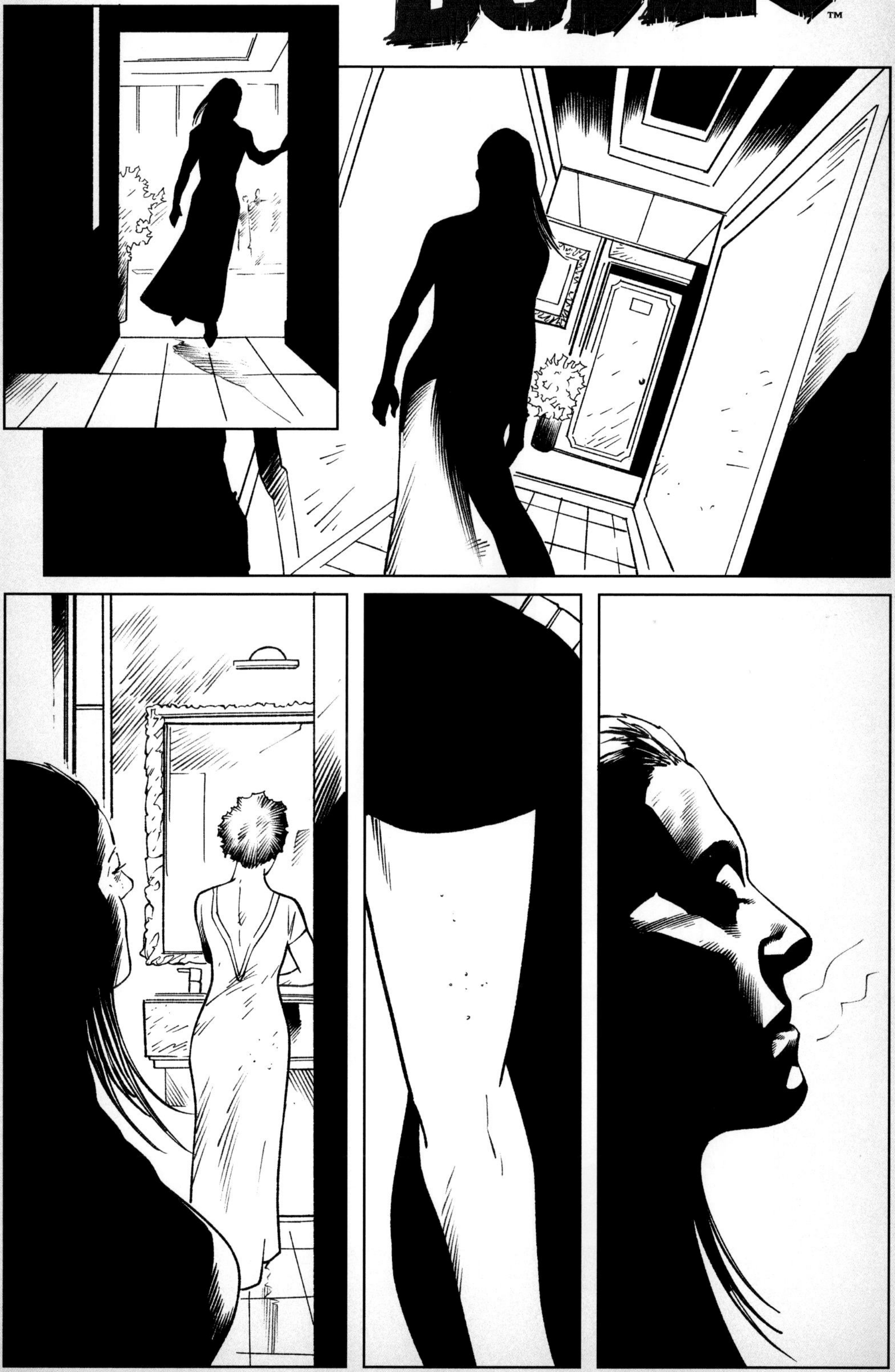

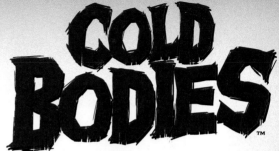

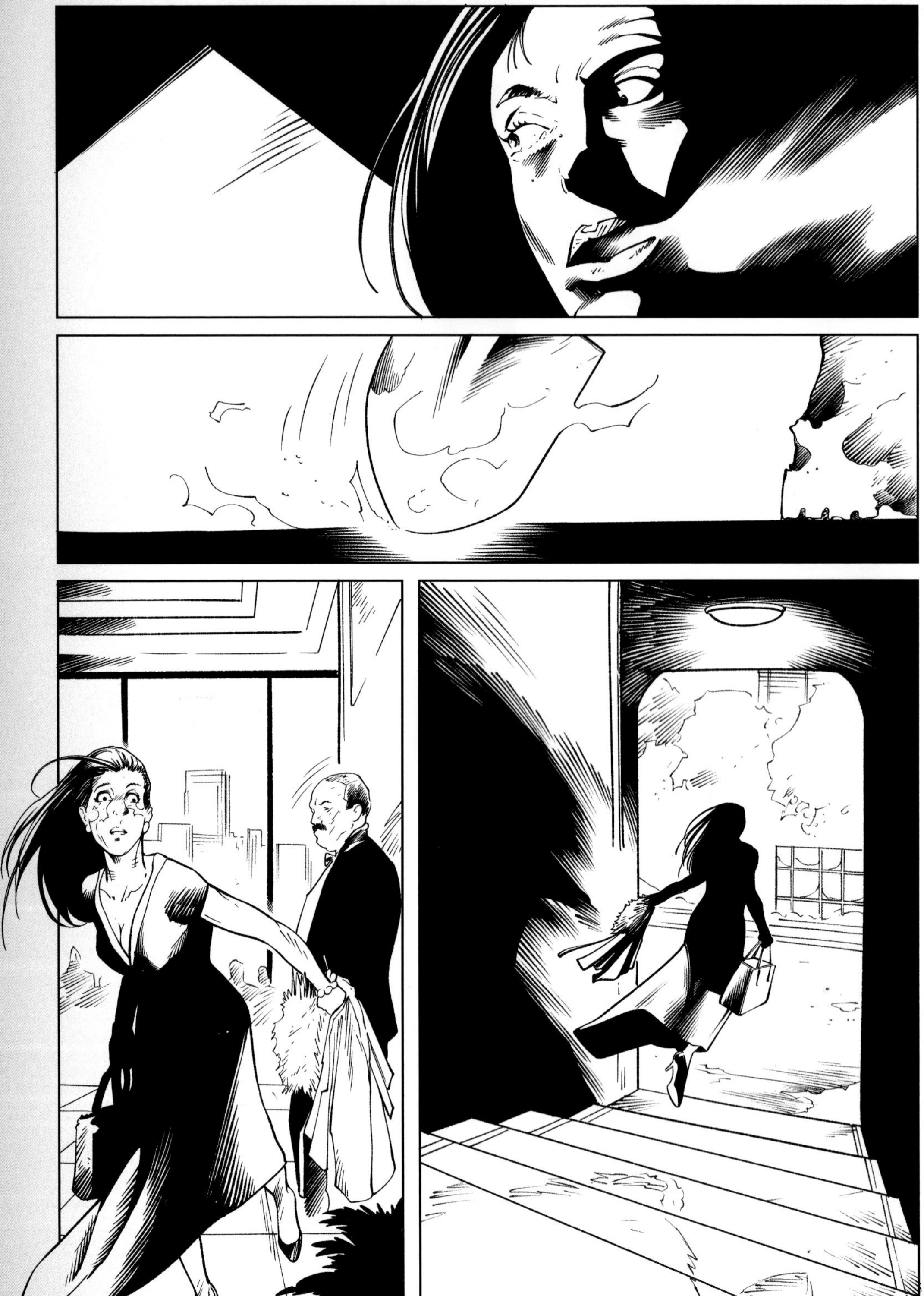

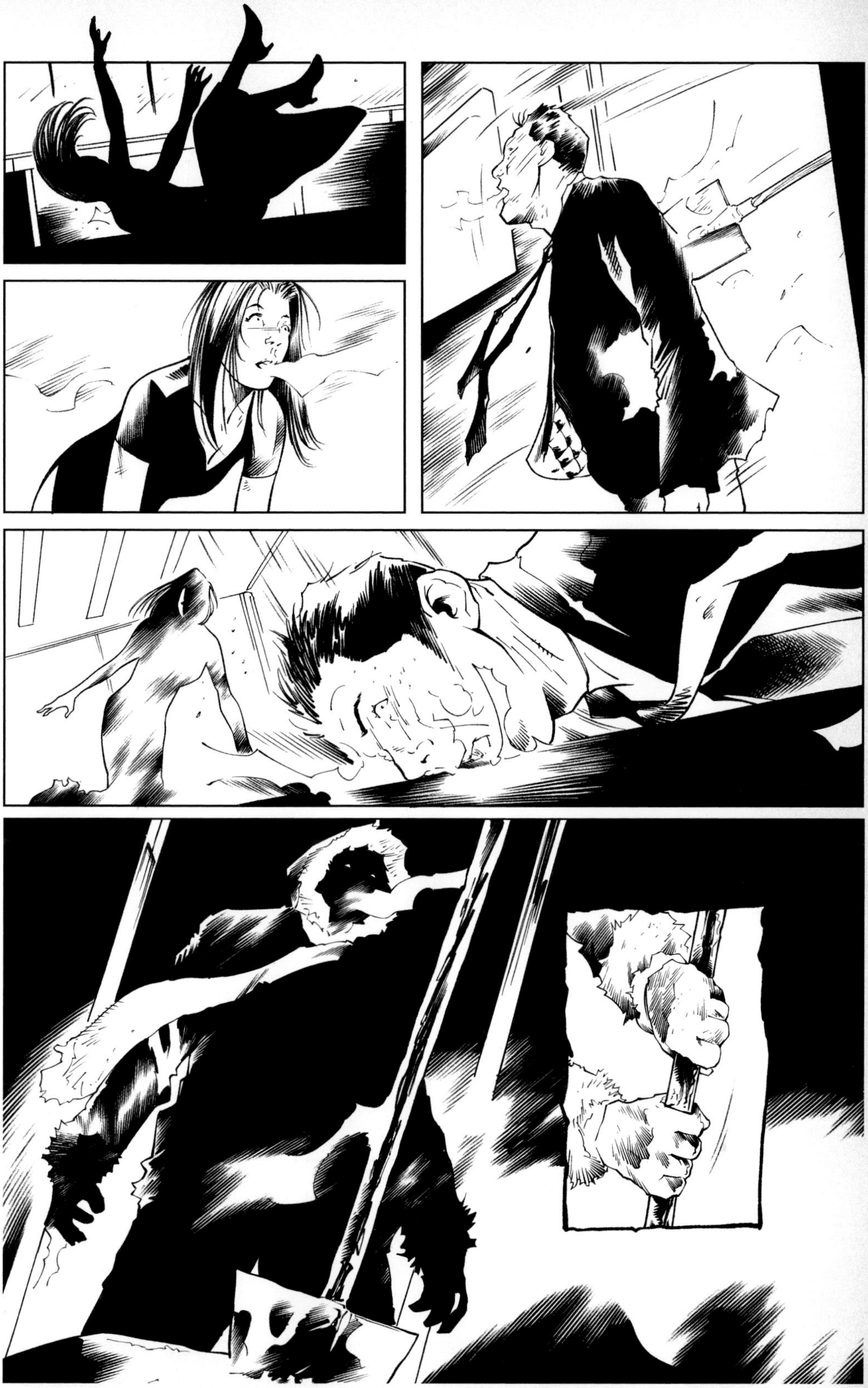

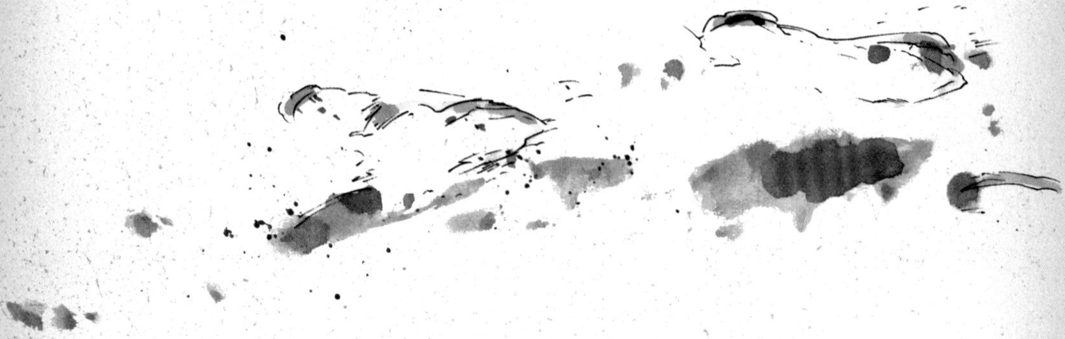